JINX
Hell's Handlers MC FL Chapter Book 4

Lilly Atlas

All rights reserved. This book or any portion thereof may not be reproduced or used in any manner whatsoever without the express written permission of the author except for the use of brief quotations in a book review.

Copyright © 2023 Lilly Atlas

All rights reserved.

ISBN-13: **978-1-946068-45-3**

Other books by Lilly Atlas

No Prisoners MC
Hook: A No Prisoners Novella
Striker
Jester
Acer
Lucky
Snake

Trident Ink
Escapades

Hell's Handlers MC
Zach
Maverick
Jigsaw
Copper
Rocket
Little Jack
Joy
Screw
Viper
Thunder

Hell's Handlers Florida Chapter
Curly
Spec
Tracker
Frost
Jinx

* * *

Mayhem Makers Series
Solo Rider

Blue Collar Bensons
First Comes Loathe
Shock and Aww

Audiobooks
Audio

Join Lilly's mailing list for a **FREE** No Prisoners short story.
www.lillyatlas.com
Facebook
Instagram
TikTok

Table of Contents

Prologue	1
Chapter One	10
Chapter Two	22
Chapter Three	31
Chapter Four	41
Chapter Five	50
Chapter Six	61
Chapter Seven	71
Chapter Eight	83
Chapter Nine	92
Chapter Ten	103
Chapter Eleven	111
Chapter Twelve	120
Chapter Thirteen	128
Chapter Fourteen	141
Chapter Fifteen	154
Chapter Sixteen	161
Chapter Seventeen	175
Chapter Eighteen	186
Chapter Nineteen	200

Chapter Twenty	210
Chapter Twenty-One	218
Chapter Twenty-Two	228
Chapter Twenty-Three	234
Chapter Twenty-Four	244
Chapter Twenty-Five	255
Chapter Twenty-Six	267
Chapter Twenty-Seven	274
Chapter Twenty-Eight	284
Epilogue	291
Zach Preview	298

I'm coining a new genre: Romantic Snarkedy.

Romantic Snarkedy: a work of romantic fiction featuring a protagonist who exhibits a sharp and witty tone, often marked by sarcasm or irony. This type of character is known for their bold and confident attitude, which adds a playful and entertaining dimension to the novel's plot.

Enjoy Jinx in his Romantic Snarkedy :)

Prologue

Something wasn't right.

Harper couldn't put her finger on it, but a persistent tingle at the back of her neck, coupled with a queasy stomach, had her nerves on edge. Tonight wasn't different from so many before it, but it still felt off.

And the uneasiness was starting to mess with her head.

Friday night in the passenger seat of her boyfriend's cherry-red Ford Mustang with his friends crammed in the back typically meant they were heading to a party that would end sometime long after midnight. When it finally wound down, they'd drop his friends at their respective homes, drive to their favorite make-out spot, and spend the next hour or so making good use of that back seat. Eventually, they'd have no choice but to return to their homes. Harper, to her family's crappy trailer on the wrong side of the tracks, and Aaron to, his attorney father's posh mansion.

"I told Ryan we'd pick up some beer. He said his house is fucking packed, and he's running out already." Aaron glanced in the rearview mirror as he spoke. Something in his voice had her frowning. A hint of excitement that seemed over-the-top considering the situation.

The last time he'd been asked to pick up some alcohol for a party, he'd practically thrown a fit. Now, as he pulled into a gas station parking lot, there was almost eager anticipation to him.

"Let's do this."

Harper turned around to find Simon, Aaron's best friend, smirking. Usually, the guy spent these rides with his tongue down his girlfriend's throat, but tonight, he was flying solo. Harper didn't like him or his girlfriend enough to ask if they'd broken up.

Stuffed in the back, four of Aaron's closest frat brothers spent most of the trip chatting about what lucky girl they planned to fuck that evening.

So much for his girlfriend.

Maybe they *had* broken up.

She shifted her gaze to Aaron. As usual, her stomach fluttered with excitement and disbelief that the richest, most popular, and downright hottest guy in school wanted her—quiet, poor, awkward Harper—but he did. And they'd been dating for most of her senior year.

Of course, he'd graduated high school over a year ago, so his popularity no longer mattered, but he'd been at the top of the food chain for as long as she could remember. Even now, he dominated at college, making the transition easily and picking up friends wherever he went.

He attracted women as well. They threw themselves at him whether she was there or not. Something about those blond locks and piercing blue eyes. The football-honed muscles didn't hurt, either. Nor did his wit and charm.

He was college-girl catnip.

Yet he still wanted her after nearly a year of dating.

And she fully trusted him. He said he loved her, after all.

She couldn't help the smile that curled her lips.

He loved her.

Aaron reached across the console and grabbed her hand. She turned her head to find his dazzling white smile aimed at her. "Ready, Harp?"

She shook her head. "You guys go in. I'll wait in the car. I don't care what you buy." No one had ever questioned Aaron or his friends' fake IDs, but she didn't have one and wouldn't be responsible for spoiling everyone's night if she got carded along with them.

He waved away her concern. "Nah, come one. You're not gonna want to miss this."

"Yeah, Harp," Simon said from the back seat. "You will not want to miss this."

One of the other guys snickered.

She eyed Aaron. "Okay, I guess, but I don't have an ID. What if they card me and won't serve you."

"You worry too much," her boyfriend said, squeezing her hand.

Carl, her least favorite of all Aaron's *bros* snorted. "Yeah, won't be a problem."

The others snickered.

She crinkled her forehead. "Why are you guys being weird?"

Aaron winked. "Ignore them. You know they're stupid. Come on. It'll be fine and fun. I promise."

Fun?

Aaron lived for fun. Truth be told, she'd have much preferred the two of them to spend their Friday nights snuggling on a couch, watching Netflix with a giant bowl of popcorn and some sodas. But skipping a college party was sacrilege to Aaron and his friends.

And she might as well soak up the experiences while she could. She certainly couldn't afford full-time college. Every dollar she earned went into a savings account for the community college classes she planned to take in the fall, and even then, she'd be stretched thin. Working as an Applebee's server didn't exactly rake in cash.

"All right, fine." She sighed. It was cold, and she'd dressed for a crowded, sweaty party, not the outdoors.

"That's my girl." Aaron leaned in and kissed her, sending a zing of happiness through her stomach. "Love you," he whispered.

Her heart sang. Was there anything better than hearing those three words? "Love you too."

It was enough to make her ignore the unease still pecking at her.

Cold air blasted her as soon as she opened the door. Her light, sparkly sweater did nothing to keep out the chill. Within seconds, she was shivering. "Why'd you park so far from the entrance? We're the only ones here."

He'd parked the car at the very end of the single row of spots in front of the building.

"You'll see." He cackled.

Ice ran down her spine, and she turned to see what that eerie laugh was all about. "Why—" She gasped. "What the hell are you doing?" The five guys stood in front of Aaron's flashy red Mustang, yanking ski masks over their faces. "Guys? W-what's going on?"

Her mind reeled. What on earth were they doing? Why weren't they answering her?

"What is happening right now?" she barked as her patience ran thin.

The unease disappeared as shock and dread moved in.

Aaron strode to her. "We're having some fucking fun," he said. "This town is so boring I can't fucking stand it anymore. Time to shake shit up and make our own fun."

"But..." She took three steps away from them as she shook her head. She couldn't even find words. "You're not gonna..." she lowered her voice to a whisper, glancing around the empty lot, "... *rob* the store, are you?"

He winked, then slid a ski mask over her head. "Like I

said. We're gonna have some fun."

"No," she said as she took another step away. "No, wait… Aaron, no. This is crazy. It's wrong."

"Knew she'd be a fucking wet blanket," someone mumbled. Probably Carl.

Aaron stepped into her space and cupped her face between his hands. "Harp, this is no big deal. Just some fun and games."

"Aaron, it's a crime."

Had he lost his mind? Was she dreaming? Stuck in a nightmare?

"Fun and games, Harp. Nothing bad is going to happen. We'll take a couple of fucking beers and be on our way. The gas station will be out fifty bucks max. What's the big damn deal?"

"It's wr—"

"Don't you trust me?" he asked with a frown.

She scoffed. "Yes, of course. You know I do, but—"

"Then you need to show me." He pulled a ski mask down over her head before she could react. "Let's do it."

"Wait, A—"

He grabbed her hand and towed her toward the door with his buddies laughing and cheering as they followed.

"I really don't want to do this," she said as she ran to keep up with him. His crushing grip couldn't be broken, and she worried he'd pull her shoulder out of the socket if she stopped. Her fingers started to ache from trying to escape his hold. "Aaron," she whispered with panic in her voice. "Just… let me sit in the car. Please."

Or run away. Let me run away.

She'd never go back to the car. If he released her, she'd flee and run all the way home.

"Too late," he said as he pulled the door open.

Carl gave her a shove from behind, making her stumble

forward.

Into the store.

"Party time, motherfucker," Aaron yelled as he entered the store behind her.

Harper stared at her boyfriend as he ran to a shelf and swept random items into a backpack.

Who is this man? Certainly not her boyfriend of the past eleven months.

Her gaze flicked between Aaron's friends as she tried to keep up with the shocking events. "Stop." She tried to shout it, but nothing more than a squeak left her throat.

"All right, asshole, open the register nice and slow."

Open the register.

Her jaw dropped behind the mask as she whipped her gaze around to find Carl standing in front of a trembling gas station attendant. He held a gun to the terrified man, who lifted his hands in the air.

A gun.

She took a step back on instinct. Where had a gun come from? Had he had it the whole time?

Her eyes locked on the weapon, unable to focus on anything else.

"A g-gun. He has a gun," she whispered.

"Just a little motivation."

She jumped and spun to the right to find Aaron standing beside her with a backpack stuffed to the brim.

"Hold this. I'm gonna fill another one." He thrust the backpack at her, but her arms wouldn't cooperate, and it crashed to the floor.

"Hey, snap the fuck out of it," he barked.

She jolted and shook her head, standing with arms limp at her sides.

Aaron growled, then ran down one of the aisles.

"Put the money in the fucking bag." Carl's shout had her

swinging her gaze to the register again like she was watching a tennis ball cross the net. He stood at the counter, gun trained on the poor man, who shook so hard he dropped a handful of bills as he tried to stuff them in the bag.

"Faster," Carl shouted.

"Stop," she whispered again. What the hell was wrong with her voice? Why couldn't she scream? Why couldn't she do anything?

Her legs felt like they were attached to two led anvils, rooting her in place. God, what the hell was happening? Would Carl shoot that man if he didn't move fast enough?

"No," she said aloud as her voice finally kicked in gear. No one paid her any attention. Her boyfriend and his friends were too busy filling backpacks with booze. "I can't do this."

She used all the strength she possessed to lift her heavy legs, turned around, and took a step toward the door. Right as her palms hit the cool glass, a shot rang out, and she jerked as though she'd been the one hit.

But she hadn't.

Air rushed from her lungs.

Turn. Find out if Carl shot the man behind the counter.

Her muscles had gone rigid. Her joints locked. She couldn't move.

"Oh shit. Oh fuck. We have to go. Now."

Carl's panicked voice pinged around in her head, and she forced herself to turn around with a pit of dread in her stomach. The gas station attendant slumped against a wall of cigarettes, clutching his side.

"Oh God." She gasped.

"Go, go. We gotta fucking move," Aaron shouted.

Instinct kicked in, and Harper rushed toward the injured man with her pulse pounding in her ears.

"What the fuck are you doing? We need to go," Simon shouted at her.

She stopped, gaping at the wounded man. "We have to help him," she said, voice pleading.

"For fuck's sake, A. Get your fucking girlfriend before she lands us all in jail." Carl ran past her and out into the night.

Aaron appeared before her. He crouched to her eye level and gripped her shoulders. Stark fear shone in his usually glittering blue eyes.

"H-he shot him," she said, staring over Aaron's shoulder at the groaning man.

"Hey," he screamed in her face.

His fingertips dug into her shoulders, but she didn't react.

"We have to get the fuck out of here before the police show up and all our lives are ruined."

She blinked at her boyfriend. This man she thought she loved had gotten bored and dragged her into an armed robbery for shits and giggles. "Don't touch me," she whispered, trying to wrench from his hold. "I have to help him. What if he dies?"

Aaron released her with a harsh burst of laughter. "Who the fuck cares? He's nobody. I'm the one who loves you."

When she didn't take her eyes off the bleeding man, Aaron shook his head. "Fuck this." He ran toward the door, turning around at the last second. "You're in here wearing a mask. Same as us. If you're still here when the police come, you're going to jail for a long time." He pushed out the door as it jangled above his head.

Jail?

Harper started to shake.

She couldn't go to jail.

Who would help take care of her mom? Who would keep their home clean? Who'd feed the dog? How would she finish high school?

"I'm s-sorry," she whispered as the man met her gaze. Her heart sat like lead in her chest. "I didn't know. I'm sorry," she mumbled.

She walked backward, shaking her head as tears soaked into the fabric of the ski mask.

"I'm sorry," she whispered again.

Her back collided with the door, jolting her out of her semitrance. She took one last lingering look at the man Carl shot. All color drained from his face, and he panted as he stared back at her.

The realization that her life would never be the same crashed over her like a tsunami. No matter what happened, this would be the defining moment that ruled for years, maybe forever. The night she pushed aside her misgivings and trusted a man who'd never care about anything but himself. The night she participated in an armed robbery where a man was shot.

A choked sob ripped from her throat.

"I'm sorry."

She turned and fled the scene of the crime.

Chapter One

She should change her outfit.

Maybe. Should she change it?

Again?

No. These clothes worked fine—tan linen slacks she'd purchased at a thrift store paired with a maroon button-up that still fit her from before. The outfit wouldn't make anyone look at her twice, but it was professional, clean, Florida-appropriate, and pressed, though a few years dated style-wise. Not that she knew anything about current fashion trends.

Bottom line, the outfit would do.

"No," she said aloud to her reflection in the mirror. "The skirt would have been better."

She turned and took two steps toward her closet, then shook her head.

"No. This is fine."

She spun to the mirror for another glance.

"No." She shook her head again. "It's boring. Too stuffy. Too old."

Another few steps toward her closet.

"No. Argh."

Back to the mirror.

Harper huffed in frustration. The woman staring back at

her wore a harried expression.

She had skin shades paler than *before*.

Hair shorter than *before*.

Eyes devoid of the youthful sparkle they'd twinkled with *before*.

And a mind full of doubt, nerves, and insecurities she'd never had *before*.

Everything in her life could be divided into two simple categories by a harsh line.

Before and after that night.

Harper sighed. "Get your shit together," she whispered to the mirror. She hated this wishy-washy self-doubting mess she'd become. Hopefully, time would shore up her backbone and give her some confidence. Though, what the hell did she have to feel confident about?

No job. No friends. No family. Nothing to feel pride about.

"It will come," she said to the mirror.

It has to come.

Since her release from prison five short days ago, she'd found herself exhausted by the constant stream of choices. There were huge, life-altering choices, such as what to do with her mother's mobile home and belongings, her mother's ashes, and should she attempt to locate her wayward father?

Options that kept her up at night, ruminating and obsessing.

Then there were the choices that should have been easy. And they would have been *before*—what to wear, what to eat, what to do with her hair, what soap to buy among the five hundred varieties at the drug store. Simple everyday selections she hadn't made for seven long years. And even then, she had barely hit adulthood or taken responsibility for her own life.

The prison had mandated societal reintegration classes for those with impending release dates. Workshops on job interviewing, banking, résumé writing, and financial management—basic life skills she and many of the other women should have gained the typical way but missed out on.

But no one had prepared her for the overwhelming task of choosing. Even the simplest choices she'd taken for granted *before* felt monumental today.

Earlier that morning, she'd spent twenty-five minutes standing in the cereal aisle trying to decide between Chocolate Cheerios or Honey Bunches of Oats. Ultimately, she'd purchased both, mixed them in her bowl, and cried after taking the first satisfying bite.

The overwhelming joy of freedom came at the most random times.

"You can do this," she whispered. "One minute at a time."

It'd been her mantra since taking her first step outside the prison.

Hell, sometimes even that felt too heavy, and she needed to take life one breath at a time.

The outfit was fine. Even if it wasn't, it beat prison orange a million times over.

"Time to go."

She had a job interview scheduled in twenty-five minutes and wanted to arrive early. After one final glance and nod of encouragement to her reflection, Harper grabbed her keys, locked the studio apartment she'd rented on top of a fabric shop, and headed down to the car she'd purchased with the meager money in her deceased mother's savings account. The vehicle was a hunk of junk manufactured years before she'd been arrested, but it worked to get her from point A to point B.

If she didn't crash, that was. Driving was another post-prison challenge she hadn't anticipated. She'd only been eighteen when she went to jail, so she hadn't had many years of driving experience. After seven years of never traveling in a car, she found herself tense beyond reason whenever she climbed behind the wheel.

Even though no one in this town knew her or her history, she felt like a spectacle as she walked to her car. The few people she passed didn't bother to glance her way, yet she still felt their stares of judgment and condemnation.

Look, there's that woman who served time.
What's she going to do now?
Does she think we don't know what she did?

Her internal guilt and fears were pushed to the surface.

Movement to her left caught her attention. She glanced toward the distraction, peering through the window of a tattoo shop next to the fabric shop she resided above. A heavily inked man sat hunched over a prone body, working away on an elaborate back tattoo. His client wore earbuds and closed his eyes as he endured the needle.

Maybe she should get some ink. Something to commemorate her freedom and a second chance at life. Something about starting over.

The thought had her chuckling. If she couldn't pick between breakfast cereals, how the hell would she decide what permanent mark to leave on her body?

She whirled from the shop and made her way to her car.

Fifteen minutes later, she went down a dirt driveway with a frown.

"Is this right?" she spoke aloud. The place looked more like a farm than a women's shelter.

"You will arrive at your destination in one thousand feet," the GPS announced in a monotone voice.

"Guess this is it," she mumbled, though not entirely convinced.

Sure enough, in about a thousand feet, she pulled up to a gorgeous farmhouse that appeared recently renovated.

A row of motorcycles lined up outside had her brow furrowing. This couldn't be right. What would all those bikes be doing outside a women's shelter? Maybe they provided some type of protection. Still, it seemed odd.

A large German Shepherd scampered around with what appeared to be a yellow lab and another one that looked like a lab mix.

Harper glanced down at the paper where she'd jotted the address. It matched what she'd entered into the GPS, so there was no mistake there. The online job advertisement clearly stated the open position for a counselor was at a women's shelter.

She might as well find out where she'd landed. Hopefully, whoever was inside could point her in the correct direction.

Nerves danced in her stomach as she opened the car door. Thick, steamy Florida air assaulted her, making her once again question her outfit choice. Short sleeves would have been wiser. Showing up with sweat stains wouldn't make the best first impression.

The door to the farmhouse opened, and a woman wearing jean cutoffs and a ribbed white tank top stepped outside. Her brown hair was high on her head in a messy bun, and flip-flops adorned her feet.

"Are you Harper?" she called out.

Upon hearing the woman's voice, the German Shepherd let out a joyful woof, then trotted toward her.

Harper schooled her features. "Yes, ma'am. I'm Harper." Her reply had all three dogs stopping in their tracks and then making a beeline for her.

Tension straightened her spine. Seven years of not being around an animal made her forget she used to love them and how to behave in their presence.

"They're insanely sweet and very friendly," the woman yelled out. "But I can call them back if you're not in the mood for slobber."

"No. It's okay." If she was going to work here, she had to make friends with everyone, even the four-legged creatures.

The yellow Lab reached her first. Harper held out a quivering hand. When all she received was a sniff and a lick, she blew out all the tension she hadn't realized she'd been carrying. The other two dogs treated her to the same inspection and affectionate lick. Each seemed to love ear scratches and chin rubs. Within seconds, the yellow lab was flopping onto her back, waiting for a vigorous belly rub. Hopefully, the woman who ran the shelter would be as easy to win over.

"Welcome. I'm Brooke."

Harper glanced up from the panting German Shepherd to find Brooke standing in front of her with a hand extended. "Nice to meet you, Brooke." She shook the offered hand.

"You too. From your expression, I can tell you're confused." Brooke gestured to the sprawling farm around them.

"Ah, yeah," Harper said. "A little. This place looks more like John Deere meets *Sons of Anarchy* than a safe haven for women."

Brooke burst out laughing. "Oh my God, that's perfect." She slapped a hand against her hip. "Seriously, perfect. I think I'm going to have to get the guys John Deere hats with a bike on them instead of a tractor. Shit, you're brilliant."

"Uh…" *The guys?*

With a wave of her hand, Brooke sobered. "Sorry, I'm not doing a good job of explaining anything, am I? Come walk with me, and I'll catch you up to speed on our situation."

Harper might not have much work experience beyond her years running the prison's library, but so far, this job interview wasn't anything like the ones she'd been coached on. Yet she had no plans to disrespect a potential boss, so she said "Sure" and fell in step beside Brooke, who was already walking.

"I suppose the job listing was a little misleading, and I apologize for that. There is still a lot of judgment out there regarding the Handlers, so I wasn't descriptive about the location."

"The Handlers?"

Brooke gazed at her from the corner of her eye. A wary expression crossed her face. "Yes. They're a motorcycle club, and they own this property. My ol' m—" she stopped, then continued with "… significant other is the president. That going to be a problem?" She'd lost the easygoing tone and sounded ready to defend her man by tossing Harper out on her ass if necessary.

One thing Harper had learned from her time behind bars was not to judge anyone. The stories she'd heard and the people she'd met taught her that lesson early on. No one was all good or all bad. Well, most people weren't. A few rotten apples were just born plain evil, but ninety-nine percent of the women she'd met while incarcerated had a story with two sides. Women who'd killed their abusers, sold drugs to feed their hungry children, or fell victim to the unfortunate circumstances of their life, forcing them to make impossible choices.

Harper vowed to reserve judgment until she got to know someone, and that courtesy would extend to this motorcycle club. "No. Not a problem."

"Great." Brooke's smile returned. "Olivia, my business partner, wanted to be here, but she had an appointment with our contractor. She might try to meet up with us later."

"Okay."

"I'm guessing you're wondering where the shelter is."

"It had crossed my mind."

Brooke chuckled. "We're in the construction phase right

now." As she spoke, a partially framed building came into view. Brooke stopped walking. "Ta-da! Welcome to what will be the Handling Life Shelter in three to six months if all goes according to plan."

Harper's heart sank. *Three to six months?* After renting an apartment, buying a car, and furnishing that apartment, she had a tiny amount of cash left but not enough to sustain her for six months. Selling her mother's mobile home would help, but seven years of neglect hadn't been kind to the place. Pennies were all it'd garner. She needed a paying job, and she needed it soon.

"Oh," she said. The word was tinged with disappointment. "So the job wouldn't be until then?"

"Actually, no," Brooke said with a smile. "Sorry, I should have led with that. We're looking for a counselor to start as soon as possible. We want someone to develop programs and assist in designing the facility so we can hit the ground running when construction is complete. We're really looking for someone to work with us through this whole planning phase."

Harper sucked in a breath. Now that sounded like a dream come true—developing her own program for women, and presumably children, in need of sanctuary, healing, and helping.

"What do you think?" Brook's eyes sparkled. The passion for her project shone through clearly.

Harper stared at the construction site, her wheels turning. If she got this job, she could give life to all the ideas she'd harbored since she started working toward her degree. Her dream was to run a program that helped women regain control of their lives after they'd been stolen from them. She wanted nothing more than to help other women realize their full potential and watch them spread their wings and fly.

It didn't take a licensed professional to understand why

this had become her mission. Too many women suffered under a patriarchal system without resources, guidance, or help. Some of the stories she'd heard in prison would forever haunt her nightmares. If she could help even a few find peace and happiness, she'd finally feel like her life was on the right track.

Peace and happiness. Two things she longed for.

"I think it sounds perfect," she said, trying not to sound breathless with excitement.

"Oh, great." Brooke clapped her hands three times. "I was worried no one would be interested once they learned we weren't up and running yet, and that the facility is on club property. By the way, we're adding an access road so we don't have to enter and exit through the club's entrance. I realize having a bunch of big-ass, grumpy bikers around isn't going to work for many of the women we'll serve. On a day-to-day basis, there won't be a reason for them to run across any of the guys."

"That's good," Harper said. "The most important thing will be making these women and children feel safe. Many of them will have deep-seated and very justified fears of men."

Brooke chewed her lip. "Yeah. I'd be lying if I said I wasn't worried about that. Do you think we're still too close to the clubhouse? We'll be putting a privacy fence around the entire back area so our clients can be outside without fear of being seen by anyone in the club."

Harper glanced over her shoulder. The clubhouse was visible in the distance but far enough away, in her opinion, that the women shouldn't feel threatened. "I think it's all right. The fence will be an enormous help. On the flip side, having the security of a bunch of bikers might be beneficial should someone's shitbag of an ex come slithering around." She slapped a hand over her mouth. "Sorry. That was unprofessional."

Brooke laughed. "You'll quickly learn no one stands on ceremony around here, and if you're not swearing, you're not talking. Besides, I fully agree with you."

Phew. Day to day, language wasn't exactly censored in prison. It'd take her a few weeks to break the colloquial swearing habit.

Like a bucket of icy water being dumped over her head, her past came to the forefront of her mind, making her trip over her feet. Thankfully, she self-corrected, and Brooke didn't seem to notice.

"Let's head over to that trailer," Brooke said, pointing to a white trailer next to the framed-out building. "It's been serving as our temporary office. It's air-conditioned, so we'll be more comfortable for the interview."

Harper swallowed. She had a huge hurdle to jump if she wanted this or any job, and she refused to sit through an entire uncomfortable interview, waiting to be rejected the moment an employer investigated her background. If Brooke didn't want her because of her time in prison, Harper needed to know immediately so she could tuck her tail between her legs and slink away now.

"Um… Brooke?"

"Yeah?" The woman faced her with that damn welcoming grin.

"Before we get into the nitty-gritty of the interview, there's something I have to tell you."

Brooke frowned. "Oh, okay. What is it?"

"Um…" She'd practiced in front of her mirror for hours yesterday. The words came easier with each trial, but now that the moment had come, she couldn't push them out. The last thing she wanted was to see Brooke's expression twist into disgust and distrust. But they couldn't stand there in awkward silence forever, so she took a breath, shored up her fleeting courage, and spoke while wringing her hands so hard her skin burned.

"Um... I, uh... wanted to let you know I spent the last seven years in prison for armed robbery. I served my full time and was released five days ago. That's where I got my degree and counseling certificate. In, um... prison, I mean."

The other woman's eyes flared, and she sucked in a breath. Those were the only visible indications she'd heard Harper's confession.

She was going to rub her hands raw at this point. "I just thought you should know now so I don't waste your time if that's a deal breaker."

"Hmm..." Brooke tilted her head. "Five days ago?"

Heart in her throat, she nodded. "Yes."

"Shit, hon, you must be seriously overwhelmed."

Brooke had no idea. "Um... yes, it's a little... daunting. And, look, I completely understand if this is too much for you."

"Armed robbery, you said?"

Harper swallowed with a wince. "Yes."

"Did you do it?"

"W-what?" Now her palms were sweaty, making her hands slip and slide on each other.

"Did you do it?" Brooke asked again.

Harper swallowed. "Yes." She flinched. "Well, kind of. Not by choice."

A small grin flickered across Brooke's lips, but it disappeared instantly. "Aah... there's a story there. A painful one, I bet."

She nodded. So painful.

"I have a story too, Harper." She extended her arm toward the farmhouse behind them. "Everyone here does. Some of them would give you nightmares. All the women we serve will have painful stories too."

They would. And some of their stories would break hearts.

"If you were looking for judgment and disapproval, you came to the wrong place. Someday, I'd love to hear your story, and maybe you'd want to listen to mine. Until that day, know that you are welcome here regardless of your past." She hummed a small chuckle. "Or maybe because of your past. Now, come on, let's head into the office and get to the boring part of the interview. Watch your step. The stairs are shit. Curly was supposed to fix them, but something came up last weekend."

She squeezed Harper's shoulder, then started for the trailer.

Harper couldn't move. She stood there, tears in her eyes, blinking at the partially constructed building that would become a beacon of hope for many women.

Brooke hadn't rejected her. In fact, she acted as though Harper's past could be an asset—a way to empathize and connect with the women they served.

Exactly why Harper worked so hard for her degree.

Today, that degree was a symbol of her renewed life.

With that thought, she spun around and hurried after Brooke.

Chapter Two

"Sup?" Jinx stuck his head into the prez's office. "You wanted me?" The big man sat behind his desk while his grinning sister sat across from him.

Half sister, actually.

That had been quite a surprise to the prez. A few months ago, Rachel appeared from nowhere, having learned of her relation to Curly after her mother's death. They had the same scumbag father who hadn't been a part of Rachel's life. Rachel's mother had been nothing more than a passing sweet butt to him.

She fit well with their group and had even started up with Frost, their newest patched member. But she had issues, especially surrounding large men, and at six foot six, Jinx was the largest, so he always tried to be careful not to spook her.

"Yeah," Curly said. "Need a favor if you've got time."

"Yeah, got all afternoon. I'm not working until tomorrow."

"Hey, Jinx," Rachel said with a shy smile.

"Hey, sweetie. How you doing? Frost treating you right?"

Her entire face lit up at the mention of her ol' man. "He is."

"Good. You let me know if he gets outta line. He might have patched in, but I'll still kick his ass for you."

Rachel laughed. "I'll keep that in mind. Thanks."

He loved making her laugh. She'd been petrified of him

when they met. Earning a laugh always felt like a victory in the mission to make her as comfortable around him as she was with the others.

He winked, then focused on the prez again. "So what do you need? Some cash?"

Rachel snorted, and Curly rolled his eyes. Thanks to his wrongful imprisonment suit, everyone knew Curly had more money than God. "Need some help with the ol' lady? Date ideas?"

"Got it covered, thanks."

Jinx cupped a hand around his mouth and stage-whispered, "Sex tips? You are getting close to fifty, man. No shame in needing a blue pill every now and then to keep your woman happy."

A strangled noise came from Rachel while Curly seared him with a death look. "Worry about your own dick. Mine's fine."

"Oooh..." Jinx ducked like he was dodging a punch. "Nice shot. But my dick is primo, my friends. In fact, I call him—"

"I just need you to take this fucking box to Brooke for me." Curly scowled as he pointed to a box on the edge of his desk. It wasn't big, about the size of a large shoebox.

"Oh. Well, that's boring. Sure you don't want my secret to making the ladies scream my name. Promise you'll thank me later."

Rachel burst out laughing. "You are ridiculous," she said, shaking her head.

He winked, loving the way her cheeks turned pink. Prez's sister was fun to play with. Frost would probably rip him a new one later for flirting with his woman, but it was harmless. Rachel only had eyes for the chilly bastard and was far too fragile for the likes of Jinx. He liked women itching for a hard fuck and no repeats. Rachel's past made it so she'd never want a man like him, and he'd never want anything more than friendship from her.

"For fuck's sake, just take the damn box," Curly muttered.

Jinx shot him a grin. "Where's the ol' lady?"

"She's out at the She Shed, interviewing a potential hire." The guys had come to call the future shelter the She Shed after Jinx had jokingly accused the ladies of wanting their own version of a clubhouse. Of course, it was all in good fun. He loved Brooke, Olivia, and Jo for their desire to help women who'd been through similar traumas as they'd suffered.

He was just the asshole who liked to tease everyone. Ragging on his family was his love language.

"Easy day," he said as he grabbed the box. He'd expected to pick it up with ease and faltered when the thing required more muscle than he'd planned. "Holy shit. This is fucking heavy. What the hell's in this thing? Bricks?"

Rachel snickered, and Curly snorted. "Basically. It's full of tile samples the ladies picked out for the She Shed."

"Fuck. You really gonna make me lug this monster halfway across the farm?"

"You can take the ATV if it's too much for you. I just assumed it'd be nothing for a big guy like you."

"Yeah, yeah, yeah." He hefted the box under one arm. It wasn't that bad. The surprise of its weight had gotten to him more than the actual mass. "Rachel, you have a lovely day. Prez, hope there's an alligator in your pool when you get home." He flipped off a laughing Curly, then blew Rachel a kiss before lugging the damn box out of the office.

His long legs ate up the distance to the She Shed, making the multiple-acre trip pass by in a blink. Though quite warm, the weather hadn't heated to summertime scorching, and the humidity wasn't quite drenching. That would all change in a few weeks, but for now, he enjoyed the milder days and comfortable nights. Soon, he'd be sweating his ass off at all hours of the day.

"Knock, knock," he called out as he reached the trailer.

He hopped onto the tiny landing, skipping the three steps to the door. The damn things were rickety as fuck and made him feel like a damn moose. They barely held his weight. His brothers would never let him live it down if he crashed through them.

Without waiting for Brooke to admit him, he opened the door and stuck his head inside. "Special delivery for one Miss Brooke."

Two heads swiveled in his direction. One easily recognizable as Brooke's and another a brown so chocolatey he salivated.

Yum.

"Well, hello there." He strode into the building.

Brooke grinned. "Those my tile samples?"

He nodded. "Where do you want them?"

"Hmm… is the box heavy?"

With a grunt, he lifted it over his head, making sure to pop his biceps. "Do the ladies love me?"

Brooke rolled her eyes.

"Yeah, it's fucking heavy. You order tiles made of lead?"

She pointed to a spot on the floor. "Just set it there, please. And no, I didn't. But I did order about fifty samples. I couldn't narrow it down."

"That's great," he said as he set down the box, then shook out his tired arms. "But there are more important things to talk about." He straightened, pasted on his most panty-dropping smile, and sauntered toward the desk where the two ladies sat. "Such as who are you and do you like men with big—"

"Jinx." Brooke held up a hand. "Can you maybe not get me slapped with a sexual harassment suit before I even hire someone?"

"What?" he asked with as innocent a shrug as he could muster. "Personalities. I was going to say personalities. Don't know what you were thinking, but get your mind out of the gutter, woman."

"Of course," Brooke said with a sigh. "*I'm* the problem. Jinx, this is Harper. She's interviewing, and very well, I might add, to be our counselor. Harper, this is Jinx. Don't believe a word he tells you. He's never serious and comes on to any female with a pulse. That includes the dogs."

"Hey, what the hell? You're making me sound like a player."

Brooke cocked her head but didn't say anything.

"Oh, you're mean, woman." He turned to Harper. "I am a damn fine catch." He winked, then held out a hand. "Nice to meet you, Harper."

Now that he could get a good look at her, he clenched his teeth to keep his tongue from lolling out. The woman was pretty as hell, with shoulder length, dark brown hair, pale skin that would darken quickly in the Florida sun, and those milk-chocolate eyes. Then there were her unpainted lips—pink, plush, and perfect.

"Nice to meet you too, uh... Jinx?" she said, but it came out as more of a question.

"Road name."

Her nose wrinkled in confusion.

"It's a club nickname," Brooke clarified. "He's superstitious. Hates the number thirteen. Freaks out when he sees a black cat, that kind of thing. Hence the name Jinx."

What the hell? Give away all my secrets, why don't you?

"Ooh... gotcha." Harper gave him a polite smile, then placed her hand in his. Electricity shot from her soft palm into his and straight up his arm. He couldn't help but suck in a harsh breath before releasing her. It was either that or yank her against him and see if those lips tasted as good as they looked. Brooke would skin him alive if he did that.

The only indication that she felt any spark was the quick flare of her pupils. She covered it by turning to Brooke. "Any other questions for me?"

"No, I think we've covered everything. I'm going to chat with my partners, and we'll get a hold of you within the next few days if that works."

Harper nodded. Though her attention was on Brooke, Jinx couldn't tear his eyes away from the soft line of her jaw as her head moved up and down. Damn, he'd like to take a bite. Just a little nip right below her ear. Would she like that? Did she appreciate a little roughness with her fucking? He sure as hell did, which was part of the reason he went for softer women with curves and some thickness. Made it easier to let himself go without worrying about hurting them.

From what he could see, Harper was much more slender than his normal type but not scrawny. Maybe more of an athletic build, like she spent time in the gym. If he was lucky, he could manage to stick around until she stood up so he could get the full picture for his spank bank.

"Do you have any questions for me?" Brooke asked.

They acted as though he wasn't there, so he saw himself outside to wait for Harper to emerge.

Ray, Brooke's German Shepherd and most loyal protector, bounded up to him with a tennis ball lodged firmly between his teeth. "You wanna play, buddy? Okay, drop it."

The ball landed at Jinx's feet.

"What a good boy." He picked up the ball and sent it sailing across the wide-open farmland.

Ray shot off after it and was back in seconds. This time, Jinx didn't need to ask for the hound to drop the ball—it landed with a small bounce. The big dog sat panting, and, Jinx would swear, smiling in gratitude. "You love this, don't you?" he asked as he threw the ball again.

An uncomfortable catch in his shoulder took him back a decade and a half to his high school days. Damn, he'd thought he was hot shit back then—captain of the baseball team, cute cheerleader girlfriend, and scouts watching him at every game. He ate, slept, and breathed baseball when he wasn't banging Jenna. With his dream of playing pro growing more of a reality each day, he'd been on top of the damn world.

Sucked for him that life had other plans.

Dream-crushing, soul-destroying, life-ruining plans.

Shit. He cracked his neck as Ray skidded to a stop in front of him. It'd been a while since he'd fallen down the trap door of his past. What the hell was the point? The car accident changed everything. Every single aspect of his life changed that night, and once he'd worked through the worst of the grief and loss, he'd vowed to leave that event where it belonged.

Far behind him.

He had a good fucking life he loved and a family he'd die for. He'd kill for them too. No point in dwelling on what used to be.

The ball left his hand for the third time as the trailer door opened. A quick peek over his shoulder revealed Harper. She closed her eyes and inhaled a deep breath with a slight smile on her plump lips, then blew it out long and slow, probably ridding herself of any lingering interview nerves.

She hadn't noticed him, so he took a moment to study her. As expected, she didn't have the lush curves he typically preferred, but his dick didn't care. It twitched as she lifted her arms overhead in a tension-relieving stretch. Truth be told, her baggy pants and business-fitting top didn't let him get a good view of her figure, but something told him she was strong under those clothes. Maybe it was the way she carried herself, but he'd bet money she was fit as a fucking trainer.

It could be some damn good fun to spend a few sweaty hours with a buff chick. Sure, she'd never come close to his strength. He was six foot six, and two hundred seventy pounds of solid muscles. Lugging tires at work, combined with hours he spent lifting weights in the gym, saw to that. But he bet Harper had some damn good stamina and strength for long, sweaty, pleasurable nights.

Lucky for him, he had a leg up on his brothers as the first to meet her.

"Interview go well?"

She jumped about a mile and let out a little yip. "Oh, shit. You scared me." With her hand pressed to her heart, she glared at him.

He lifted his arms in surrender. "Sorry, sweetie. Wasn't my intention."

"Sweetie?" She rolled her eyes, making him laugh.

So, she was one of those women who didn't like pet names from random men. Who could blame her?

"Meant no offense, ma'am," he said, tipping an imaginary hat.

She didn't laugh, but her lips twitched.

"The interview went really well, thank you." She took two steps forward before he rushed over.

"Careful. Those steps are shit. Give me your hand, and I'll help you down."

Instead of reaching for him, she shook her head. "I got it."

"Not trying to be fresh." He kept his arm extended, but she still refused to take it. "Seriously, they're so unstable that I just jump over them."

"I got it," she said again.

"I don't bite."

"I. Got. It." She white-knuckled the railing as she descended the three wobbly steps. "See?" she said with a smirk once on solid ground.

Huh. So serious. Independent.

"I do see. My apologies for doubting you."

Again, no laugh. Not even a grin. Maybe he was losing his touch. Or maybe she didn't like giant tattooed bikers with in-your-face personalities.

Nah, that couldn't be it.

All women loved him.

He wasn't deterred. "Let me walk you to your car. Never know who you'll run into along the way."

She pursed her lips and looked over her shoulder toward the clubhouse. "There's literally an empty field between me and my car. I think I'll be okay." With that, she started across the field. After about five steps, she turned. "But thank you for the offer," she said as she walked backward. "It was kind of you."

Kind.

He almost laughed out loud, but then she turned again, affording him a good look at her ass. He swallowed his tongue.

Hot damn, that thing was made for squeezing. Firm, high, and round as fuck. The woman must do two hundred squats a day to get a booty like that. *Dayum.* He wanted a bite. Maybe two. Hell, he'd like to devour that whole peach.

What a fun development in his life.

Here's what he knew about Harper so far—she was uptight, serious, and didn't seem to want a lick of attention from him.

He grinned.

Challenge accepted.

Chapter Three

How could a day that started on a high end in such an infuriating disaster?

Harper scowled at her flattened tire as though her annoyance could magically patch the hole and reinflate the tube.

Running over a nail. That's how a day could turn to shit in the blink of an eye.

She'd woken at six thirty, worked out for an hour, meditated for ten minutes, guzzled coffee, and polished off her new favorite mixed-cereal breakfast just as the phone rang. It'd been three days since her interview with Brooke, who'd called with an official job offer. Harper managed to keep her squeal of delight inside until they arranged a time to meet, fill out paperwork, and introduce her to Brook's two business partners. As soon as she hung up, she let out a joyful whoop and spent the next ten minutes dancing around the apartment like a loon.

Because she could.

Because she was alone.

Because there weren't any guards to tell her to shut up or inmates to heckle her.

She had true privacy for the first time in ages. It was the most incredible feeling in the world, even if it did come with a hearty side of loneliness.

So far, she'd successfully shoved those feelings of isolation aside and focused on the excitement of autonomy and space.

The news had called for a celebration. Since she had no one to celebrate with and only pennies to spare, taking herself for ice cream would have to do. Ever since she'd been a child, ice cream had been her weakness. She'd never admit to a soul how much she'd consumed in the week since her release from prison. The staff at her new favorite ice cream shop already knew her face and favorite flavor.

At least she'd managed to scarf her chocolate peanut butter fudge sundae before a three-inch piece of sharp metal ruined her day.

"Okay," she said to her phone as she opened the search engine. "How to change a tire." Her fingers crawled over the keyboard. The teenager she'd seen in the ice cream shop texted faster than she could think, but with this being the first phone she'd owned in a long time, she was slow as hell to learn the new technology.

Sure enough, YouTube had thousands of videos on DIY tire changing. "Let's try you with your seven million views," she said as she tapped on the screen.

Calling a tow truck would be divine, but it'd suck her account dry. As it was, getting the tire patched would run her more than she could spare.

She watched the five-minute-and-sixteen-second video three times before getting to work. In the end, she succeeded in removing the busted tire and securing the donut, but it took thirty-six minutes, and by the time she finished, sweat drenched her clothing.

"Ugh," she complained as she pinched a chunk of fabric and peeled it away from her stomach. It slapped back against her skin with a wet *sploosh* when she let go. "Gross. Damn Florida heat."

With a tired sigh, she tossed the tire iron, jack, and deflated tire in the trunk before getting behind the wheel. After googling the nearest tire shop, she set on her way.

"Hell yeah," she said with a satisfied grin as she pulled into the parking lot. "The donut stayed in place." Part of her had been convinced the thing would pop off as soon as she got on the road.

A loud rumble had her peering over her shoulder as she stepped out of the car. She watched as a noisy-as-hell motorcycle coasted into the lot and stopped in a spot near the side of the building. The man astride the bike was huge with muscular tattooed arms and a leather vest. His face couldn't be seen behind a full-face helmet, but something about his size and stature reminded her of…

"Oh shit," she breathed out.

The hulk pulled off his helmet, revealing he was, in fact, Jinx. The enormous biker she'd met a few days ago in Brooke's office.

Harper swallowed as her throat went dry. The man was like no other she'd ever seen, and that wasn't only because she had spent the last seven years surrounded by women. The universe didn't make many men like him. It couldn't possibly subsist if millions of Jinx's were running around. Women everywhere would stop doing anything productive in favor of following them with their tongues hanging out.

He was that damn sexy with his shaggy blond hair that was messy enough to be roguish but not so much that he seemed sloppy. The muscles required no explanation—those babies spoke for themselves—but the mischief in his eyes had her stomach flipping. Like he knew he was trouble and loved it.

And if she wasn't mistaken—which could be due to less than zero experience—he'd flirted with her the other day. Her heart had raced so hard as she walked away from him she worried she might collapse in the field. Thankfully, she'd made it, but what the hell did a man like him see in her?

She sure hadn't flirted back, nor did she give off some kind of subconscious *come-hither* vibe. She knew less than nothing about sex and men. At eighteen, she'd slept with her boyfriend a handful of times, which was the entirety of her experience with men. It'd been so long since anyone had touched her or even glanced at her with desire that she didn't know what to do with it. After so many years of going without touch, privacy, or romantic human contact, she'd let that side of herself go dormant. Within days, Jinx was awakening a primal need she'd forsaken. As much as it excited her, it terrified her.

According to Brooke, Jinx was the type of man who flirted with anyone and everyone. That information helped some to quell her anxiety. Writing it off as just something he did took the pressure off her. If she was going to be working on the MC's property every day, she couldn't have a man chasing her. No matter how her stomach flipped at the sight of him or her long-neglected nether regions sparked to life, that was a complication she couldn't afford.

It was too much on top of trying to build a life from nothing. If the attraction became distracting, she'd buy a vibrator and deal with it herself. Maybe she should get one anyway now that she had the privacy and solitude to explore.

For now, the plan was to focus on herself.

And someday, she'd admit to and deal with the mountain of trust issues she had from being screwed over by the only man she'd ever been with. Unfortunately, denial would have to do for the foreseeable future.

Jinx climbed off his bike and rested his helmet on the seat. As he turned her way, her cheeks heated.

Crap. How long had she stood staring at the man like he was one of her favorite sundaes?

Too long.

Harper lifted a hand in an awkward greeting—something to salvage the moment—then turned to her trunk again. As she popped it, she could feel his substantial presence coming closer. Her pulse fluttered, and she froze.

Go inside. Go inside. Go inside.

"Need a hand?"

Dammit. He didn't go inside.

"Ah... no thanks. I got it." She reached into the trunk and hefted out the tire. The thing was more awkward than heavy, and she'd love to let the mammoth of a man carry it, but she didn't need him to.

She'd do it herself.

He leaned his very nice ass against her car and folded those inked arms across his chest as he watched her struggle with the tire. "You sure? It's heavier than you'd think."

"I'm sure. I got it."

"Last chance," he offered, dark eyes sparkling.

Harper resisted the urge to growl at him. "I took the damn thing off myself. I can manage to carry it inside, where I'm sure a very nice attendant will help me out. You are free to go about your business, but thank you for your concern."

His lips quirked. "All right. I'll walk with you."

She faltered. What the hell were they supposed to talk about in the forty-five seconds it would take to walk into the building? She had no clue how to talk to a man like him. She had no clue how to talk to any man.

His presence was so huge that even without speaking, he sucked in all the air from the atmosphere. Not to mention, Harper's insane reaction to him transported her back nearly a decade to a time when she was a teenager crushing on the hottest boy in school. The boy who fucked up her life and landed her in jail.

"Thinking hard over there."

She glanced up at him. "Huh?"

"I can practically hear your gears grinding."

"Oh, uh…" She'd die before admitting her thoughts to him. "Just trying to figure out the rest of my day. This messed me up."

"Need a ride somewhere while your tire gets fixed?"

"Oh, uh… no. I got it." Prolong this torture by getting on a death machine with him? Hell no.

He grunted.

By the time they reached the door, her arms burned, and she probably had a bruise on her thigh from where the tired banged her leg with every step. But she'd rather lose the leg than confess she couldn't handle it. She could handle anything.

Changing a tire.

Living alone.

Reintegration after prison.

She slowed to allow him to go first and get the door, but only because her hands were full, and it'd be plain stupid to set the tire down, open the door, then make an ass of herself wrestling the thing into the shop.

Instead of getting the door as she'd expected, he stopped next to her. Harper frowned and risked a glance up at him. Was he going to make her ask?

He arched an eyebrow. "Figure if I offer to hold the door for you, you'll just say, 'I got it.' Seems to be your favorite phrase."

*Touché. Snarky bastard. Now s*he was forced to ask for his help or make a fool of herself trying to open the door while juggling the damn tire.

She bristled for a moment, then sighed. "Jinx, would you please open the door for me?"

His victorious grin drove her up a wall.

"Of course. After you, darlin'."

Darlin'. She was no one's darlin'. Never again. *Damn backstabbing men.*

"Thank you," she said through clenched teeth.

He followed her into the tire shop. The scent of rubber and motor oil flooded her nose, as she would expect of an automotive business. Jinx strode past her with long, sure steps, then rounded the counter.

She frowned as she watched him take off his motorcycle vest, stash it under the counter, then straighten. His T-shirt bore the logo displayed on the sign for the shop. "Wait…"

He typed a few keystrokes into a computer, then glanced up at her. "Morning, ma'am. Welcome to Ty's Tires. Looks like you got a busted one there. You wanting to patch it or replace it?"

If he was trying to hide his smirk, he was doing a terrible job. "You work here?"

"I do. Ever since it opened. Ten years and running. The owner, Ty, is a member of my club. I'm the second in command. So, you see, while you were busy thinking I was a big ol' sexist who thought a woman couldn't carry a tire, I was really demonstrating the stellar customer service our company prides itself on."

His smile stretched so wide it nearly reached his tanned ears.

Ugh, why did he have to look so *yummy*? It flustered her, and she had no idea how to handle being flustered by a man, especially one laughing at her expense, so she fell back on the safe and comfortable. The steely backbone she'd formed over the years was unbreakable. If it kept her going through prison, it could push her through anything. "I'd have turned you down either way. As you saw, I'm perfectly capable of taking care of myself."

He chuckled while shaking his head. "Anyone ever told you you're a bit prickly?"

Her heart sank.

Before, she'd never been described as prickly.

Before, she'd been warm, open, outgoing, and fun, even if on the awkward side.

But *before,* she'd also been a naïve child. She was now a grown woman who'd never fall prey to a smooth-talking man again. "Look, I just need my tire fixed."

With a grunt, he lifted the tire from the counter. Of course, he made the damn thing look as light as a box of tissues. "So, you'd rather us patch it?"

Well, no, she'd rather get a new tire. But a random hundred or so dollars wasn't in the budget. "Yes. If it's possible."

"Tell you what." He swung the tire up to his shoulder. "Can't have you missing days at your new job because your tire's shitty. I'll throw in a new one for the price of a patch. Whatdya say?"

She blinked. "Why would you do that?" What was the catch? Was he about to ask for a favor, sexual or otherwise? Would he want to collect sometime down the line? She was bound to run into him occasionally, working on the MC's property. Would he hold this over her head until he needed something from her?

"Consider it congrats on the job. Or a welcome to the family." He shrugged. "Take your pick."

Why would he... "I don't understand. Is there something you want from me?"

"For fuck's sake. You always this suspicious? You're like a damn cactus. Just say 'Thank you, Jinx' and take the damn tire. Promise I won't be asking for your firstborn in return. Contrary to what you seem to think, I'm not an asshole."

That remained to be seen. In Harper's experience, most people had a healthy dose of asshole in them. Then again, she hadn't exactly spent the last few years with society's poster children for perfection.

"Uh, okay. Then, thank you, I guess."

Chuckling, he slung the tire on the top of a pile. "So, when's your first day?"

"I start Monday. But I was supposed to stop by to complete some paperwork this afternoon."

He returned to the computer and was typing when a second man emerged from what she assumed was the garage area. "Hey, Jinx, didn't realize you'd gotten in."

"Just taking care of this lovely customer. Harper, this is Ty, the owner."

She lifted a hand in greeting. The man was older than Jinx by maybe twenty years or so, probably in his mid-forties. If she had to guess, she'd say Jinx was around the same as her—mid-twenties.

"Hey, hon," Ty said with a welcoming smile. "Jinx'll take good care of you." Then with a wave, he disappeared through the door again.

"I'll get a guy on this immediately so you can get out to see Brooke. You good to wait?"

"Yeah, sure." She had no way to get anywhere else.

"All right. Have a seat, grab some coffee, imitate a cactus, and we'll have you out of here in no time."

She tilted her head. "A cactus?"

"Yeah, all prickly and shit." He winked and strode through the door Ty had gone through.

A cactus?

He nailed her personality on the first try. Despite her distrust of this situation and the giant, sexy man, Harper couldn't stop a burst of laughter.

She froze in the center of the tire shop.

Damn, that laugh felt good. It was also the first genuine one since she'd been released from prison.

And it happened because a sexy biker teased her.

Ridiculous.

But as she sat to wait for her car, she found herself smiling and wondering if Jinx would be the one to ring her up at the end.

Chapter Four

"We've got a problem," Curly said as he sat at the head of the gorgeous hand-carved table his sister gifted the club at Christmas. "Actually, two problems."

Well, shit, so much for the good day he'd been having. He'd woken at six, hit the gym, then clocked in for work, where he'd gotten to see the thorny yet intriguing Miss Harper. For some reason, her neon flashing *fuck- off* sign only drew him more to her. Didn't hurt that she was hot as fuck.

He'd been right about her being fit as hell. Those arm muscles she'd been rocking in her tank top had him struggling to keep his dick in line. Never before had he found himself so attracted to a woman. It wasn't only her looks that got to him, but her standoffish personality also intrigued him. Discovering if he could knock down her walls and land in her bed would be a fun challenge.

One he didn't plan to fail at.

"What's up, Prez?" Scott asked with a frown. As the club's enforcer, he tended to be the first to sniff out signs of trouble.

The prez's curly hair had grown past shoulder length, and he pulled it up into a stellar man bun as he spoke. "First problem is internal and hopefully fixable."

"Lock," Pulse said in his customary softer voice.

Curly nodded. "Lock. He's fucking spiraling. He missed

church the last few times, he's apparently flaking on clients, and he looks worn-out as fuck."

A few months ago, Lock's sister had died of an overdose while eight months pregnant. Being her only family, he'd retained custody of the infant, but what the fuck did Lock or any of them, know about raising a kid? Add the grief the man suffered from losing his sister, and it was no wonder the guy was a mess.

Jinx didn't have any siblings to leave him a surprise child, not anymore, but he'd slept with more than his fair share of women. He was twenty-five, good with his dick, big, and in a motorcycle club. He couldn't throw a stick without hitting a few ready and willing women.

Just how he liked it.

But he *always* wrapped his shit up. Ever since Lock became an overnight insta-dad, Jinx had been gun-shy when it came to getting his dick wet. Lock's life went from good to shit in the blink of an eye. Jinx didn't know what he'd do if a woman he'd banged showed up with his baby cooking in her belly. The fear was enough to keep him celibate for almost two months, which was unheard of for him.

He shuddered. Just the thought of all that responsibility had him sweating.

"So, how do we help him?" Tracker asked. "I know fuck all about kids."

"Same here," Ty added. He shivered. "I don't even like 'em."

Jinx grinned. He might be deathly afraid of ending up responsible for one, but he liked the little buggers. Kids were fun. They were loud, messy, and didn't give two shits about anything beyond their toys and snacks. What wasn't to like? He could hang as long as he could give them back at the end of the day. "I'll get in touch with him before I head home. See what he needs from us."

With a nod, Curly added, "The ladies have been helping him out as much as he'll let them. He's been cagy about them going to his place, but I think they're working on a schedule to help him with babysitting so he can work and get some rest."

"I suck with kids, but I'm happy to help any other way," Ty said as he lifted a beer to his lips. "I'll take him out, get him laid."

Spec laughed. "Seriously, has the poor bastard gotten any ass since he became Daddy Lock?"

"That how you romance your woman?" Jinx asked with a laugh. "Yo, Liv, give me some ass."

Spec flipped him off. "Hell no. Don't gotta. My ol' lady can't keep her hands off my shit. But you can borrow the line. Ain't seen you with a woman in a hot minute."

"Ain't seen you with a woman in a hot minute," Jinx mocked in a childish voice.

"Ooh... gonna need some aloe for that burn." Spec smirked. "I think the lack of sex is fucking with your sense of humor. You used to be funny."

"You know what will be funny?" Jinx asked. "When I tell Liv you used her fancy-ass, expensive-as-fuck towels to wipe your hands after you changed the oil in your bike."

Spec paled. "You wouldn't."

"In a heartbeat," Jinx said. He leaned back in his chair and folded his arms across his chest as he smirked.

Game. Set. Match.

"All right, guys. Can we get to the next order of business?"

Poor Curly. Jinx didn't envy him having to wrangle this group of undomesticated animals.

He blew Spec a kiss, earning another one-fingered salute. "Okay, boss, what's our next hurdle?"

Curly flicked a glance toward Tracker, who nodded. The small move made Jinx's stomach turn. Whatever they were about to say, it'd suck for sure.

"Shit," Spec mumbled. "Something's wrong."

"Tracker's shop was vandalized last night."

That had Jinx's spine straightening. "What do you mean, vandalized?"

"Someone threw a brick through the front window," Curly said.

"Shit." Spec jumped up from his chair. "Why the fuck didn't you call me?" he asked, glaring at Tracker.

"Simmer, Spec." Curly held up a hand.

"There was no reason to call you right when it happened," Tracker spoke directly to the hot-headed enforcer. "I didn't catch anyone in the act. My security system alerted me around three in the morning, and Jo and I drove right over. We cleaned up the glass and boarded the window, and I got a guy coming later today to measure for a replacement. There wasn't any point in waking everyone up at the ass crack of dawn."

"Okay, sounds like some stupid kids. Maybe customers who didn't listen to their tattoo aftercare and got an infection, and they now want to blame it on you. Is it more than that? What am I missing?" Jinx's attention shifted between Tracker and Curly, who seemed to be communicating with their eyes. Their little back and forth did nothing to kill his anxiety.

"This." Tracker tossed a picture onto the table.

Gut swirling, Jinx was the first to grab it. "Fuck," he said on an exhale as he scanned the picture. Brooke, Live, Jo, and Rachel sat in a circle on the sand at the beach. Their carefree smiles let Jinx know the ladies had no idea they'd been photographed.

Stalked.

"Lobo?" he asked as he lifted his head and passed the picture to Spec.

No surprise. The enforcer's reaction was swift, loud, and

violent.

"Motherfucker," he shouted as he hopped to his feet again. "Is this fucking Lobo?" Fiery anger shot from his eyes, and his ears nearly smoked.

Jinx understood the fury and didn't even have a woman being threatened.

"Turn it over," Curly ordered.

Spec flipped the photo as Jinx leaned over to see better. Sure enough, a rough sketch of a wolf marked the back of the picture.

"God-fucking-dammit," Spec yelled.

"He's back," Jinx stated the obvious, but his mind raced with the implications instead of measuring his words.

Lobo was a low-level drug runner who'd hit the big-time recruiting members of Curly's former MC to his side. He'd been the president of a different club back in the day. A nasty organization that ran drugs, guns, women, basically anything that would earn them a buck. Loyalty ran thin among Curly's former brothers, which played a big part in his landing in prison for a crime he didn't commit.

After the state overturned his conviction and released him, Curly returned to his hometown in Florida to start a chapter of the Hell's Handlers MC. He'd steered clear of men from his past due to their involvement in his wrongful arrest and the ruthless and often brutal way his former club had been run. He'd wanted a fresh start with a new brotherhood. Like most of them, Curly would never completely dance on the right side of the law, but he wasn't a monster and lived by a strict outlaw code.

As a younger man, he hadn't cared who he stomped on to grab a slice of power. His views changed after thirteen years behind bars for a crime he didn't commit. One that he'd been framed for by the police with the help of some of his former clubs. Once he'd returned with a fat wallet from a wrongful imprisonment settlement, his old club brothers came sniffing around for a piece of the pie. They hadn't taken the rejection well when he'd turned them down.

Lobo, the piece of shit that he was, capitalized on their fury and hatred of Curly. He'd formed his own band of merry assholes who profited from dealing fentanyl-laced drugs all over town.

The same drugs responsible for the death of Lock's sister.

About eight months ago, the MC burned down Lobo's factory. They hadn't heard a peep from the wolf since that day. All signs indicated he'd slunk with his tail between his legs to lick his wounds somewhere else.

Until today.

"He's back," Curly repeated with a nod.

"Do we know if he resumed his meth operation?" Jinx asked.

"I haven't heard anything from my sources, but I haven't checked in as often lately." Spec prowled back and forth behind the table, agitation rolling off him in waves. He'd be itching to fuck up the wolf.

Jinx understood the feeling, and he wasn't half the violent fucker Spec was. "Think he has the resources to fuck with us beyond annoying pranks?" he asked as he pointed to the photo lying on the table.

"Don't know." Curly blew out a breath. "Not willing to risk it, though. We need to make sure the women are protected.

"Good luck with that," Pulse muttered.

Jinx snorted. "Can I be there when you tell them you're locking them down?"

Tracker flipped him off. "We could put you on babysitting duty? Have *you* follow them around twenty-four-seven until we get this shit sorted."

"Fuck that. I'm better served on the street digging up

information." Jinx shoved a sleeve up to his shoulder and flexed his hard-earned bicep. "All I gotta do is show 'em my guns. The ladies start drooling, and the men shit themselves in fear. Either way, they'll tell me whatever I want to know." He kissed his upper arm with a dramatic flair.

Tracker turned to Pulse, their resident trauma nurse. "What do we need to do to get him held on a seventy-two-hour psychiatric hold?"

"I don't think it'll be too hard. He's suffering from some pretty major delusions right now." Pulse rubbed his chin as though considering his options.

"Whatever," Jinx said. "All you scrawny fuckers are just jealous." Not a single man in the club qualified as scrawny. Even Tracker, who was the leanest, was packed with muscle. He just didn't put on the bulk that Jinx did. Though Jinx worked out, he couldn't take full credit for his enormous size. He was born big and sprouted muscles like it was his job.

Got to love genetics. His asshole father was just as big.

And ten times as mean. Damn, those fists could leave a mark.

"Reign it in, guys." Curly's words broke Jinx from a past he never allowed himself to return to. He mustn't have had enough sleep the night before.

"For now, stay vigilant at home and in your businesses. Make sure your security is functioning. Keep your eyes peeled and ears to the ground. I'll work out a schedule with the ladies and make sure they understand how important this is. Might call upon you guys to help escort them occasionally."

"Anything you need, brother," Ty said.

"Same," Jinx added.

The rest of the guys muttered their agreement.

"Good. Anything else?" Curly asked. He stood, planting his palms on the table. "If not, then... oh wait, almost forgot.

Brooke hired a counselor to work with the ladies out at the She Shed. She'll be starting right away. I think a few of you have already met her, but those of you who haven't, her name is Harper. You'll be seeing her around. She's extended family, so she gets treated the same as any of the ol' ladies." He narrowed his eyes. "Get me?"

Jinx lifted his hands and bit off his chuckle. "Why you looking at me, Prez?"

"Cuz you're the most likely to try and fuck her," Tracker said with a grunt.

"She does look quite tasty." Jinx licked his lips and rubbed his hands together. Quite tasty, indeed. In fact, he'd imagined getting a sample last night while stroking himself to completion.

Then again in the shower after his workout.

"No free samples." Curly pointed at him. "Brooke loves her, and she'll murder you in your sleep if you fuck this up for her because you can't control your dick."

"Ha ha." Spec pointed to him. "He's got your number."

"Screw you all." Jinx stood and did a sensual body roll, running his hands down his torso as he gyrated. "It's not my fault that women can't resist all this."

Ty snorted. "From what I saw the other day, she had no problem resisting your giant ass."

Spec rested his elbows on the table. "Ooh... do tell."

"She came in for a tire yesterday. Romeo here was laying it on thick. Harper might as well have been made of rubber with how hard his cheesy lines bounced off her. His dick won't be getting anything from her."

"What the hell?" Jinx stumbled back with a hand over his heart. "I thought you guys were my brothers." He moved his hand downward, covering his crotch. "It's okay, Conny. Don't listen to them. We'll get you a nice warm pussy real soon."

"Conny?" Frost said around a grunt of laughter. "You call

your dick Conny?"

"Sure do. Short for Anaconda." He winked and gave his cock a jiggle.

"Get the fuck outta here with that shit." Frost mimed vomiting.

Something pinged off the side of Jinx's head. He glanced down to find one of Spec's favorite protein bars lying on the table. "Thanks, man." He ripped it open and took a giant bite. The thing tasted like chocolate-flavored cardboard.

"Hey, I was gonna eat that before I worked out."

"Too bad. Later, assholes." Jinx forced the dry-as-hell bite down his throat as he waved.

They all yelled and tossed things at him as he walked out of the room laughing.

Christ, he loved those guys.

Hopefully, the trouble with Lobo fizzled out into nothing serious. They'd been through a lot in the short time the club had been together. A few years of peace would hit the spot.

On the other hand, if things became too stressful, he had the perfect image in his head to call up anytime he needed it.

Chapter Five

"Okay, that's it. I can't take it anymore." Olivia shoved away from her desk and rubbed circles on her temples. "If I have to listen to this construction for another minute, I will lose my mind. We've been here since nine. What do you say we call it a day, ladies?"

"Sounds good to me," Brooke added while Jo nodded and shut her laptop. "I'll still be hearing hammering in my sleep."

Harper glanced up from her laptop, where she'd been reviewing an article on recommended strategies for structuring group therapy sessions for domestic violence survivors. She planned to offer a program combining individualized and group therapy. The article offered a slightly less traditional approach incorporating various technologies, and she loved it.

"What do you say, Harper? You in?" Liv asked.

She blinked. "Sorry? What? I zoned out."

"No worries. We're going to head over to Brooke's for some drinks and a float in the pool. You in?"

Three sets of eyes stared at her as the words 'I'd love to' died in her throat. It felt like they could see through her pressed clothes and freshly styled hair to the raw nerves popping beneath her skin.

Drinks with the girls?

She'd been eighteen when the cops arrested her. There had never been drinks with the girls. Sure, she'd had some wine coolers and hard lemonades at a few parties. And there was that one time her boyfriend convinced her she'd love tequila shots.

She hadn't loved them nor the hours spent hugging the toilet as a result of sucking back four in thirty minutes.

How the hell did she explain to these girls that even though she'd spent the past seven years surrounded by women, she had no idea how to socialize as an adult? Occasionally, some contraband had popped up in the form of prison-made wine, but after a few sips, she'd steered clear because it was always disgusting. She'd had friends behind bars, but the relationships were one-hundred-and-eighty degrees different from what she'd witnessed in her few days working with these women. Those friendships had been more about survival, connecting with people who could do something for you, and befriending those she'd been forced to share a space with. None of them had been free. Most of the women had been angry and some downright dangerous.

Not the same as these ladies who clearly loved each other.

What would she even have to talk about? Yard time? Her thrilling job in the library? The cell-block fights that used to break out over nothing more than some side-eye? Would they grill her? Pepper her with questions about her time behind bars? While, so far, she was enjoying the days spent working with these women more than she'd imagined, she wasn't quite ready to vomit her sad history all over their evening.

"Harper?" Brooke asked in a soft voice.

She blinked. "Um… I'll probably pass. But thank you for including me."

Liv crouched in front of her, placing a hand on her knee. "We'd really love for you to join us. It's totally casual." Her eyes held understanding and empathy, though Harper could only hope none of these women would ever understand what it'd been like to be in her shoes.

Her face burned. "I'm just a… uh… a little rusty when it comes to hanging out." Of course, they all knew her history, at least on paper. Brooke had run a formal background check, after all.

"There's no pressure at all." Brooke's open smile eased some of Harper's embarrassment. "We do this all the time, so there will be plenty of opportunities, but if you're interested, we eat, drink a little too much, gossip about the guys, and share stories. As little or as much as we're comfortable with. Promise none of us will ask you to talk about anything you're not willing to discuss."

"Trust me when I tell you we may all look damn good…" Liv said with a chuckle.

She could say that again. Harper was quickly learning Liv never had a hair out of place and wore clothes that cost more than Harper's car.

"But we are all a hot freaking mess under the surface."

"Ain't that the truth," Brooke muttered.

"Some of us more than others," Jo said, raising her hand.

Oh, what the hell. "Okay," she said with a tentative smile. Her stomach fluttered with more nerves than when she'd stepped outside the prison for the first time.

"Yay!" Liv clapped.

"I've got a bathing suit you can borrow," Brooke said as she stood and grabbed her purse. "You can follow me home. My house borders the farm property. Usually, I take an ATV and cut across the property, but I have my car parked outside the clubhouse today."

"Sounds great," Harper said, and she halfway meant it. Part of her felt a warm happiness at the invitation and the fact the women wanted her company. The other part felt like the start of fear and the sure belief that she'd do or say something stupid to embarrass herself, then have to quit her job rather than show her face ever again.

Less than twenty minutes later, Harper sat in a donut-shaped float, wearing a borrowed black bikini with her feet dangling in warm water, an icy-red drink in her hand, and laughter all around.

The moment felt so surreal Harper found it difficult to concentrate on the conversation. When was the last time she'd worn a bathing suit? Ten days ago, she'd been wearing an orange-colored jumpsuit, sleeping on a two-inch mattress, and hoping no one stole her shower shoes because the shower floor in prison was beyond disgusting.

Oddly enough, this experience brought her back to her early days of being incarcerated. She didn't have the fear she did then, but the feeling of landing on another planet was the same. Worry over saying the wrong thing. Concern about how she'd be accepted. Some level of anxiety all day, every day.

"You doing okay?" Rachel paddled over to Harper in a similar pool float. "You seem a little overwhelmed."

"Oh, I, uh... maybe." Harper gave her a small smile. Tonight was the first time she'd met Rachel, who was apparently Curly's half sister. And Curly was Brooke's boyfriend, or ol' man as this group seemed to call it. Hopefully, soon she'd have all the players memorized as well as some of the lingo.

Actually, it wasn't the first time she'd heard the term ol' lady, and she wasn't completely unfamiliar with MC life. A few of the women she'd served time with had been tied to motorcycle clubs.

"I hear you." Rachel was maybe a year or so younger but presented herself as older than her age. She looked cute in a red bikini with her hair in a high ponytail. "Though I've been here for months, I'm the newest member of this rag-tag family, and I still need a minute to catch my breath sometimes."

"Yeah, it's not what I'm used to."

Rachel laughed. "Who is used to this? I don't know anything about what brought you to us, but if you're here, fitting in so well, it probably means you've had some… let's call them, challenges in your past."

It was Harper's turn to laugh. "Yeah, you could say that."

"Well then, you've come to the right place. We're a fucked-up but stellar group if you ask me. Best part is the lack of judgment you'll get from these ladies and the guys too. Have you met the guys in the club?"

Shaking her head, Harper took a sip of her drink. As the tangy zip of fruit, sugar, and alcohol hit her tongue, she smiled. Having a drink with the girls was such a normal activity, yet to her, it was monumental. "I've met a few, not many."

"You will."

Would Rachel ever know what those two simple words, said with such acceptance and surety, did to Harper? Someday, if this worked out, if she kept this job and became actual friends with these ladies, she'd open up. She'd tell them about her time in prison, the full story of how she ended up there, and she'd make sure they understood how their kindness helped in these early days of reintegrating into the world.

"Yeah, I'm looking forward to it."

"You should be," Rachel said with a mischievous wink. "They're all fun to look at."

"You talking about how hot our men are?" Liv called out as Harper laughed. "Cuz I want in on that conversation."

The rest of the women swam over, and before she knew it, Harper found herself smack in the middle of a hilarious debate about who had the hottest boyfriend. She listened and laughed for most of the conversation without participating since she'd only met Spec, Liv's ol' man, and the very single Jinx. By the time they called a draw, she had a mental picture of the Hell's Handlers' men that was basically the cast of *Magic Mike*.

It'd been a wild night when they played that movie in the women's prison.

She laughed at her new friends' antics so hard her sides ached, though that could have been the monumental amount of chips and guacamole she'd shoved in her face.

Yawning, she accepted the towel Brooke handed her after they'd all climbed out of the pool. It was only six thirty, not even dark, but the long day caught up to her. The alcohol probably helped with the fatigue.

"Anyone ready for another drink?" Brooke asked as she wrapped her towel around her waist. Clad in a bright blue bikini, she looked a decade younger than her forty-two years. However, Harper might not be the best judge. Most of the women she'd spent time around packed on years before their time. Prison aged a person at what felt like double the rate.

"Nah, I gotta get home," Jo said, a crocheted coverup over her perfect body. "Tracker and I are going to take Betty White to the beach and let her run in the waves before it gets too dark."

Harper choked on her spit. "Betty White? Didn't she pass away recently?"

Giggling, Jo shook her head. "Yes, God rest her incredible soul, but I was referring to Tracker's dog. Her name is Betty White."

"Oh." Her face heated. "Well, that sounds fun."

"It's a blast. You should come sometime. Betty goes nuts for the water."

With each passing day, Harper thought more about getting a pet. Living in an apartment alone after having a roommate for so long took more getting used to than she'd anticipated. Having another beating heart around the place might help stave off some loneliness. A dog might be more than she could handle as she learned to keep herself alive and thriving.

A cat could be good—a more independent pet.

"I'd like that," she said to Jo. Then she turned to the other women. "I think I'm going to take off as well."

"We're so glad you hung out with us," Liv said as she walked over with her arms outstretched.

"Oh," Harper said as she received a wet hug. "Thanks. I'm glad I came. Uh... I'll see you at work tomorrow."

"Definitely. See you in the morning."

The rest of the women called their goodbyes as she walked into the house.

Harper changed into her clothes in Brooke's bathroom, then made her way out to her car.

As she drove home in silence, pondering the success of the evening, she couldn't stop smiling. It'd been a great night. The only thing that could improve it would be a pint of ice cream. It took a little self-convincing since she truly was tired, but the five-minute delay in stopping and grabbing a pint would be well worth it.

She drove into the parking lot of the first convenience store she came across. Hopefully, they'd have a selection of ice cream because she wasn't sure she'd be willing to stop again. After parking under a light—the lot was nearly empty, and she had enough street smarts to seek out the brightest spot—she went inside.

Three minutes later, she exited with a pint of Ben & Jerry's Half Baked and a smile.

Until she noticed the light she'd parked under had gone out. "Of course it did," she mumbled as she fished her phone from her purse. The flashlight would help a little. Maybe she should invest in some pepper spray or one of those keychain weapons. Hell, maybe even a taser. She should be prepared to protect herself if need be. A single woman needed to make intelligent choices.

She lived alone, shopped alone, and spent most of her non-working time alone.

Always alone.

"Wow. Great time to get all maudlin," Harper muttered as she walked across the dark parking lot. Her flashlight provided a small triangle of light, guiding her path.

"Dammit," she whispered as she reached the car. It would have also been smarter to take the keys out before she arrived at the dark car in the deserted parking lot. "Idiot."

A shiver of awareness ran down her spine as she fished in her purse, attempting to hold the phone and ice cream while rummaging.

She froze. The hair on the back of her neck rose.

Someone was behind her.

Hot breath hit her ear. "Which one of those animals are you fucking?"

Harper screamed and dropped everything she'd been holding as she whipped around, slamming her hip into the side mirror. It'd leave a bruise for sure, but the pain barely registered above the terror.

"Get the fuck away from me." Could he hear the command? Or only the sound of her pounding heart? It hammered so loud it sounded like the drum section of a marching band.

"I just wanna talk." He reached toward her face.

Harper jerked her head away and tried to back up, but the car behind her kept her from escaping.

He pushed a lock of hair behind her ear. His touch made her shudder in fear.

She couldn't make out his features in the dark, especially

since he wore all black, including a sweatshirt with the hood pulled up over his head. But she could tell he had a short beard, dark in color. His nails were also painted black, and he wore multiple rings on his fingers.

She was too afraid to look away from his face to try and discover more.

"I'll scream," she warned. "Loud."

He chuckled as he made a show of looking around the empty parking lot. "Knock yourself out. You think the guy working in there will help you?" He leaned in. "He won't. So, tell me, which one are you fucking? Whose *ol' lady* are you?" He said the word in a mocking tone.

The MC. This had to do with the MC.

"N-none of them."

He tsked. "Don't lie. Makes a pretty girl like you so ugly." He trailed a finger along her jaw, making her shudder. "I know you were with the rest of those bitches today. I just wanna know which biker you're letting dick you down. Maybe he's willing to share."

She sucked in a breath.

A bead of sweat rolled down her back.

His finger continued its journey, coasting across her lips.

Harper was fit as fuck. She'd started working out in prison to pass the time and help control her anxiety. Now lifting was as necessary as breathing. Maybe she couldn't take this man, but she'd rather die than go down without a fight.

Quick as a snake striking, she opened her mouth and bit his finger.

Hard.

"You fucking bitch." The crack of his palm across her cheek stunned her immobile.

Until he grabbed her shoulders and slammed her against the car.

"No," she cried as he tried to wrench her legs apart with

his knee. With a grunt of effort, she slammed her head forward into his nose.

A harsh cry of pain immediately followed a sickening crunch of bone, and his hands disappeared from her body. Harper didn't have time to think. She reacted on pure instinct. She rammed a knee into his junk as hard as she could —thanks to a daily kickboxing class in the prison's gym, she had a wicked knee kick—then shoved him away. He crumpled to the ground with a pained groan.

Harper didn't wait around to assess the damage or find out if he could chase her.

She grabbed her phone off the ground and ran.

Fast and hard as she could.

And she kept running.

Past the abandoned gas station next to the convenience store. Through the parking lot of an adjacent shopping center where all the stores were closed. Only when her legs wobbled and her lungs burned did she search for a place to hide.

She rounded the corner at the far end of a strip mall and saw three large dumpsters. She wedged between two of them and didn't stop moving until she hit brick. She was far enough in and shadowed enough that the guy wouldn't be able to see her if he'd followed.

Though he might hear her heavy panting. And the screaming in her head.

Harper focused on quieting her breath and slowing her heart rate for the next few minutes. Her entire body trembled, and she realized she was crying. Big, fat, terrified tears. How long should she wait before going back to her car? What would she do if he found her? Should she call the cops?

Harper wasn't a fan of the police.

If only she knew someone who could help.

Slow your breathing. Feel the air around you. Listen to the quiet night. Smell the stench of the garbage. Ground yourself.

Maybe she did have someone to call. Her new friends and coworkers seemed to genuinely like her. Would they come to her rescue? Maybe, especially if she told them this involved their boyfriends' motorcycle club.

With shaking hands, she pulled up her recent calls. Liv's name sat at the top of the list. Harper sent up a prayer as she tapped on the name.

Please answer.

The second the phone rang, her heart jackhammered again.

"Hello? Harper?"

Chapter Six

"Jinx, you can go. I'm sure you have better things to do than babysit me." Liv hit pause on the god-awful reality show she'd forced him to watch the past forty-five minutes.

A hoard of dumb but admittedly sexy people were dropped on a tropical island to see who fell in love or some shit. The only saving grace was how hot the women were and how everyone was horny as fuck.

"I'm sure Spec will be back soon, and I'm in my own home. Perfectly safe." She grinned and sipped her wine.

"Nice try, Livvy, but I promised my brother I'd hang out until he got here. By the way, he said he's sorry your plans for a night ride were canceled."

Spec had gotten caught up in a *conversation* with a guy who'd borrowed money from the club, then decided he didn't have to pay it back on the agreed-upon date. Some young social media influencer wannabe with the audacity to ask Spec, "Do you know who I am?" So this evening, the idiot was getting a crash course in loan repayment ala Spec's fists.

Liv waved away the apology. "Oh, that's fine. We could use a night in just to hang."

"And bang?" Jinx said, straight-faced.

Liv choked on her wine. "You ever worry about the fact that your humor never made it past an eighth-grade level?"

He stuck his tongue out at her, making her laugh.

"I mean, there's gotta be a reason for it. Tell me about your middle school years, Jinx."

"Keep it up, woman."

Liv stood, still laughing. "Well, if you're gonna be stuck here, you might as well get a snack outta the deal. I'm gonna throw a pizza in the oven. Sound good?"

"Sounds perfect."

She disappeared into her kitchen, leaving him alone and very tempted to change the show. After about thirty seconds, Liv's phone rang.

When she didn't reappear after two rings, he called out, "Livvy, that's your phone."

"Can you see who it is?" she yelled back.

He picked up the sparkly rose-gold phone and couldn't hold back the massive grin.

Well, well, well...

"It's Harper."

"Shit. Can you answer it? I'll be there in a minute."

Hell yeah, he could answer it. In fact, he insisted. "Yeah, I got it. Hello?" he said as he lifted the phone to his ear.

All he heard was rapid breathing. He straightened. "Harper?"

"Uh... S-pec?" Her whisper sounded heavy with fear, and his senses immediately went on red alert.

"No, it's Jinx. Liv asked me to grab the phone. What's wrong?" Something was wrong. He could feel it in his bones.

"I, uh... there... there was a man. He said something about the club. I don't know. He, uh—"

"Harper, where are you?'

"I—" She choked out a sob. "I don't know. I ran and hid. Um..."

"Okay, sweetie, it's okay."

Liv walked back into the room. She took one look at Jinx

and rushed over. "Is she okay?" she mouthed.

He shook his head as he said, "Where were you before you ran?"

"Um… a store. The one off Atlantic. 24-Hour Market or something like that?" she whispered between breaths.

"24-Hour Mart? I know it. Good job, sweetie. Where did you run?"

"Through an empty gas station, then a strip mall. I'm hiding between some dumpsters at the end of the strip mall."

He shot to his feet. "I know the area. We'll find you. I'm giving the phone to Liv so I can drive. We'll be there soon. Hang tight, okay?"

"Thank you." She started to cry in earnest.

It killed him to pass off the phone, but Liv would be better at calming her friend, and he'd be better at driving like a maniac to get to her. "Let's go, Liv. You're coming with."

"Damn straight, I'm coming with you," she responded as she shoved her feet in slip-ons while lifting the phone to her ear. "Harper? I'm here. I'll stay on the line while Jinx drives. We're coming for you."

"Move fast, Liv."

They raced to Liv's car since Jinx only had his bike.

"Here." Liv tossed him her keys.

"Christ," he mumbled as he swiped them out of the air.

This was Lobo. Maybe not the motherfucker himself, but one of his minions. It had to be. Why the hell hadn't they considered Harper's safety? They should have. They should've known he'd be watching and waiting to strike at anyone he could. And who better than the new, unprotected employee barely connected to the club? She'd been the low-hanging fruit, and Lobo tried to pluck her.

If that fucker hurt her, Jinx didn't know what he'd do. But it would be cataclysmic.

The second Liv slammed her door, he was peeling out of

the driveway. Spec would have his ass if he left a black streak on the driveway, but he didn't give a fuck. He'd have the damn thing repaved if necessary. All he cared about was getting to Harper before Lobo or his fucking goons found her.

As he weaved in and out of traffic, he gripped the wheel so hard it creaked under his hands. Liv's voice registered every few seconds as she said something soothing to Harper, but he couldn't make out the words over the rush of blood in his ears.

He barely knew this woman, and yet finding out she'd been scared and could be hurt had his blood boiling in his veins. God help him if he came across the man who assaulted her.

"Jinx? Hey, Jinx?"

He blinked and risked a quick glance at Liv before depressing the gas harder. "What?"

"She's gonna be okay. She's hidden, and we'll find her."

Please let that be true.

"She still on the phone?"

"Yes," Liv said. "I just muted for a second."

The light in front of him turned yellow. *Goddammit.* This light took for-fucking-ever. Not wasting time stuck there, he floored the pedal and soared through the light a second after it turned red. Liv gripped the oh-shit bar but, thankfully, didn't berate him. Hell, she was probably as anxious to get to Harper, even if she did a better job keeping her cool.

"There's the market," Liv yelled, pointing as though he didn't know exactly where they were. "We're almost there, Harper."

He blew past the store and the rundown gas station and screeched into the strip mall's parking lot on two wheels.

Liv yelped and grabbed the handle again. Jinx skidded to a hard stop at the end of the row of stores, not bothering to shut the engine off or wait for Liv. He flew out the door and charged for the dumpsters.

"Jinx, wait," Liv called. Her softer footfalls sounded behind him as he ran.

It was so goddamn dark. Harper had to be terrified, hiding and not knowing what was around the corner. "Harper?" he called out in a low voice. "Harper, it's Jinx. Liv and I are here. You're safe."

"H-here," she yelled.

He followed the sound of her voice to the small space between two dumpsters, where he found Harper wiggling herself out.

"Let me help," he said, reaching out a hand.

She took it, letting him guide her out into the night. Liv reached them just as Harper worked herself free.

"Harper," Liv cried. The two women embraced. Actually, Harper threw herself into Liv's outstretched arms with a harsh sob. "Shh… it's okay. We've got you." Liv met Jinx's gaze over Harper's head, and he couldn't help but feel a stab of what could only be jealousy as he watched Liv hold Harper.

He wanted to be the one with his arms around her, which was insane. What the hell did he know about comforting a traumatized woman? Absolutely nothing. He knew sex and jokes but not tender care. Much as he'd love to feel her all pressed up against him and settle his mind that she was truly okay, Liv was the better choice for comfort, and he'd have to suck it up. His job was to get them all out of there safely.

"I'm sorry I got you involved in this mess," Harper said, still squeezing the life out of Liv.

Jinx clenched his teeth. Either the ladies did a shit job of letting her know she was one of them now and she could call anytime for anything, or she had some serious self-worth issues. Knowing the ol' ladies, he'd bet the latter.

Which was bullshit.

"Don't even start with that," Liv said in a firm tone. "I am so glad you called." She glanced at Jinx again. "C'mon, let's get out of here." She guided Harper toward the idling vehicle.

"My car is parked over there." She pointed in the direction of the market.

Jinx whipped out his phone. "I'll have someone get it." A quick text to their new prospect would take care of that. He also texted Curly and Spec to fill them in. Spec wrote back immediately, letting him know he and Curly would meet them at the clubhouse.

"The keys are on the ground with my purse. I dropped them when he startled me."

Jinx clutched his phone. It was either that or punching the side of Liv's car, imagining Harper being startled so bad she dropped her stuff fucked with his head. "We'll grab them before we leave. Prospect's gonna meet us at the clubhouse, and someone will ride him out to pick up your car."

"Thank you."

She needed to stop with that shit. He didn't want her thanks. He didn't fucking need it. He wanted her snark and sass back. He wanted the prickly woman who'd look him in the eye and say, "I got it" if he offered to hold her damn door.

But she'd been so rattled tonight that the woman went into hiding.

And he didn't fucking like it.

"I'll sit in the back with Harper," Liv said before she climbed into the rear seat of her car.

Jinx grunted. He felt like a spring being coiled tighter and tighter. Something was bound to make him snap and shoot into the damn stratosphere. The worst part of it was he couldn't figure out why. He'd be upset if any woman he knew went through what Harper did, but this hit him so deep he wanted to tear the car apart and howl at the moon.

As he settled in the driver's seat, he glanced in the rearview mirror. Harper sat with her head resting back and her eyes closed with Liv holding her hand. The dome light illuminated the exhaustion on her face. And then his eyes caught sight of the bruise forming on her cheek, and he growled.

Fucking growled.

"Jinx," Liv said in a soft voice.

He met her eyes in the mirror. She shook her head while mouthing, "Not now."

His nostrils flared as he breathed through his nose to keep from hyperventilating. Liv was right. This wasn't the time for him to lose his shit. Harper needed him calm so she could relax and come down from the adrenaline rush. All the questions would be asked and answered back at the clubhouse.

"Thank you," he mouthed back.

Liv smiled, but it didn't meet her eyes. She knew what this meant. That Lobo had targeted Harper, and shit would hit the fan once her man found out.

Ten minutes later, they drove onto Handlers' property. Liv escorted Harper into the clubhouse while Jinx trailed behind, carrying Harper's purse and phone. The first thing he did once inside was head to the bar, pour himself a double shot of whiskey, and down it in one gulp.

"You good, brother?" Spec asked as he walked up beside him.

"I don't fucking know," Jinx said. He grabbed a second glass and poured two drinks this time. He had no idea if Harper drank whiskey, but if a night ever called for it, tonight was that night.

Spec grunted a half laugh. "Know that feeling well, man."

"Where'd Liv take Harper?"

"Bunkroom. She wanted to shower and have a few

minutes to collect herself."

Made sense.

"When she's ready, we'll talk about what happened. You thinking Lobo?"

Jinx took a swig straight from the bottle. "Don't know what was said, but I know the fucker brought up the club, so I'm guessing yes."

Spec bit off a vicious curse. "Yeah, this shit's got his name all over it. Can't believe we didn't anticipate Harper would be a target."

His thought exactly—one that would eat at him for a while. Especially if it turned out he'd been right and the discoloring on her face came from a man's hand.

"You did good tonight, brother." Spec clapped him on the shoulder. "Glad you were there with Liv. You know my girl, if you hadn't been there, she'd have gone after Harper herself."

"She's got balls."

With a snort, Spec shifted his gaze to his woman, who sat at a table with Brooke and two large glasses of wine. Both women wore expressions of worry as they whispered to each other.

"She does. Gonna give me gray hairs." Spec slapped his back again, then meandered over to Liv, who stood, allowing him to sit, then plopped down on his lap. After a few more words, Brooke took her wine glass and walked toward Curly's office, giving the lovebirds space.

Spec kissed Liv long and slow. When it was over, he rested his forehead on Liv's and whispered God knows what to her. Probably something sickeningly sweet.

An unfamiliar twinge twisted in Jinx's chest. He couldn't conjure up his typical snarky comment or witty innuendo. Probably leftover adrenaline from the drama fucking with him.

He left the lovers to their schmoop and started for the

bunkroom, drinks in hand. Harper could do with a stiff one, which was why he sought her out. Not because of any need to reassure himself she was okay. Not because he wanted to touch her. And definitely not because of that strange twinge in his chest.

A second after he knocked, she called out, "It's open."

He strode into the bunkroom to find her seated on the edge of a bed, wearing a pair of thin sweatpants and an animal rescue T-shirt. Clearly, Brooke had been the one to lend the clothes.

"Hey," she said as he strode over to the bed.

"Thought you could use this, though if I'd really been thinking, I'd have brought the whole bottle." He clenched the glass to keep from reaching out and running a finger along her purple cheek.

Christ, he wanted to get his hands on Lobo. Only he wouldn't limit himself to one punch. He'd beat the fucking life out of the man. Normally, he loved that Spec was the enforcer and was happy to leave the violence to his brother. But not this time.

Harper accepted the drink. "Thanks for thinking of me, but I'm fine. Good, actually." She smiled at him.

She looked cute and tiny, with her wet hair hanging down past her chin. Gone was the woman who'd been visibly upset twenty minutes ago. If it weren't for that bruise, Jinx would never know she'd been through a fucking ordeal tonight. Well, the bruise and the fact that her smile was as plastic as a damn Barbie Doll's smile.

He cocked his head, studying her. "Good, huh? You got it?"

Her huff of laughter at least had a semirealistic quality to it. "Exactly. I got it. I'm fine. But thanks for the drink." She sipped and winced as the liquid went down. "Yikes. That is strong."

"Bullshit."

"What?" Her eyes bugged. "No, it really is stro—" Her gaze met his, cutting off her words, and she paled.

Yeah, I'm on to you.

She wasn't *fine*. She sure as hell wasn't *good*. And she didn't *got* anything. She was rattled as shit, and tonight he wasn't in the mood to indulge her I-don't-need-anyone attitude.

Chapter Seven

If she ground her teeth any harder, she'd be chewing her food with nubs for the rest of her life.

Jinx bent down until he was at her eye level, and her breath caught at the heat swirling in his gaze. "Bull. Shit," he whispered so close to her lips that she caught the scent of whiskey on his breath.

God, he smelled good. Fresh and woodsy as though he'd showered recently with the faintest undertone of rubber and motor oil—two smells that probably never fully left his body, considering his job. Also, two things she'd never have thought would smell so sexy, but then, she'd been surrounded by women for the past seven years. What the hell did she know about what she found sexy on a man?

"Wh-ah, what?" His close proximity jumbled her brain, made her stomach flutter, and gave her the insane urge to squeeze her thighs together to relieve the mysterious ache.

She resisted.

Barely.

"I'm calling bullshit. You are not fine. You are not good. You're a fucking mess."

Her breath caught. How could he tell? She'd been practicing her I'm-fine face for so long she didn't have to think about it anymore. No one had ever called her on it. Not her cellmates. Not the corrections officers. Not even her attorney. And since her release and move to Florida, no one knew her well enough to pick up on when she was pretending.

But this frustrating and gorgeous man saw through her after only a few short encounters.

Did he know? Was he aware of her past? Brooke and Liv swore up, down, and backward that they wouldn't share the information on her background check with anyone, but Jinx wasn't just anyone. He was part of their family.

She cleared her throat. Might as well give it one last go. Denial worked some of the time. "Not sure what you mean. My face is a little sore, but aside from that, I'm doing well."

He grunted and shook his head. She'd have to be blind to miss the disappointment in his expression. "All right, tough guy. Stick to your story." He straightened to his full towering height and threw back his drink in one hearty swallow before dropping next to her on the mattress.

Harper peered down at the brown liquid in her glass. She couldn't shoot the thing as well as he had, but maybe getting it down the hatch as fast as possible would minimize the torture and speed up the relaxing effects of the alcohol.

"Here goes nothing," she muttered, tilting her head and taking a huge gulp of the liquid. Fire burned its way down her esophagus, but she ignored it in favor of a second swallow, which polished off the rest of the disgusting whiskey. "Jesus." She coughed, and her eyes watered.

"Damn, woman." Jinx took the empty glass from her hand and set it down next to his on the floor. "Didn't expect that."

"Told you," she said with an actual grin this time. "I got it."

He threw back his head and let out a booming laugh. "Yeah. You did tell me that."

Silence descended thick and heavy but not bad. Something

about his bulky body next to hers made her feel safer than she had since long before prison. While she felt safe with him, she also felt an unfamiliar agitation. As though she wasn't fully comfortable but also wasn't uncomfortable. Her skin felt alive. Slightly tingly. Her breasts felt heavy and her sex empty.

The best way to describe the sensations his presence brought out was needy, but she had no idea what it was she needed from him.

"You feel up to talking to my club about what happened tonight?"

Ugh, no.

She nodded. "Yeah. I asked for a few minutes to collect my thoughts, but I guess I've been in here a while, huh?"

"Nah. You could take all night, and they wouldn't care. Even if they did, Liv and Brooke are keeping their asses under control. They're worried about you."

Her reply came automatically, as though she read it from a script. "They don't need to be. I'm f—" God. How many times had she said that since her release? How many times during her incarceration? Countless.

Jinx watched her with a raised eyebrow.

With a sigh, she stared at the white ceiling, then back at Jinx.

Fuck it.

"I just got out of a seven-year stint in prison. I was eighteen when I went in. A kid. Now I'm twenty-five and free. Every single thing in my life is new and different. Everything. From having a job to driving a car to drinking that whiskey. I missed it all. And suddenly, I'm expected to jump into all this shit I've never done. One day I lived behind bars, and now I live..." She shrugged. "Now I live. I survived the arrest. I survived a bullshit trial. I survived my mother dying while I was in prison. And I survived my sentence.

Now I'm surviving this enormous change. And tonight, I'll survive this. I'm fine because I have to be. There is no other option." She stood as emotion began to well up inside her. She'd never forgive herself if she broke down again in front of this man. "I'm ready to talk."

She turned her back on him, but before she could take a step, a warm, calloused hand circled her wrist, preventing her from walking away. Questions had to be bouncing in his brain. There was no way he wouldn't want to know the details of what she'd word-vomited all over him. What she'd been apprehended for, and if she'd done it. Why? All the dirty details people would be curious about for the rest of her life. Would he ask? Would he demand she unload more of her secrets?

"You left out a word."

Harper tilted her head. Shock kept her from forming words. His eyes held a somber sympathy she hoped didn't extend into pity. Pity sucked, and she didn't want it from anyone. Especially not a big, strong man who made her knees weak.

"Alone. You survived all those things alone, Harper. You're not alone anymore. You're never alone when you're part of this club. And we never need you to be *fine*."

His words should have made her feel better, but instead, they were a knife to the heart. Brooke and Liv employed her. She wasn't actually part of this club and would never be anything more than the girl on the outside looking in. The employee. She wouldn't let herself be more. Never again would she trust someone enough to influence her life like she'd trusted her boyfriend all those years ago.

But she'd revealed enough of her sad truth for one night, so she gave him a small smile. "Let's get this over with. I'm tired."

He frowned as though her answer left him unsatisfied,

which it probably did, but she couldn't give him anything else. Not tonight, and maybe not ever.

"Your call," he grumbled as he stood.

It *was* her call. She had control over her own life for the first time in years and was able to make her own decisions. It was a precious gift she wouldn't sacrifice for anyone. Not even a gorgeous man claiming his shoulder was one she could lean on.

She nodded, after which he released her wrist. The urge to circle it with her fingers to prolong the feeling of connection hit strongly, but she ignored it as she did so many impulses.

Not five minutes later, she sat at a table in the clubhouse with Curly, Spec, Tracker, Jinx, and their women. A second drink sat on the table in front of her. She tipped it back and drank as quickly as she'd downed the first. Liquid courage, they called it.

"I'm a bit of an ice cream fiend," she said with a self-deprecating smile. "Now that I can go to the store whenever I want, I can't seem to buy enough."

Tracker and Spec's brows furrowed like he couldn't figure out why the hell she wouldn't have been able to go to the store previously. Nice to know their girlfriends hadn't spilled her secrets. Curly knew, but he was the one to help Brooke with the background check. She didn't have the energy to divulge her depressing truth again, so she pushed on before anyone could pick up on the odd phrasing.

"I stopped to buy some on my way home. I'm not stupid," she said when Spec side-eyed her. "I parked under a light and paid attention to my surroundings. Anyway, I couldn't have been in the store more than five minutes, but when I returned, the light had gone out. I used the flashlight on my phone so I'd have some illumination as I walked to my car."

"Smart," Tracker said with respect in his gaze.

Her lips twitched into a small smile. "Thank you. I'll admit

I was uneasy, but what could I do? I had to get back to my car. Anyway, when I reached it, a man came up behind me. He was so damn quiet." She shuddered as the memory of his hot breath scaring the life out of her came rushing back.

"Take your time." Jinx rubbed one of his monster-sized hands up and down her back. At first contact, she stiffened but after a second, forced herself to relax. His palm was warm and so comforting she almost gave in to the urge to sink into the touch. But not after this. She'd return home. Allowing him to soothe her would feel great for a few moments, but it'd be gone before she could blink, making it that much harder to calm herself next time something unsettling happened. No, she had to continue to rely solely on herself as she'd done in prison.

"Uh… he whispered to me. It startled me so bad that I dropped everything… keys, phone, purse, ice cream." God, she could definitely use that ice cream after she got home tonight. By the time Jinx and Liv drove her to pick up her belongings, it'd been a melted mess on the pavement. "Think I'm most upset about the ruined ice cream," she added in a lame attempt to lighten the heavy conversation.

Beside her, Jinx frowned, then pulled out his phone and typed furiously for a moment.

"What did he say?" The question came from Curly, who had Brooke in his lap and the most solemn expression she'd seen him wear.

"Um…" Her face heated. "He asked which of the guys in the MC I was sleeping with." She stared at the table, unable to look any of them in the eye. "That's not a direct quote, but it's what he wanted to know."

Spec leaned forward in his chair. Of all the men she'd met, he was by far the most intense. Maybe even the scariest. But he seemed head over heels for Liv, which helped ease her discomfort around him a smidge. Now, his eyes shot fire, but he smiled as though trying to make himself appear harmless. "Do you remember exactly what he said? Could be important to know word for word."

Ugh, she was going to have to say it.

Kill me now.

"Uh... yeah, he said, 'Which of those animals are you fucking?'" Her face burned, and she kept her gaze down.

Brooke winced. "I'm so sorry, Harper."

Jinx snorted. "Well, that's a load of horse shit."

"Right?" Liv added, nodding.

"No, I mean, it would clearly be me."

Harper blinked as her head snapped up. "Uh... what?"

He gestured to the rest of the people at the table. "All these jokers are taken, and clearly, I'm the sexiest *animal* of the single ones. So, it'd be me. I don't even understand why he'd ask. Stupid question."

She stared at his dead-serious expression for a beat, then burst out laughing. The rest of them followed a second later. The man was ridiculous, but oh my God, had she needed something to laugh about at that moment.

Also, he wasn't wrong. In her mind, he'd claimed the title of sexiest biker, even among the couples. Not that she'd ever let anyone know that little secret thought.

"You're an idiot." Tracker flicked the side of Jinx's head with his finger.

"Ow. What the fuck, man?" he shouted, cradling his temple.

Brooke sighed. "Sorry, Harper. I'd tell you they aren't usually like this, but it'd be a lie."

"Yeah," Jo said with a wry grin. "They are always like this. Big children riding their big bikes."

"Don't hate, baby." Tracker smacked an audible kiss on Jo's cheek. She swatted him away, but the wide smile stretching her face showed how much she adored her playful man.

"How did he know you were connected to the club?" Curly asked. Though she barely knew the club's president, Harper's respect for Curly grew with each conversation they'd had.

He'd been in prison, almost twice as long as she had, all while being innocent of the crime he'd been convicted of. As much as Harper felt her sentence was unjust, and though she knew in her gut her ex-boyfriend's attorney-father called in some serious favors to have the blame placed on her, she couldn't ever claim complete innocence as Curly could. She'd been there. She'd witnessed the crime and had done nothing to help the injured man.

She *was* guilty.

Within a matter of minutes after meeting him, Curly had become her role model. He'd found his way back into society. He was thriving in all aspects of his life. Sure, not in a conventional way, but Harper understood that too. She wasn't the person she'd been before her incarceration. She'd seen, heard, and lived through too much.

No matter how normal her life eventually became, she'd always have firsthand knowledge of the darker side of humanity. Maybe it was why she hadn't blinked at the thought of working so closely with an outlaw MC.

A dull ache throbbed behind her eyes. "He said I wouldn't have been hanging out with the ol' ladies if I wasn't sleeping with one of you."

"Fuck. So he had eyes on the house?" Spec asked as he pulled Liv out of her chair and onto his lap as though needing to touch her to reassure himself she was safe.

"That's the impression I got," Harper said.

"But what did he want?" Liv asked with a frown. "Was this just a ploy to scare you?"

"I think so," Harper answered. "He said he wanted to know who I was with to see if they'd be willing to, uh…" she cleared her throat, "… to, uh… share."

"Fucking pig," Jo muttered.

"When I said it was no one, he grabbed me and ran a finger over my mouth, so I…"

Would they think she was crazy? Disgusting?

"You what?" Liv leaned forward, eyes practically glowing. "Tell me you did what I'm thinking you did."

Harper's face might never cool down. "I bit him."

"Fuck yeah, you did!" Liv cheered and pumped an arm in the air.

"So vicious, baby," Spec murmured in her ear.

"Yeah, I bit him hard. That's when he did this." She pointed to her tender cheek. "After that, he pushed me against the car and tried to pry my legs apart, so I headbutted his nose, kneed him in the junk, and got the hell outta there. Once I was far enough away and hidden, I called Liv. And you all know the rest."

No one said a word. They sat staring at her with varying levels of shock, and was that admiration?

She risked a sideways glance at Jinx and almost swallowed her tongue at the heat in his gaze. He was looking at her like he'd never seen her before. Like she'd blown his mind. Like he wanted her, but that couldn't be possible. Sure, he'd flirted, but as she'd heard, flirting was in his nature. What was it Jo had said? Jinx never met a woman he didn't flirt with.

His eyes told a different story right then.

They were liquid fire, burning hot with desire.

For her?

A shiver ran down her spine that had nothing to do with reliving the traumatic evening. Her body felt hot, flushed with unfamiliar sensations. She could feel her nipples beneath her bra. Suddenly, the fabric felt *erotic* against her skin. If he didn't stop staring at her like she was his favorite dessert, she would have to stick her head in the freezer.

"So that's what happened."

Lame.

"You are fucking badass," Jinx said.

"Seriously," Jo chimed in. "You're my hero."

"What she said," Liv added, jerking her thumb in Jo's direction.

But Harper couldn't tear her gaze away from Jinx. What was it that had her so captivated by the man?

"Harper, on behalf of the club, I want to apologize for what you went through tonight. We are having some... difficulty with a local drug dealer. We want him gone and thought we successfully ran him out of town a few months ago." Curly shook his head. "Seems we were wrong. I am sorry we didn't protect you from what happened tonight. Moving forward, you have my personal guarantee nothing like this will happen again."

"Oookay?" She frowned and rubbed a hand across her aching head. "What does that mean exactly?"

"It means we'll beef up your security system or give you one if you don't have one."

"Security system?" she questioned with a weak laugh. "I have a deadbolt."

Beside her, a rumble of displeasure came from Jinx.

"Okay, so we'll get you set up. We can also have someone escort you when you drive—"

Escort me? "Uh... no." Hell no, to be exact.

"Excuse me?" Jinx growled from next to her.

She glared at him. "I said no. I do not want a babysitter, and I don't give my consent to have one."

He scoffed. "That is the stupidest thing I've ever heard."

"Jinx..." Brooke warned, her tone heavy.

Harper straightened. He might be hot, and he might make her stomach flip, but in no way would she bend on this.

"No, Brooke, this is serious." He turned to Harper again. "You could have been really hurt tonight. He could have fucking raped you. We can make sure this doesn't happen again, and you're refusing? Why? Because it'd be annoying to have someone drive behind you?"

She stood and got in his face. God, the man was nearly at her eye level when sitting. "You know what, Jinx? I'm not stupid. I'd love help with a security system. But I just got my freedom back, and I'll be dammed if someone is going to take it away again, even for my own safety," she shouted the words in his face, then froze.

An ant sneezing would have sounded like thunder in the dead quiet. All eyes focused on her with varying levels of shock, confusion, pity, and in Curly's case, understanding.

"What—" Spec started until Liv squeezed his arm.

"Excuse me." Harper cleared her throat. She felt naked beneath their stares, as though they could see beneath the steely mask she wore to the vulnerable woman beneath, and she hated it more than she hated hearing that guilty verdict all those years ago. "Curly, I'll call you tomorrow about the security system, if that's okay?"

"Of course, Harper. One of our prospects brought your car here. The keys are in it."

Right. Her car.

How humiliating would it have been if she stormed out of there only to have to slink in again and ask for a ride home?

"Thank you." Tears burned in her eyes, but she'd be damned if she started crying on top of her little outburst. A few more seconds and she'd be outside. She could keep it together for that long.

"You've been through a lot tonight."

Yes, she sure as hell had.

"Would you like an escort home?" Curly asked.

She shook her head. "No. I got it."

Waves of fury radiated off Jinx, so thick she could feel them. He opened his mouth, probably to blast her stupidity again, but Curly lifted a hand, cutting him off. His mouth snapped closed, and he settled for glaring at her.

She nodded once to the group, then mumbled "Good night" and left.

Walking with her head held high took more energy than she had, but she powered through. These people did not need to know how much the night had rattled her. They didn't need to know she wanted to curl up in a ball and cry herself to sleep. They didn't need to know how much she'd love to let them take over and iron out this chaos for her.

No one had the power to organize her life anymore.

She had it, and that meant taking the hard times with the easy.

But when she arrived at her car and discovered an ice-cold pint of ice cream sitting on the driver's seat, she wondered if it would be so bad to let these people in a little.

Chapter Eight

His back ached, his eyes felt like they'd been blasted with sand, and his hip had a knot that twinged whenever he moved from sitting to standing.

That's what he got for spending the entire night sitting in his car on the street below Harper's apartment.

The area remained quiet all night, thankfully. After the drama he'd caused yesterday, Lobo had to know the Handlers would ramp up security. Jinx forced a new prospect to keep watch with him. They switched off every so often so they could grab a few hours of shut-eye.

Hadn't worked, though. Jinx spent most of his off time staring at the car's ceiling and mulling over the bomb Harper dropped on him.

The woman had spent seven years in prison.

Holy fuck.

No wonder she had impenetrable steel walls twenty feet high and five feet thick. How on earth did that woman—hell, girl at the time of her arrest—end up behind bars for the better part of a decade? What she'd done didn't actually matter. He didn't condemn her for it. Jinx had been arrested a handful of times for a variety of misdemeanors in his younger days and risked another longer stint every time he conducted business for the club. But even with a slew of arrests under his belt, he'd never spent more than a few consecutive weeks locked up.

Seven years? That was a life-destroying time.

The way she'd told the story, the tone in her voice, led him to believe it wasn't so straightforward as her being punished for a crime she'd committed. He'd love to know the details, but she tended to be as closed as a clam most days.

She'd blown his mind with the little bit she'd opened up last night.

He wanted her.

Rather, his dick wanted her. It had from the first time he'd laid eyes on her. And with each meeting, she intrigued him even further, to the point that he'd spent the entire damn night sitting outside her house, thinking about her.

Would Lobo have sent someone to her home?

Probably not.

Most likely not.

But even a point-five percent chance had been too much, so he'd gone against her wishes and set up camp on the street below her apartment. And damn, did that prospect snore like a fucking chainsaw. He'd been tempted to rip out the guy's throat to spare himself the constant noise.

To top off his fantastic night, now he was standing outside Lock's home at seven in the morning with two vats of coffee while listening to the baby scream his face off.

Fuck my life.

Since his hands were full of God's nectar, he kicked the door with his foot a few times.

"It's open," Lock called from inside.

Great. Jinx juggled the coffees, hugging one against his chest to free a hand. He opened the door and stepped inside, only to be smacked in the face with the most putrid odor he'd ever smelled. "What the fuck? Did something die in here?" he called out as he tried not to gag.

"That'd probably smell better." Lock's voice came from down the hallway, along with the unhappy wails of an infant.

"Please tell me that stench is not coming from my godson," Jinx said as he walked into the room only to discover the smell was, in fact, baby in origin. "Goddamn, that's unnatural."

Lock snorted as he tossed a wadded-up diaper in a weird-looking trash can. "You have no idea."

The baby stopped crying and locked his curious eyes on Jinx. "Hey, little dude. How's it hanging this morning."

"Godfather?" Lock asked. He secured a fresh diaper on the baby and picked him up.

Jinx nearly stumbled at the sight of his friend. He looked… well, he looked like death—pale skin, dark under-eye circles, beaten-down expression. *What the hell?*

"Uh, yeah. Godfather."

"He doesn't have one. I'm not religious." Lock shifted the baby to his hip and grabbed a bottle. The little guy practically ripped it out of his father's hands and shoved it in his mouth.

"Me neither." He spread his arms wide. "But come on. I'm clearly godfather material."

The joke didn't earn even a flicker of a smile. "Then knock yourself out." His focus was back on Caleb, whom he'd dressed in a Harley Davidson onesie. "Did you need me for something? Curly asked me to swing by and beef up his locks this morning."

"Nah, man, I don't need anything. Figured I'd give you a break and take the rug rat while you're at Curly's."

Lock glanced up at him, and the relief on his face would have had Jinx teasing him if he didn't look so damn haggard. "Really?"

"Really. Even brought you some coffee." He jiggled the to-go cup filled to the brim with plain black coffee as Lock's eyes finally lit.

"Oh, shit, thanks. I ran out yesterday and haven't had time to get more."

"Well, here, brother. Trade you a coffee for a baby." He set both cups on the changing table.

Lock lifted the eight-month-old, who still held the bottle for dear life. "He's all yours."

"Well, if it isn't my favorite little man." Jinx settled the baby in the crook of his arm. "Shit, he's getting heavy."

"Yeah, growing fast. Um… I'm gonna get dressed, then I'll give you all his shit."

"No rush, I'm not working today, so the little dude and I can hang as long as you need. Isn't that right, buddy?" The baby gurgled and gave him a milky smile. "He fucking loves me."

Lock snorted and left the room.

"Let's snoop around, huh?" It felt like ages since he'd been in Lock's house. Jinx wandered out into the hallway toward the kitchen. His jaw dropped as soon as he entered the space that opened into the den. It was a fucking disaster—dishes overflowed in the sink, unwashed bottles were on every surface, and a stack of pizza boxes lay on the floor. But what had his stomach sinking was the massive amount of empty beer bottles strewn all around. Even the den had become a recycling can for empties.

"What the fuck? Shit, buddy, I had no idea your daddy was struggling this bad." The first stop when he left would be a visit to the ol' ladies. They needed a plan of action, and they needed it fast.

"You say something?" Lock wandered into the kitchen, dressed and coffee in hand. He strolled past Jinx to the table where a big bag full of baby shit sat.

Jinx swore he got hit with a whiff of alcohol as he moved.

Had he doctored his coffee?

Fuck, it wasn't even seven thirty in the morning.

"Uh… no, brother. Just talking to the little man."

Lock nodded. "Here's his stuff… diapers, wipes, formula, bottles. You know what you're doing?"

Jinx snorted. "Fuck no. But I'm gonna bring this handsome dude to the She Shed so the ladies can fawn all over him. They'll show me what to do."

"Okay."

His brother was so flat this morning. Sure, he'd been seeing to the baby's needs, but there barely seemed to be a connection to his son. Didn't new dads act all mushy and speak in baby tones while telling the kid how it was the cutest kid of all the kids?

Maybe not. Maybe he'd just seen too many movies. Jinx sure as hell didn't know babies in real life, but Lock was not Lock today. He was a hollow shell of Jinx's friend.

Possibly a drunk one.

"You wanna ride with me?"

"What?" Lock gave him a look that said he was crazy. "No. Why the fuck would I do that?"

"You smell like booze, brother."

He waved a hand at his pigsty of a kitchen. "Just this shit. I haven't cleaned in a while."

Should he push it?

Lock was a grown-ass man who didn't need his club brother harping on him. But maybe he needed something to shock him out of this rut. Not that a downward spiral wasn't justified. He'd lost his twin sister and had become an unprepared father on the same day just a few short months ago, but as a father, Lock didn't have the luxury of hitting bottom.

Another thing he'd discuss with Brooke and the ladies.

"You sure?" One more check, just in case.

Lock's expression grew thunderous. "Yes, I'm fucking sure. I don't need a father, Jinx. I am one."

He lifted his eyebrows. "Sorry, man, I'll stay out of your shit." *For now.* "C'mon, show me how to get his seat thing in my car and buckle him in."

Ten minutes later, Jinx cruised toward the clubhouse with a sleeping infant in the back seat of his car. He snorted. Who the hell would have ever thought that'd happen? At least the kid wasn't his.

He shuddered.

Fuck, no, it wasn't his. Never would be. That shit was way too fucking scary.

The second he'd hit the highway, the kid passed out as though he'd been shot with a tranquilizer.

"Wish I could do that," he muttered. Instead, he stressed about the little guy's father on the drive. At least he'd been able to keep his mind off Harper for a few minutes.

And there she was, front and center once again, sharing her secret with sad eyes and enormous courage, making him want to ask a million questions on top of wanting to fuck her senseless.

"Holy shit," he whispered as a thought hit him like a battering ram. She'd been out of prison for mere weeks. She'd gone in at eighteen.

Was she a virgin?

If not, there was a very high chance, like ninety percent, that she hadn't had sex in more than seven years.

The woman had to be starving for it.

His dick hardened.

God, why was the thought of reintroducing her to the wonder of dick so damn hot? Typically, he ran from inexperienced women faster than an Olympic track star. Didn't all women fall in love with their first? At least a little bit?

No, thank you.

Even women who'd fucked before, but only a few times,

didn't interest him—too needy, unsure, and lacking confidence. He wanted a woman who knew what she liked and how to give him what he liked.

Unless she was a prickly cactus of a woman who'd spent the last seven years behind bars. One with walls so thick he'd need a tank to blow through them. One with deep, soulful eyes, a rare smile, and an independent streak so wide no one could cross it.

Then, apparently, he was all for being a sexual tour guide.

Fuck, they wouldn't just burn up the sheets, they'd incinerate the entire house.

The bumpy farm road woke Caleb as he pulled onto the club's property. Jinx held his breath, waiting for the screams of an unhappy baby, but instead, all he heard was a damn adorable coo.

"That's right, my man. You stay nice and happy for Uncle Jinx." He killed the engine and went around to unhook the baby from the medieval contraption Lock called a car seat. As he'd done earlier, Caleb fixed his gaze on Jinx. He gave a gummy smile that only a complete ogre wouldn't respond to. "You're cute, buddy. I'll give you that." He unhooked the baby and pulled him close, resting his tiny bum on his forearm. "You ready for this, dude? Those ladies always go bananas when they see you, so prepare yourself."

He took his time strolling across the farm to the She Shed. The day hadn't heated to uncomfortable yet, so Caleb happily sat in Jinx's arms, playing with the patches on his cut. About halfway to the shed, Ray came bounding across the field with his foot-long tongue lolling out. Caleb squealed and kicked his legs, making his whole body jerk in Jinx's arm.

"Whoa, buddy, careful there," he said as he supported the infant's back with his free hand. "You like the dog?"

Brooke's German Shepherd was such a damn good dog Jinx had no concerns about how he'd interact with the baby.

He crouched down on one knee, settling Caleb on his leg. The little guy squealed again as he flapped his arms and legs.

"C'mere, Ray. Good boy. Sit down." The German Shepherd plopped his butt down right in front of Jinx. Caleb reached out and grabbed Ray's ear with his chubby fist. "Easy, buddy. Let's do it like this." He pried the tiny hand off the dog's ear and ran it over his soft head. "See? Nice and gentle." He released Caleb's hand, and the baby tried to mimic the move. It was uncoordinated and ended up being more of a bop on Ray's head but a gentle one. "Good job."

Caleb gave him a huge drooly smile Jinx couldn't help but laugh at.

He rose to his feet. "Let's go, Ray. We're going to see your mama." The mention of the word 'mama' made his heart clench for the baby in his arms. The baby who'd never know his mother, thanks to Lobo selling fentanyl-laced meth on the streets.

"Fuck, now I'm getting dark. Let's go." He looked up and stopped midstride. Standing on the rickety steps to the She Shed stood Harper. She wore a simple yellow dress, revealing more skin than he'd seen her bare.

Her eyes were wide with shock and maybe longing as she stared at him holding the baby. He couldn't look away or tear his gaze from her. She was so pretty. Insanely fragile, yet she worked so damn hard to hide it from the world.

Why?

Because she's been terribly hurt.

It had to be the reason. Why would you always wear a mask if it wasn't to keep a painful past from repeating itself? He'd bet money on the reason being tied to her prison sentence.

And he'd give nearly anything to hear her whole story.

Brooke might know. Maybe all the ladies knew. He could ask and probably charm them into revealing Harper's secrets, but he didn't want to. He wanted the woman to come to him with her secrets and give them up freely.

Harper blinked, then ripped her gaze away as though realizing they'd been staring for too long. After one final glance at Caleb, Harper scurried into the shed.

You can run, but you can't hide.

He grinned and strode her way with the most adorable kryptonite in his arms.

Chapter Nine

He has a child.
He has a child.
Jinx has a child.
How did she not know this?

With all the things her new friends had told her—he was a master flirter, hilarious, kind, protective as hell, and all that—all those things, and they couldn't have mentioned he had a child?

A recent child too.

A baby, for crying out loud.

Her heart went berserk in her chest, trying to escape and hide under her desk because, for all her protests, the sight of that big man being so gentle and sweet with a baby and a dog did something dangerous inside her.

She went straight to her desk, bypassing the coffee maker and tray of muffins someone generously brought. The last thing she needed was extra caffeine to charge her system even more.

He has a baby.

A future including children wasn't something Harper had ever given much thought to. What was the point? She spent many of her meet-a-man-and-have-a-child years in prison and couldn't imagine trusting someone enough to create a life with them now. Why waste time envisioning that kind of future when she could barely picture herself allowing a man close enough to kiss her, let alone knock her up? It seemed like a recipe for heartache and pain, so she didn't indulge in the fantasy.

At all.

But all it took was one glance at a gorgeous man holding an adorable baby while petting a dog, and her brain couldn't help but go all white picket fence on her.

No.

It would never happen, so she needed to stop thinking about it.

Focus instead on the fact that he hid the small detail of being a new father.

Where was the baby's mother? Were they close?

Oh God, were they in a relationship?

Her stomach cramped.

Why was she more shaken this morning than she'd been after being attacked last night?

The toilet flushed, and a moment later, Brooke walked out of the bathroom. "Morning, Harper." She walked straight to Harper's desk, leaned over, and hugged her tight. "How are you feeling this morning."

"Uh… I mean, I'm a little shocked but okay. I just wish someone had clued me in. Now I feel a little foolish."

Brooke pulled away and frowned. "Clued you in? What do you mean? I was referring to everything that happened last night."

Harper's face burned.

You're an idiot.

Of course, Brooke wasn't referring to Jinx and the baby.

What the hell is wrong with you?

She needed to screw her head on straight. With a forced laugh, she waved a hand in front of her face. "Sorry, I'm off my game this morning. Of course, that's what you meant. I'm okay, thanks."

Brooke still wore a funny expression, but she let it drop. "You sleep okay?"

"Uh... no." She chuckled. "That I did not do." She tapped her temple. "Lots of spinning up in here."

With a sigh, Brooke nodded. "Been there, hon. Boy, have I been there. You know we are all here anytime you need—"

A sharp rap on the door had both their gazes shifting. A second later, Jinx strode into the trailer, baby in arms.

Brooke straightened and beamed at him. "Gimme." She charged over to Jinx, who unloaded the baby into her arms. "How is the most handsome boy in the world?"

"Doing well, thanks," Jinx answered.

He winked at Harper as Brooke rolled her eyes.

"Muffins, yes. You, ladies, are amazing." Without being invited, he grabbed one and bit through half of it in one bite. "Mm."

Once again, Brooke rolled her eyes. "He's a pig, isn't he?" she asked the baby in a sing-song voice.

"Morning, everyone." Liv walked through the door with her usual flourish, then squealed. "I'm next. I'm next."

Brooke hugged the baby close to her chest. "Don't even think about it."

"Come on." Liv pouted. "Jinx," she said with an exaggerated whine. "I wanna hold the baby."

"Not getting in the middle of that fight," he said, mouth full of muffin. He swallowed, then turned his gaze on her. "Looking hot today, Harper. That dress is killer."

She couldn't find her voice. They all acted as though this was so normal. Was she the only one whose mind was blown by the giant man flirting with her while he had a new baby? Why didn't they care?

All three of them narrowed their focus on her as she did

nothing but sit there staring at Jinx like he'd sprouted another head.

"Harper? You in there?" Liv teased.

She blinked. "Uh… yes. Sorry. Didn't sleep well."

Jinx's expression grew dark. Of course, he knew why she didn't sleep well. She'd die before admitting she'd been scared out of her mind alone in her home last night.

Maybe she'd talk to Brooke about getting a dog after all. Something to give her a measure of security. Not that she knew the first thing about raising a dog.

They were still watching her, waiting for some contribution to the conversation.

God, she hated being the center of attention.

"Anyway, uh… I didn't realize you had a son," she said.

Did that sound weird? Like she was accusing him of something? Like she cared?

Because she didn't—shouldn't. They barely knew each other and meant nothing to each other. He owed her no details of his life even though she was feeling all kinds of weird about this revelation.

A strangled sound came from Brooke, but Liv burst out laughing. She placed a hand over her stomach as she doubled over. "Holy shit."

Jinx stood there with a horrified expression as he held the muffin halfway to his mouth. "No. No, *no*." His denial came out in a rush and followed with an adamant no.

Liv laughed even harder, and Brooke joined her.

"It's not that funny," he grumbled.

"Oh, it's so, so funny," Liv said around her laughter.

Harper's gaze bounced between them.

"What am I missing?"

"Oh, for fuck's sake." Rolling his eyes, Jinx stormed over to Brooke and snatched the baby from her arms. "He's not my kid. And since you two are mean, you can't hold him now."

The baby giggled and waved his arms.

"Hey," Liv cried.

Not his kid?

Not his kid.

"Harper, have you met Lock yet?"

She looked at Brooke. "No, I don't think so."

"Yeah, he hasn't been around much lately. Anyway, this is his kiddo. Actually, his sister's." Her expression grew somber. "He had a twin who was pregnant. Unfortunately, she had a drug problem and died when she was about eight months along with Caleb here after she took some bad meth."

Harper gasped. "Oh my God. That's horrible. I'm so sorry."

Liv nodded. "It was awful, especially for Lock. As you can see, they were able to save this little cutie, and now Lock has custody. But it's been hard for him, so we try to help out where we can." She shifted her attention to Jinx. "How was he when you saw him?"

Jinx swallowed the last bite of his muffin. Harper couldn't help but watch how his Adam's apple rose and fell with the movement. When had she ever found something like that fascinating?

"Looks like fucking shit. Something's gotta give, or he's gonna crack. His place is a goddamn disaster. Hell, he's a disaster."

Brooke frowned. "Shit. I'll head over after work today. Get it cleaned up a bit and see if I can get him to talk."

"Good luck with that," Jinx said with a grunt. "Think he's drinking too."

"What do you mean?"

"Had to be fifty empty beer bottles lying around the kitchen. I don't know. Just a gut feeling. I think he's worse off than we realized."

"You talk to Curly?" Liv asked as she walked over to him

with her hands held out.

He shook his head, handing over the baby, who practically leaped into Liv's arms. "Not yet. He's my next stop."

"I'll come with you." Brooke grabbed her phone from her desk.

"Don't take him away from me," Liv said as she bounced the baby on her hip. He grabbed a hunk of her hair and brought it to his mouth. "Oh, no, buddy. That's yucky. You don't want to eat that."

"I'll leave him with you if you don't mind. There are some toys in his bag."

"I don't mind at all. Do I?" she asked, focusing her high-pitched tone on the baby. "No, I don't. No, I don't."

"Jesus." Jinx made a gagging noise. "Do you have to talk to him like that?"

"Yes, I do. Oh, yes, I do," Liv cooed.

"Thank God you're Spec's problem," he muttered.

"Hey," she cried.

Harper couldn't help the laugh that burst from her.

Jinx's face lit up, and he winked. "You gonna be around when I come to pick him up?"

What? Why does he care? "I work here."

He grinned. "Yes, you do." He grew serious for a moment and strode toward her, not seeming to care at all that Liv and Brooke watched with rapt attention. He cupped her face in his large hand, tilting her chin up. "You in pain?"

Her throat thickened at the concern in his voice, and she refused to acknowledge the electricity buzzing under his finger where it stroked her jawline. "Uh… not much. I took some ibuprofen."

"Good." With a huff, he shook his head. "Wish to fuck I coulda had two minutes with the bastard."

"I'm fine, Jinx."

His wry grin only added a few more butterflies to her

stomach. "Yeah, hon, you are." With a touch so gentle—she wouldn't have thought it possible for such a big man—he ran a finger across her bruised cheek. "Still wanna kill him. Ready, Brooke?"

Her head spun from the quick subject change.

"Sure am." Brooke's voice held a note of humor, but Harper ignored it.

"Oh, Jinx?" Harper called out as her brain came back to her.

He raised an eyebrow.

"Thank you. Uh… for the ice cream."

Ugh, that smile could melt the icebergs.

"No idea what you're talking about. Ladies first." He gestured for Brooke to precede him, then followed her outside, tossing one final wink Harper's way before he disappeared.

"Whoa," Liv said with a chuckle.

"What?"

"Is the air conditioner broken, or was that seriously hot?" She smirked, still bouncing the baby on her hip. He'd discovered her long necklace and seemed as fascinated with it as Harper was with Jinx.

Which meant a scary level of fascination.

"I don't know what you mean."

"Okay," Liv said. "If that's how you wanna play it, let me spell it out for you. That yummy man wants you."

"He's just a flirt. You guys have said so dozens of times. He wants every woman."

"That may be, but this feels different. More significant. Trust me when I tell you that man wants *you*. Not just what's between your legs, though I'm sure he wouldn't turn it down." She cleared her throat. "If you know what I'm saying."

"Yeah, pretty sure I saw through that subtlety."

Liv laughed. "I like you a lot, Harper. You fit well here."

She looked to the door as though Jinx still stood there. "I don't know how to handle all that."

"Neither does he, sweetie." The baby brought the necklace to his mouth so Liv walked over to the diaper bag. After a quick search, she pulled out a rubber giraffe and replaced the necklace in the baby's hands. The toy immediately went into his mouth. "Might be fun to learn together, don't you think?" She waggled her eyebrows.

Fun? No.

Terrifying? Yes.

But she wasn't ready to admit that, so she conceded. "Maybe."

"Oh, crap, I forgot to tell you I stopped by the PO Box on my way in. There was something for you."

"Great, thanks. I'm waiting for some books I ordered."

"This was just a letter. Here, let me get it." She walked to her desk, where she'd set her purse before getting an arm full of baby. "Here you go," she said as she held it out.

Harper took it. One look at the return address had her blood running cold.

North Carolina State Penitentiary.

How?

She glanced up to find Liv watching her with kind eyes. She had to have seen where this came from. "Um…"

"You okay?"

"Not sure yet." Her gaze drifted down to the letter lying on her open palm. *How did he get the address?* Stupid question. Probably from his father. He must have been keeping tabs on her.

"I'll give you some privacy to read it, but Harper?"

"Yes?" She lifted her gaze.

"Whatever it is, good or bad, please know you can trust us both with your secrets and with you. We're your friends."

She blinked as moisture prickled the edges of her eyes. There would be no crying. "I don't know how to do that either."

"Neither did I when I first came here. But this place has a way of winning you over. Come on, Caleb, let's go find some big bikers to get all mushy over you." She smiled and gave Harper's arm a squeeze before heading out the way Jinx and Brooke had gone.

Harper's hands shook as she opened the envelope and unfolded the letter.

The crinkling of the paper sounded ten times louder than it should have in the quiet office. Familiar handwriting greeted her as this wasn't Aaron's first letter. Over the years, he'd sent many to her in prison. She'd hoped her release would mean the end of his communications, but it seemed his father had passed along a way to get in touch with her. God, how she loathed that man.

Aaron was the reason she'd been arrested, but his father had been the reason she'd gone to prison for so long. He was a slimy defense attorney who'd pulled every dirty trick he could to make her look as guilty as the others.

The jury had eaten it up, dazzled by his thousand-dollar suits, fancy manipulation techniques, and charming smile. Harper's inexperienced public defender hadn't stood a chance against that shark. Aaron should have been given fifteen to twenty years for being the mastermind of the armed robbery. His father's team painted him as a lovesick victim reeled in by her. They made the jury sympathize with him, giving him a ten-year sentence instead of what he deserved and giving her seven years. Seven years for trusting that asshole.

He started each letter the same and made her ill each time.

My Harper,

You're out. I am so happy for you, and as always, I miss you so much it hurts. Now that you are out, I have two wishes. I wish you happiness. You deserve it after what we have been through since our trials. I also wish you would come to visit me. I'll be out in three years, and we can be together again, but a visit would go a long way toward soothing my soul.

I love you.
Your Aaron.

Her Aaron.

God.

As much as she despised these quarterly letters, this was the bucket of ice water she needed to destroy any errant thoughts about Jinx. This was why she didn't plan to get close to anyone again. Hell, this should be enough of a reminder to keep the ladies at an arm's distance as well. The one time she'd chosen to give herself to someone, he'd ruined her life and didn't even have the decency to leave her alone years later. There was no way in hell she'd visit Aaron. If she had a gun to her head, she'd take the bullet over being in the same room as that man ever again.

Either she was such easy prey a sociopath like Aaron had targeted her, or she was too blind to have seen him for who he was. Neither held any appeal, so why try again?

Even flirting with Jinx was dangerous because she softened toward him each time he flashed that panty-melting smile. From now on, she'd steer clear of the man to the best of her control, starting with not being present when he came to fetch the baby.

She stuffed the letter in her purse and scrawled a note letting the ladies know she'd gone to check out some furniture for the therapy room. It was on her to-do list anyway, so it wasn't a lie. Then she practically ran out of the trailer. Thankfully, Jinx was nowhere to be seen.

It'd be hard to avoid him entirely, but she'd do her best. She'd maintain a professional relationship with the women but end all the extra socializing. It would be tough at times, but she could do it.

I got this.

Chapter Ten

Jinx was hornier than he'd been in ages. He loved to fuck—what man didn't?—but he typically had solid control over his dick. It'd been years since he popped random boners all day, but there he was, reliving his teenage torment whenever thoughts of Harper floated through his mind.

Like now, while he stood at the front of the line in his favorite ice cream parlor. All it took was one fantasy of Harper's tongue licking the cold treat off a spoon, and he was almost willing to hump the counter for relief.

Christ, he needed to get laid.

Most confounding was how his dick got hard ninety times a day for Harper but didn't so much as twitch for another woman. Just a few moments ago, walking from his bike into the shop, he ran into a woman who frequented the Handlers' parties. She was fun, hot as hell, and had slept with a few of his single brothers. Now, she'd set her sights on him, and not five minutes ago, she let him know she would be at the clubhouse tomorrow night and was down for any damn thing his dirty mind could drum up.

And he was a guy with a fantastic imagination.

She'd worn shorts so short her ass cheeks could feel the breeze and a top that was little more than a bra. Pre-Harper, he'd have been all over that shit, suggesting they skip waiting until tomorrow and sneak around the building for a quick pregame. Instead, he found himself wishing she would talk faster so he could get on to surprising Harper.

Harper, who had no clue he was on his way to her house.

Harper, whose eyes screamed she wanted him but whose posture never relaxed.

Harper, who tried so damn hard to be an island unto herself.

Today was the day he started building a bridge connecting her lonely island to his big, boisterous MC family.

The lanky teen working the counter set Jinx's order down. "That'll be thirteen-sixty-four."

He handed over a twenty. "Thanks, man. Keep it all."

The kid's eyes bugged. "Wow, thank you, sir."

Chuckling, Jinx shook his head. "Here's a second tip. Do not call someone who looks like me, sir. Gives us hives." He scooped up his ice cream cups and nodded. "Have a good one, kid."

"Y-you too, sir, uh... dude."

The best ice cream shop in Florida happened to be three stores down from Tracker's tattoo shop, which meant it was two doors away from the flower shop Harper lived above. He strolled her way, ignoring the wide-eyed attention he drew everywhere he went.

At twenty-four, he'd been dealing with it since he hit his teen growth spurt almost a decade ago. What could he say? People liked gawking at a big, intimidating dude.

The strangest fucking thing happened as he climbed the steps behind the flower shop. His stomach flipped. *What the actual fuck?* He couldn't be nervous. He hadn't gotten nervous around a woman since he'd been eighteen and fucked his landlord, a thirty-four-year-old vixen who taught him some *things*.

Women didn't make him nervous. Sex was easy and

something he excelled at.

Yet, there he was, standing outside Harper's door with some weird fucking quiver in his gut.

Maybe he shouldn't have had that fourth cup of coffee.

He knocked and stood, ice cream in hand, waiting.

A few seconds later, he heard a tentative, "Uh… yeah? Who is it?"

Good girl, not answering without knowing who darkened her doorstep. "Hey, Prickles, it's Jinx."

The locks disengaged, and she pulled the door open with the frown he was coming to love. "I hate that name."

He grinned. "Why? It fits you so well. My prickly little cactus." Damn, she was smoking hot in short cotton shorts and a cropped tank top that revealed a swatch of silky skin along her stomach. Forget the ice cream. He found something else to lick.

"Ugh," she said, rolling her eyes. "What are you doing here? Wait, did you bring me ice cream?" Her face lit up like a damn Christmas tree.

"I did."

Her eyes widened. "From Frost Bitten?"

"Yes, ma'am, I know where to get the good stuff."

Her smile broadened so wide it made her eyes sparkle, and he'd swear under oath she let out a little squeak of delight before schooling her expression. A range of emotions passed through her eyes in a matter of seconds—reluctance, uncertainty, and a measure of fear.

Would she let him in or kick him out on his sorry ass?

He'd never tell a soul, but he held his breath, waiting for her decision.

Finally, he saw acceptance in her expression.

She reached for the cup he held out. "Thank you. Uh… did you want to come in? It's nothing special in here."

"I'd love to."

He entered her small apartment to find the truth in her words. A simple twin bed without a headboard rested against the far wall, while a love seat sat to the left. To the right, a tiny kitchenette with a two-burner stove, a mini fridge, and a microwave was pristine. She had a small television mounted on the wall opposite the couch with a four-drawer chest beneath it. That was it. No other furniture, no decorations, knickknacks, or photos. It might as well have been a hotel room for all the personalizing she'd done.

"How long have you been here?" he asked as he took in the bare walls.

Her cheeks pinked. "Uh... a few weeks. I know I haven't done much to it. I just don't really have anything since I was in... well, you know."

Right. Since she'd been in prison. Fuck, he was an ass. Of course, she didn't have tons of personal belongings. She'd been locked up for seven years. The last time she owned anything for herself, she'd been eighteen and a kid.

He cleared his throat to dislodge the golf ball wedged in it. "You should have the ol' ladies take you shopping. Trust me when I tell you they are Olympic-level shoppers, especially Liv." He made a mental note to mention it to them.

She snickered. "Yeah, I could see that, but I'm pretty sure her tastes exceed my budget."

With a grunt, he nodded. "Her tastes exceed all our budgets combined. But you'd be surprised how down-to-earth she really is. She'd never put you in an uncomfortable position you couldn't afford."

"Hmm... I'll think about it. Now shut up so I can eat."

He chuckled, then stared, transfixed, as she dug into the ice cream and slid the spoon between her gloss-free lips. It was a very short leap to imagine his cock taking the same journey. It would be so damn hot.

An involuntary groan escaped as said cock plumped.

Christ, this woman did it for him. Thankfully, she didn't notice his slip since she was busy making her own obscene noises.

"Mm… this is so good. Like insanely good. How on earth did you know chocolate peanut butter was my favorite?"

"Lucky guess," he said with a wink. "It's mine as well. Guess we have similar tastes."

"Oh." She swallowed, which did nothing to help his awkward hard dick situation. "Sorry, I'm being rude. Please sit. This couch is tiny, but it's what I have." She shrugged.

"Oh, you mean I'll have to sit super close to you? Well, damn. What a hardship."

She let out a nervous laugh. "Yeah, sorry. I promise I showered today."

He swallowed his spoonful of ice cream, then said, "Holy shit, did you just joke with me?"

"I can joke," she grumbled with a scowl as she walked to the couch.

He followed, sitting a second after she did. As promised, the couch was itty bitty, and he took up more than his half. He angled himself to face her as much as possible.

Harper drew her legs up and crossed them, wedging herself between the armrest and his bulky body. With limited space, her knees pressed into his thighs.

He had no complaints about the casual contact.

"This okay?" she asked with pink cheeks. "I can sit on the floor."

"You're not sitting on the fucking floor. I'd offer my lap if I didn't think you'd kick me in the nuts."

Making her laugh, a reluctant but genuine laugh, was better than any high he'd ever experienced.

"Thank you for this," she said with a shy smile. "I'd say it was a mistake to tell you my biggest weakness, but it seems to be working out for me."

Damn, he liked this side of her. Was it being in her own space that had her lowering her walls a few inches? Enough to tease and be teased?

"I guess it's only fair I tell you mine, huh?"

"Ooh, yes. That is fair. What is it? Wait, let me guess. It's motorcycles."

His head fell back on his shoulders as he laughed. "No, but that might be a close second."

"So what is it?"

"Prickly ladies with sad eyes and fierce souls."

She froze with the spoon only inches from her mouth.

"Jinx, I—" Heavy regret tinged her voice.

He waved away whatever rejection she planned to lob his way. He didn't need to hear it and wouldn't accept it.

Not today.

They were having too nice a time to ruin it with reality. Jinx preferred the fantasy where she'd polish off her ice cream, rip off her clothes, and they'd spend the next ten hours getting each other off.

Fuck the real world and its heavy issues.

"Oh." He reached into his back pocket. "Almost forgot. I found this on the ground outside the She Shed. It wasn't any of the other ladies, so I assumed it was yours." He handed over the folded paper, keeping a close eye on her reaction.

Her pupils dilated. "Shit. Thank you," she said as she snatched the letter from him. "Must have fallen out of my bag." She dug another scoop from her dish, then met his gaze. "You didn't read it, right?"

Of course, he fucking read it. It's what brought him to her door.

When he didn't answer, her back straightened. "You read it?"

"I did."

"What. The. Fuck?" She set her ice cream down, then

leaned forward, getting up in his face. "You had no right. That is my private, personal property."

Jinx followed suit, setting his dessert on the ground.

"I'm aware of what it is."

She threw her hands up in the air. "I can't believe you read my letter. How dare you? You know what? Get the hell out of my apartment."

She was mere inches from his face, yelling, and he was fucking hard. Goddamn, this woman was no shrinking violet, and he fucking loved it. He had at least a hundred pounds and a full foot on her, yet she had no problem telling him where to stick it. Unfortunately for her, it'd take a lot more than a sexy pissed-off woman to drive him out.

"No."

"No?" she shrieked. "That's not an option. Get out."

He lunged forward, caging her against the armrest of the couch. She reared back, breathing hard as he hovered inches from her face. "Yeah, I read the letter, and I'm damn glad I did. I won't fucking apologize for it. You wanna know why?"

She didn't answer, staring at him with furious, blown pupils. Her jaw ticked with the effort to keep her mouth clamped. Her chest heaved, and her lips were so close all it would take was for him to dip his head, and he'd get a taste.

As big as he was, as fucking angry as he was, and as trapped as she was, she didn't appear afraid. Mad as a wet cat, yes, but not scared.

And maybe... God, he fucking hoped... maybe a little turned on.

He sure as hell was.

"I won't apologize because that letter seems like a big fucking problem. The kind of problem that a person would need help solving. I might not know you well yet, Harper, but I know you're so stubborn and independent you won't ask for a goddamn lick of help solving your problems. And there is no fucking way I'll sit back and watch some fucker harass you while I have the power to help make it go away. Do you hear me?"

Her eyes flared wider than the tires he spent all day replacing. "I... I hear you."

"Shit like this turns into stalking, which turns into attacks, Prickles. I will not sit back and watch that happen to you."

"H-he can't hurt me. He's in prison for a few more years. I hate getting those letters, but they're not a threat."

"And then? When he gets out, and he's tired of you ignoring his letters? What happens when he decides it's time to see you in person?"

"How do you know I don't answer them?"

He barked a half laugh. "Because you're a fucking badass who wouldn't give scum like him the time of day."

A laugh bubbled out of her. Not one of humor but self-loathing and hysteria. "If only that were true. My whole life would be different if only that were true."

Her anguished admission chased away his anger. "Let me help you," he offered in a much softer tone.

Her eyes pleaded for him to drop it, but he wouldn't, not ever. He couldn't. Not when her safety was involved. So she sighed and nodded once.

"Tell me about the letter. You can trust me, Harper," he said.

"No. I can't." The whispered confession held so much sadness his heart ached. "Not because of you, but because of who I am. Mistakes I've made. I can't trust anyone."

"You will," he rumbled in a low tone. "Maybe not today but someday soon."

Chapter Eleven

In the past two minutes, Harper had gone through such a wide range of emotions her head spun, and her body tingled.

Or maybe that was the incredibly big and sexy man practically lying on top of her. His pelvis was right there. All she had to do was push her hips up a fraction of an inch and she'd be able to grind against him. To try and find some relief for the desire between her legs that only seemed to occur when he was around.

Then she remembered why they were positioned like this. He'd read Aaron's letter and wanted to know her secrets. Hot shame burned through her at the thought of revealing her darkest days to him.

No, she didn't trust him fully. And despite his confidence to the contrary, she never would. That was something Jinx probably couldn't understand, but she wouldn't let herself trust him because she didn't trust herself anymore. She did not trust herself to choose loyal and safe friends. And certainly not when it came to lovers.

He was the type of man, however, who wouldn't let this go. And he'd brought her ice cream, which she now realized was a ploy to butter her up before he dropped the bomb of Aaron's letter. But was there a chance Jinx could make it so she never received another one? If so, maybe talking a little was worth that outcome.

It meant she had to trust he'd keep his word and help. That he wouldn't use her story against her somehow or betray her. Did she trust that?

No.

Fear outweighed her ability to see beyond past mistakes, which wasn't fair to him. He'd never hurt her. And he was asking for a chance to prove he and his club were on her side.

She wanted to trust him.

She truly did.

But she couldn't get there.

What she did instead was a quick mental rundown of all the ways he could use her story against her, and in the end, the worst she could fathom was humiliation and shame if he were to run out in disgust or gossip to his entire club. If he couldn't help end the communications from Aaron, nothing would change for her. She could leave Florida and start again if he tried to use her mistakes against her. She'd only lived there a few weeks and hadn't planted deep roots.

Something inside her balked at the idea of leaving, but it could be done if necessary.

She sighed, suddenly exhausted. "I'll tell you about it," she said with a nod.

His victorious grin made her huff a tiny laugh.

Please don't make me regret this.

He levered himself off her, then tugged her up to a sitting position. For a second, she thought he would pull her onto his lap, and she both feared and wanted that in equal measure. But he returned to respecting her space and quietly waited for her to speak.

Here goes nothing.

"I had a semi-crappy childhood. Nothing insane that required CPS intervention or anything like that, but it wasn't any kid's dream. My dad left when I was five, so it was just me and my mom living in a sketchy trailer park. She worked at a call center for a marketing company during the day and spent her nights drinking and watching infomercials. She had me young, like sixteen young, and never really took much interest in my life beyond keeping me alive. Anyway, it wasn't bad, it just wasn't… good. You know?"

Solemn, he nodded. "I do know. I'm not exactly the poster boy for family stability myself." He gave her the same wry smile she'd come to expect from him, but it didn't hold the humor he was known for.

"Yeah, anyway, I guess as a teenager, I felt unloved and unwanted and all those crappy things." She shrugged, playing it like the memories didn't cut her as deeply as they did. "At least, that's what multiple therapists have told me. When I was a junior in high school, I met a guy named Aaron. In true cliché form, he was everything I wasn't… rich, outgoing, fun, and carefree. The life of the party. He was a year older, charismatic as hell, and getting ready to graduate and go to college. Everyone loved him." She chuckled. "He played football, for fuck's sake."

"And he wanted you." There wasn't an ounce of judgment coming from him.

She nodded. "He wanted me. The poor girl from the wrong side of the tracks who was so starved for attention she'd do damn near anything he asked."

Jinx put his hand over hers. She hadn't realized she'd been rubbing her knee so hard the skin became red and tender. Nearly twice the size of hers, his hand swallowed hers whole. But it was gentle and warm.

Comforting.

"Did he mistreat you?"

She gave the question some thought, as she had many times before, searching for red flags and signs she should have run from him before that life-altering night. "No. I can't say he did. We certainly weren't a match made in heaven, and what I felt for him couldn't be described as love, even if I thought it was back then. More of an idolizing, hero-worship kind of thing. He knew how to play me, that's for sure. Looking back, I can recognize all the manipulation for what it was. He knew how to leverage his position and maneuver me into getting what he wanted, but I can't say I was mistreated. Certainly not abused."

"Prickles, manipulation is mistreatment."

"Maybe. But anything I did with him, I did willingly."

He tilted his head. "Until…"

She inhaled as she met his gaze, then blew out a calming breath.

"You got this," he whispered with a wink.

That had her choking out a half laugh, half sob. "Until the night we were on our way to a party with some of his friends. A real group of douchey frat-boy idiots."

"Most college-age guys are."

"Yeah." She chuckled. He was making jokes as she revealed her most painful secret for the first time in years, but not in a mocking way. And she could have kissed him for it.

He squeezed her hand he still held. She turned her palm up, interlacing her fingers with his. If he minded, he didn't say and just let her cling to him. She didn't have the extra mental space to wonder why she sought comfort from his touch or why it felt so right to open up to him. Every ounce of focus she had went into recounting the incident without breaking down.

But there's where the story went downhill. "Um… we were supposed to bring some beer, so we stopped at a gas station. Looking back, I can see they were all acting a little weird, but I just rolled with it. I said I'd wait in the car because I didn't have a fake ID, but Aaron insisted I come in. Said it'd be fine. Kept asking if I trusted him."

"Fuck."

"Yeah. And I did trust him… or I wanted him to think I did. We got out of the car, and I turned around to find them pulling ski masks over their faces. And… and Aaron yanked one over my head as well," she whispered. "It was shocking. Didn't take a genius to realize they planned to rob the store." She huffed a self-deprecating laugh. "God, I still remember the feeling of shock and horror. I tried to get them to stop, but they were determined and promised they'd only snatch some beer… not that I was okay with that. Aaron dragged me along, literally, into the s-store." Her chest tightened as painful memories bombarded her.

"It's okay, Harper. You don't have to relive it. I can guess what happened from here."

But the dam had been broken, and the words poured out of her like a surge of rushing water.

"I barely took two steps into the store when all hell broke loose. A gun was drawn, and everyone was shouting, myself included. One of Aaron's friends shot the clerk," she whispered. The same horrified, sick feeling she'd had that night came rushing back. "I froze. I couldn't even blink. All I could do was stare at the bleeding man in complete shock. I didn't want to leave him, but I didn't want to be there. I'd never wanted to be there, and suddenly, I was involved in an armed robbery where an innocent man was shot. Shot! I wanted to help. To go to him. To call for an ambulance, but I couldn't do any of that. I was stuck. Then Aaron screamed at me about how we had to leave before the police came. I didn't move. I couldn't. I kept apologizing to the bleeding man. And then Aaron left. He left me because he didn't think I'd follow him. He'd dragged me in there but didn't drag me back out. You know, he had the audacity to tell me to forget about the clerk. 'Who cares about him?' he'd said. 'I'm the one who loves you.' Then he walked out. All I could do was repeat how sorry I was to the man. Over and over."

She buried her face in her hands, breathing heavily as tears ran down her cheeks. The words stuck in her throat, choking her. "I finally moved. I left. Just like the others. I left the bleeding man there to save my own skin." Sobs tore from deep within her soul.

She'd deserved everything she'd gotten. All seven of those years. And she deserved whatever look of disgust Jinx was about to level her way.

"CHRIST, BABY, NO," Jinx whispered, yanking her against him, crushing her in his hold.

For fuck's sake, that story ripped his heart out, but what smashed it into a million pieces was the self-loathing. She truly believed she'd done something so heinous she deserved jail, loneliness, and a lifetime of never trusting her own instincts.

Jinx understood regret. He knew that feeling of guilt over something that wasn't his fault. Many times, blame didn't matter. The mind took it one way, no matter one's involvement, and it could break a person. He hadn't let it break him, and he wouldn't let it break Harper either.

"I am so sorry that happened to you." If he could go back in time, he'd break Aaron's kneecaps to keep the fucker from ruining Harper's life.

"I should have stayed in the car. I shouldn't have gone into the store in the first place. If I'm really listing my shouldn'ts, I shouldn't have dated him."

Of course, she fucking blamed herself. "You were a kid. You were forced into being there. And you didn't participate. Baby, you are not responsible for what happened that night. You are not responsible for Aaron or his actions. You didn't do it."

"I know."

She heard the words, but believing them after she'd spent the past seven years telling herself otherwise would take much more than one conversation.

"You don't know," he said as he held her close. "But you will."

She made a disbelieving noise. Her cheek pressed against his chest, and slowly, as though she feared he'd protest, her arms came around him. No way could she reach around his whole body as he could hers, but she held tight, and he fucking loved it.

She wasn't as soft as the women he typically went for, but her toned physique mirrored her emotional strength. Jinx was in awe of her. His dick loved how she felt against him, stiffening even though the timing couldn't have been worse.

"How the hell did you end up with a seven-year sentence?" he asked. Maybe if he focused on her prison time, he could get Jinx, Jr. to calm the fuck down.

"Aaron's father is a big-time defense attorney. To win sympathy for his son, he painted me out to be pretty awful and very much on board with the robbery. I had a public defender who couldn't have been much older than I was. We didn't stand a chance against a shark like Aaron's father."

"Fuck, baby, I want to make them all pay." And he would. It'd take some time to come up with a plan, but everyone who fucked her over would feel his fury.

Her hum of approval made him smile because she had no idea how damn serious he was. "It didn't completely work. Aaron still ended up with ten years, but his father made it so he took me down with him."

"Tell me about the letters?"

"Aaron sends me a few every year. It started on my birthday, the first year we were both in prison. I've never responded, but they kept coming. I think he's fixated on returning to our relationship when he gets out as some crutch to get him through his sentence. Maybe he sees it as a way to erase these years."

That asshole wasn't allowed to erase what he'd done. He deserved to think of it every day for the rest of his miserable life. "Fuck him. That shit stops today."

Do you trust me?

Christ, the words hung from his lips, nearly falling free. He wanted her trust and hear her give it to him, but she needed time. She didn't need him forcing her through the process of healing, so he swallowed the words.

"I, uh... didn't finish my ice cream." She pointed to the half-full cup on the floor.

Her statement made him laugh, even though he saw it for what it was—deflection. She was finished talking and making herself vulnerable.

He'd give her the out.

For now.

"Well, we can't have that." He loosened his arms, and she drew away from him, but he cupped her face before she could reach for her dessert.

Her eyes widened as he leaned in and pressed his lips to hers in a chaste but lingering kiss. Sweetness hit his tongue, making him moan despite the tame kiss. She grabbed his biceps and gasped against his mouth. Instead of plunging his tongue in like he was dying to do, he moved his lips to her jaw then placed another kiss on the side of her neck.

And one more for good measure.

She shivered against his mouth.

When he drew away to admire the dazed look in her eyes, she whispered, "W-what was that for?"

"When I leave and you think about this afternoon, I want you to have something good to think about first."

"Oh." The cutest fucking flush rose on her cheeks.

She licked her lips as though savoring his taste, and he had to force himself to keep from throwing her down on the floor and ravishing her. Something had to give or his dick would get him in trouble.

"That was nice, but I already had the ice cream to think about." She blinked at him with an innocent smile.

That did it. Jinx laughed so loud she jumped. Her giggle was the best thing he'd heard in ages. He felt like he'd won a prize when she gave him these little glimpses of the woman hiding beneath the layers of pain and guilt. One day, she would live life to the fullest, and he planned to be there to see it.

His new mission in life was to make Harper realize how incredible she was and how much she deserved happiness.

And if he could help her achieve that happiness while naked?

All the fucking better.

Chapter Twelve

"Hey, Prez, you got a minute?" Jinx asked into his phone as he sat astride his bike.

After his trip to Harper's apartment, he had a five-hour shift at the tire shop. Once that was finished, he headed to the clubhouse to speak with his president.

"What's up?" Curly replied.

"Gotta run something by you, but I'd like to do it in person. You in the clubhouse?"

"I'm with Spec. We're chatting with... a new friend."

Certain things weren't said over the phone. Things like, "We're beating the fuck out of someone connected to Lobo." But Jinx didn't need the words. He could read between the lines.

A spark of energy zipped through him. After the heavy emotions of watching a woman he wanted relive her pain, getting his hands dirty sounded like a nice way to round out his day. "Spec up for sharing the fun?"

"Well, he's a selfish fucker, but I bet he'd let you get a shot or two in."

Jinx chuckled as he imagined Spec throwing a toddler tantrum over having to share his toy.

"You know where to find us."

Yes, he did. "On my way."

He hung up and strode over to a shed where the club kept several ATVs. With the amount of property they had, the four-wheelers were often the quickest way to get from point A to point B, especially when point B was the newly finished shack to be used for these very reasons.

Not long ago, the club realized they needed a secure, private place to conduct *chats* with certain individuals they didn't want in the clubhouse or around the ladies. One weekend, they whipped up a quick shack deep in the property where prying eyes couldn't see.

After a few moments of rough riding across the club's farm property, he parked the ATV beside the two others already outside the shack. The whomp of a fist smacking flesh followed by a pained grunt was the first sound to greet his ears after he killed the engine.

With a grin of anticipation that probably made him look psychotic, he rapped on the door. "It's Jinx."

The lock snicked, followed by the door swinging in. Curly moved to the side, revealing an unhappy-looking dude tied to a chair with his head lolling to the side. Spec stood in front of him, knuckles bloody and eyes shooting fire.

"Well, shit, I really am late to the party. Who's the guest of honor?" Jinx asked as he stepped into the building.

Curly wasted no time securing the door behind them. Chances were slim someone would wander onto the property and happen upon them, but slim meant there was still a chance, so no unnecessary risks would be taken.

Spec's attention swung his way. He had a feral, on-the-edge-of-control glint in his eyes Jinx rarely saw since the enforcer got together with Liv. Before she came into his life, Spec had no limit on the depths of his rage and violence. Liv stabilized him, but the wild animal still lurked just beneath the surface. It seemed today was the day he broke free.

"Liv saw this fucker five times in the last three days." The words were snarled, exactly what Jinx would expect from an untamed beast.

Nothing else needed to be said. That one sentence fully explained Spec's vicious chat with his new friend. "Oh shit." Jinx barked out a laugh. He walked over to the chair, grabbed the guy's hair, and yanked his head up. Two black eyes greeted him, along with a shitload of blood. "Stalking this crazy fucker's woman is up there in the top three stupidest things you can do. But I guess you know that now." He glanced at the battered face. "Oh, Spec, I think there's a spot here without any blood or bruising. Mind if I take care of that for you?"

Spec nodded. "Do it, brother." He stepped out of the way.

Jinx released his grip on the guy's hair, and his head immediately flopped forward. If it weren't for a grunt of pain, he'd have wondered if the guy passed out. Taking his sweet time to build the anticipation, he circled the chair and stopped directly in front of their captive. Then, without a dramatic windup, he rammed a brutal uppercut into the man's face.

His head snapped back, then drooped forward, and a long string of blood dropped from his mouth to the floor.

Yes, that sharp ache in his knuckles felt good. He couldn't deny picturing this guy as the one to have landed Harper in prison. But if he ever got his hands on that piece of shit, he wouldn't stop at one punch. "Problem solved. He's covered now."

Spec's grin bordered on evil. "Thanks for the assist."

"He tell you what you wanted to know?"

"He's about to. Ain't that right?" Spec walked closer to the chair.

The guy flinched, making both Jinx and Spec laugh. Curly remained by the door in quiet support as their leader.

"All right. Now that we're warmed up, you wanna

reconsider your answer?"

The guy groaned.

"I'll take that as a yes," Spec said. "Where the fuck is Lobo hiding out?"

The slurred response was barely audible.

"What's that?" Spec cupped his ear. "Can't hear you?"

Jinx jerked the guy's head back again. "Answer the man."

"I don't know."

With a snort, Spec shook his head. "This again? Need another round of memory jostling?"

"N-no. No."

"Then tell me what I want to fucking know," Spec screamed the words in the guy's face. He jumped so hard Jinx had to shove him down to keep him from overturning the chair.

"I'm telling the truth." He tried to yell, but it barely came out above a whisper. "I don't fucking know."

"So tell me something you do know. Why were you following my woman?"

He stared at Spec through swollen eyes as though trying to decide who was the worst threat. Spec? Or Lobo? Long seconds ticked by before he finally made the correct decision.

"Lobo ordered eyes on all of them. He's looking for weaknesses."

Jinx laughed. "He won't find them in Handlers' women. They're tough as shit."

The weakness lay with the men, not the ol' ladies. Threaten the women, and the men lost their shit. Hopefully, once they sent this asshole back to Lobo, bruised and bleeding, Lobo would see that targeting the Handlers' women wasn't wise.

"And you don't know where he's staying?"

"No. He won't tell anyone for this reason. If no one knows, we can't tell you."

"Where do you meet him?" Jinx asked.

"Changes every time."

Of course it did. This would be a whole lot easier if Lobo were a stupid fucker. But unfortunately, he seemed to have a few brain cells, even if he didn't always use them.

"Tell you one thing," the guy said. His voice grew stronger and less distorted.

Almost smug.

"He knows you guys blew up his factory, and he is fucking pissed."

"Tell us something we don't know," Jinx muttered.

"Does he have money? Someone funding him?" Spec asked.

Good question. In destroying Lobo's meth factory, the club incinerated his main source of income.

"He's got enough."

Yeah, definitely smug.

Jinx met Curly's gaze. The question he wanted to be answered shone in the prez's eyes.

Who the fuck was giving Lobo cash?

Curly jerked his head toward the door.

Jinx nodded. "I'm out, brother. Thanks for letting me crash the party."

"Any fucking time."

They bumped bruised knuckles, then Jinx followed Curly outside. He pushed his sunglasses back down on his nose as the glare assaulted his eyes.

"We need to find out who's backing him," Curly said the second the door closed.

"Yeah," Jinx agreed. "Think it's someone we know? Someone who has it out for us?"

"Fuck." Curly ran a hand down his face. "Probably. Who else would bankroll Lobo's revenge scheme?"

"So it's time to start going through our little black books and see who wants to fuck us?" Jinx asked.

Christ, with this group's fucked-up pasts, it could be one of a thousand people. Hell, it could be a ghost from one of the ol' ladies' former lives.

"Something like that."

"Christ, it's always something, isn't it?"

Curly nodded. "What did you need me for when you called?"

He wouldn't betray Harper's trust but wanted to get Curly's assistance on this one. "Without going into too many details, Harper is getting letters from someone in a men's prison who needs to leave her the fuck alone. You got any contacts who could help with that?"

"Where is he serving time?"

"North Carolina State Penitentiary."

A pensive expression crossed Curly's face, and Jinx could sense his wheels turning. "I may have someone for you," he said after a moment. "Give me a few days to feel things out. If it'll work, I'll help you come up with a plan."

"Thanks, Prez."

"Always, brother." Curly held out his hand. When Jinx grabbed it, the prez pulled him in for a back-slapping hug.

"So, you and Harper, huh?"

He grunted. "Me and Harper, nothing. Getting in there is like breaching Fort-fucking- Knox."

"What? You mean you found a woman who won't drop her panties at the sight of you?"

Laughing, Jinx flipped his president off. "Ain't what I'm talking about. She's got walls, brother. And I'm not sure I'll ever knock 'em down."

Curly's lips twitched. "I'm sorry. Are we talking about more than just you fucking her?" He blinked and shook his head. "Something's not computing."

"Oh, fuck you," Jinx said with a laugh. Of course, he didn't want more than a few good orgasms with Harper. "I can be her friend even if I want to fuck her."

Not that he'd ever done that before.

Friends and fucking. How the hell would that work? They'd hang out, eat together, have fun, *and* fuck each other's brains out.

Huh, that doesn't sound too bad.

"You realize that you're basically describing a relationship, right?"

"What?" Jinx scoffed. "No. Not the same thing at all."

Curly raised an eyebrow. "Who do you think my best friend is?"

Jinx's stomach dropped as he sensed the trap before him. "Uh… Ty?"

"Fuck no." Curly laughed. "He's my cousin, but he ain't my best friend. Try again, genius."

"Ugh, fine. It's Brooke. Point taken, okay?"

His president's smile grew way too smug for comfort.

"Look, I don't want to date Harper or anyone, okay? Can't a man just think a woman is great, want to fuck her, and… I don't know, wanna hang with her?"

"So, like, a date?"

Jinx lifted his hands in frustration. "Forget it. You just wanna bust my balls." He gave Curly his back as he strode toward the ATV.

"Life's stressful, brother. Gotta grab my fun where I can."

Yeah, at Jinx's expense, apparently.

He lifted a middle finger and couldn't help but snicker as Curly's laugh hit his ears. In the background, the music of Spec working over his new friend played like easy-to-ignore elevator music. God, he loved his crazy fucked-up family.

"I'll get back to you in a day or two about Harper's problem."

"Thanks, Prez."

"Your girl know about the party here tomorrow night?"

Curly called out.

Jinx threw a leg over the ATV. "Don't have a girl."

"I'm sure the ol' ladies invited her."

He turned the key, which got the ATV rumbling.

"What's that? Can't hear you?" he yelled as he cupped an ear.

"You're a jackass," Curly shouted.

"Huh?" He pointed between his ear and the idling ATV. "Sorry, man. Too loud."

He laughed his ass off as Curly gave him a double middle finger, then he shot off across the farm on the four-wheeler. As the warm wind whipped through his hair, he couldn't help but wonder what it'd be like to have Harper clinging to him on the back of the ATV.

Or better yet, on the back of his bike.

Fuck, the thought of it had him hard. They could ride to the beach, take nothing but a blanket and a six-pack, watch the sunset while they got tipsy, and then fuck in the sand beneath the stars.

Damn, it sounded good.

It also sounded romantic, which was enough to kill the fantasy.

Jinx didn't do romance.

He fucked and moved on.

Romance led to feelings that ended in messy emotions and devastation.

And if he ever got lonely? Well, that's what his family was for.

Except those bastards were coupling off, one by one, over the last year.

Made no difference to him.

None at all.

Chapter Thirteen

It'd been almost eight years since Harper had been to a party.

Eight years.

And then it was a college frat party with trash-can punch and boys pretending to be men, trying to get in the pants of anyone with tits.

Even though the years had been long and grueling, today, it felt like she'd skipped through time and landed at a biker party. Frat party to biker party with no holiday work gatherings, birthday bashes, or family celebrations in between. Only cell 'parties' with whatever scraps they'd pilfered from the kitchen on a Friday night.

Judging from the loud rock music and gruff men milling around the farm, she couldn't be farther from those cell block soirees.

Why the hell did I agree to come?

Right, because her bosses slash new friends begged, pleaded, and basically forced her to come. Something about her needing to make up for lost time, socialize more, and *"have some fucking fun already, girl,"* as Liv had eloquently put it.

Since her other option was sitting on her couch and stuffing her face with ice cream while she obsessed over the kiss she'd allowed to happen with Jinx, she'd chosen the party.

Her first kiss in many years. Jinx's kiss blew any memories of Aaron out of the water. Had kissing always made her entire body tingle and tighten with need? Had it always made her want to take off her clothes and rub all over the man kissing her?

Did she forget those feelings from years ago?

Or was Jinx that damn good?

For crying out loud, it hadn't even been a passionate kiss but one more for comfort. Jinx probably kissed his female friends the same way. Well, maybe not. She couldn't imagine Curly or Spec tolerating Jinx's lips on their women. A giggle burst forward as she imagined Spec's epic meltdown if one of his brothers tried to lay one on Liv.

"You know, I almost bet against you, but at the last minute, I decided to put my twenty down on you actually showing up." Speak of the devil. Liv's amused voice had Harper spinning around.

Spec ambled alongside his woman with his arm slung around her shoulder. Liv's hair wasn't as perfect as usual, with a few strands out of place. Her shimmery top was a bit rumpled as well. not to mention the small bruise on her neck. Seemed they'd had a bit of fun before leaving the house.

"You guys bet on me?" she asked as she jammed her hands on her hips. Should she be offended that they'd gambled on her chickening out?

Laughing, Liv shook her head. "No, we're not that bad. But we did have a plan to drag you out of your apartment if you didn't show. We were gonna send Rachel. She's the youngest and sweetest of us. Figured she'd have the best chance of convincing you. If that didn't work, it was Jo." Liv shuddered with dramatic flair. "That crazy bitch would tackle you, cuff you, and toss you in her trunk."

Harper laughed along with her and Spec. Maybe tonight

wouldn't be so bad. It might even be fun if she stuck close to the people she knew.

"You look good tonight, Harper," Spec said with a kind smile. It surprised her every time the slightly scary biker spoke to her without his tone matching his perpetual scowl. Well, the scowl disappeared for Liv, but almost everyone else got its full power.

She glanced down at the outfit she'd spent hours agonizing over—a black leather mini skirt from a thrift store paired with strappy black heels and a sparkly black tank top. The tank fit her like a second skin, showing off her toned upper body and even a hint of cleavage. Compared to what she'd worn in prison, she felt naked but had a sneaking suspicion she'd be more covered than most of the women attending the party.

"Thank you," she said to Spec. "I've got nothing on Liv, though."

"Oh, please," Liv said with a roll of her eyes as though she didn't look smoking hot in a white crop top and tiny sequined black shorts. She stepped away from her man and linked her arm with Harpers. "Come on, babe," she called out to Spec. "Harp and I need some drinks."

Behind them, Spec chuckled, but he didn't pull Liv back to him. "Yes, my queen."

"Ooh, I like that. Keep that up and you might get lucky later."

Harper nearly choked on her spit.

"What?" Liv shot her a frown.

"Your lipstick is smudged."

Liv didn't even have the decency to blush. She merely grinned and swiped a thumb under her lips. "Oops, guess the cat is out of the bag." She winked. "He already got lucky tonight. We both did." Then she laughed and towed Harper toward the clubhouse.

As they walked, with Spec trailing behind them, Harper

couldn't help but wonder what it'd be like to live in Olivia's shoes. To have a man she wanted and who wanted her so much they couldn't keep their hands off each other. But beyond that, they loved each other. Deeply. Liv didn't seem to have a single insecurity regarding her Spec. She knew the depth of his devotion and love for her and trusted him implicitly.

Would Harper ever get there? Would she ever be able to give herself to someone in that way without wondering when the other shoe would drop?

Without worrying if and when they'd betray her?

Without thinking they'd do something to land her back in prison?

Probably not. Not without the ability to trust. Liv trusted Spec with everything she had. That much was obvious. Harper could never take the initial leap of faith where she put her trust in someone. Taking the step toward being with someone terrified her and seemed impossible at this point in her life. No two ways about it. She'd have to make herself vulnerable. Anyone did if they wanted a relationship or even a situation to work. And that was what she wasn't sure she could handle. She worried that seven years in prison without healthy friendships, the love of family, and support had destroyed her ability to try.

What a depressing thought.

"Here we go," Liv said, shaking her from her pity party.

Spec pulled the door open, and Liv ushered everyone inside.

"Whoa," Harper said as she drew up short.

Beside her, Spec chuckled. "Yeah, it's a lot. But stick with us, and you'll be fine."

The place was packed and freaking crowded, and anxiety shimmied down her spine. "I didn't realize there'd be this many people here," she yelled to Liv above the noise.

"You good?"

No, she wasn't, but no one needed to know that.

"Oh yeah. I'm great. Just didn't realize how popular you guys were."

"It's not always like this. There are plenty of times we hang with the family. But sometimes these parties are fun too. Oh, look, there's the gang. Brooke," she shouted as she waved. She released Harper and wormed through the crowd toward her people.

"You sure you're good?" Spec asked near her ear to avoid screaming.

"Oh yeah. I got this." Lies. Total lies.

She was seconds from turning and sprinting out the door. The only thing that kept her from bolting was the promise she'd made to her friends to be there. If she wanted to develop strong friendships, the first step was keeping her word. Being someone people could trust was important to her.

It didn't take a trained professional to figure out why.

Spec chuckled. "I see why he hates that."

She frowned. "Who hates what?"

"Jinx."

What did Jinx hate?

He never clarified. "C'mon, let's go. My woman is ready to dance all over me, and I'm not missing a second of that. Plus, I know a guy who is dying to get you in his arms."

Her eyes widened, and she sputtered.

Spec winked, then followed the path his ol' lady took toward the back of the room.

Harper stared after him for a second. Then, as she shifted her gaze right, she locked eyes with Jinx.

Her throat dried up. The man captured her attention in a way she didn't even understand. His large, imposing presence dominated the room, even a huge crowded one like the Handlers' clubhouse.

Was he standing directly under a light?

He seemed to have an aura around him. His ink stood out against his suntanned skin—the skin that covered all those impressive muscles. He stood a head above almost everyone in the room, and that was saying something because the guys in the MC were all big. He carried himself with a confidence that bordered on arrogance, but it only made him hotter.

And he'd kissed her.

And now he was staring at her with an intensity that left her exposed and raw.

She had no idea what to do with a man, let alone a man like him. Or if she even wanted to do anything. She should have stayed home and skipped standing here ensnared by his gaze like a fly trapped in a spider's web.

This was too much too fast for her battered soul.

But still, she didn't look away.

And neither did he.

Until a woman wearing shorts so short her ass would chap if the wind blew too hard sidled up to him. She batted her long eyelashes, pursed her shiny lips, and slid a manicured hand up his chest in a sensual caress.

His gaze flicked to the woman. He smiled.

The spell was broken.

Harper's stomach soured.

"She's no one." A voice near her ear had her jumping in surprise. When she turned, Tracker stood next to her with a drink in each hand.

"For you. Double whiskey."

She didn't give a shit what it was. "Thanks." She grabbed the glass and chugged the liquid like it was water, and she'd run a marathon. Fire burned her throat and chased the liquid down to her stomach. Her eyes watered as her chest heaved with a violent cough.

"Easy there, champ," Tracker said with a half laugh. He snatched the glass from her hand before a violent cough could send it crashing to the floor. "Might wanna pace yourself."

After a final throat-clearing cough, she said, "I don't care who she is."

Tracker laughed for real this time. "Sure you don't. Let's go, party animal. If I don't head back to Jo with you in tow, she'll leave me. She's been looking for you."

Harper chuckled and rolled her eyes. "I told them all I'd show up," she grumbled but followed a snickering Tracker.

The few shots of whiskey she'd pounded were warming her blood and loosening her muscles. This was what she'd needed—a little something to take the edge off and bleed the tension out of her.

She smiled at the back of Tracker's head.

I got this.

And then, as though by magic, Jinx appeared in front of her, looking more delicious than her favorite bowl of ice cream. People milled around them, drinking, partying, and having a damn good time. But the rest of the clubhouse barely registered as she lost herself in his hungry look.

He wanted her. That much was clear.

But for all her tough talk and spiny exterior, she was scared.

Terrified.

Both from her lack of physical experience compared to a man like him and her lack of emotional experience. The one time she'd trusted a man with her body and heart, she had ended up missing out on a huge chunk of her life.

He walked until he was so close she had to tilt her head up to see his face. Her heart slammed against her chest.

"You look hot as fuck."

Her blood heated to near boiling. *Why was that so sexy?*

Instead of telling her she was beautiful or pretty, he'd used crude words. And it raised the temperature in the room by twenty-five degrees.

"Th-thanks. Uh… so do you."

Awkward much?

He didn't seem to mind her bumbling lack of social skills if the sexy-as-hell grin he shot her way was any indication.

Had he thought about their kiss? Did it make his head spin even a fraction of the way hers had? Probably not. It'd been nothing more than a prolonged peck. If what her friends said about his experience with women was true, it'd take her five lifetimes to match the belt notches he'd earned by his mid-twenties.

A solid reminder of how far out of her league he resided.

He held a glass of something that looked a lot like the disgusting alcohol she'd recently pounded. "You need a drink."

It didn't seem to be a question, but she answered anyway. "Not now. I'm good for a bit." Tearing her gaze away, she searched the crowd for someone she knew and could use to escape. Brooke smiled at her and waved from fifteen feet away.

"Uh… I should probably go say hi to Brooke." She didn't get two steps before a large, calloused hand circled her wrist. The innocent touch shouldn't have sent electricity skittering across her nerve endings, but it did.

Oh, how it did.

She shivered and looked up at the man who held her captive.

"Dance with me."

"Uh… I'm not much of a dancer." Shit, she hadn't danced with a man since her high school prom. And who was she kidding? It hadn't been a man, but a teenage boy. What the hell did she know about dancing? She'd probably freeze up and make a complete ass of herself.

" 'S all right," he drawled with a wink. He leaned closer and spoke next to her ear. "Don't actually give a shit about the dancing part. Just want to feel you pressed against me."

The combination of his smoky voice, warm breath tickling her ear, and the fantasy of being in his arms weakened her knees. A dance sounded so damn good she almost said yes, but at the last second, sanity won out.

"I don't think so." She tried to pull away, but he gripped her tight. Not nearly hard enough to hurt, but her only means of escape would be making a scene. "Jinx..." She pleaded with her eyes, begging him not to fuck with her.

His grin grew wicked. "C'mon, Harper. *You got this.*"

Well, fuck. The man knew her weakness, didn't he?

Gauntlet thrown.

Dare initiated.

Bluff called.

Was she as tough and confident to handle life as she claimed, or would she chicken the fuck out and run from a damn dance?

She narrowed her eyes as he chuckled. "One dance."

"Yes, ma'am." He held out a hand. Were he anyone else, she'd be tempted to smack the smug smirk off his face, but on Jinx, it only made him hotter.

Asshole.

"You haven't won anything," she grumbled as she placed her palm against his.

"Huh, then why does it feel like I did?"

As she was about to blast him with a snarky comeback, he pulled her flush against him. "Anytime you give me even an inch, I feel like I won the fucking lottery." He turned, still holding her hand, and tugged her toward the dancing bodies.

Jinx didn't give her a chance to be nervous. He yanked her against him, trapping her in place with a hand on her lower back. The other still held his drink. He spread his long fingers so the tips flirted with the waistband of her skirt.

Her breath caught in her throat. For a moment, she stood stunned with her arms hanging limply at her sides. What the hell was she supposed to do with them?

"Put your hands on me," he rumbled, low and deep.

She looked up at him.

As though he knew the question in her mind, he whispered, "Any-fucking-where, Harper."

With a hard swallow, she rested her hands on his hips in a barely-there hold. He grunted as though she'd grabbed his dick.

And then he started to move. The music pounded a heavy metal beat that didn't fit the way he held her or the sensual way he rolled his hips, but it didn't matter. In her mind, the music changed to a sultry beat only they heard.

Harper was helpless to do anything but follow where he led. As she moved with him, against him, every nerve cell in her body ignited. He was big, hard, warm, and felt so good against her that it took everything in her to keep from moaning.

Her limbs grew heavy and felt as though they were moving in slow motion. Her nipples tightened, and her sex pulsed to the imagined rhythm in her head. She had no shame, rubbing her chest to him in search of relief.

His hand moved lower, no longer pretending to be on her back. He cupped her ass, drawing her hips against him. One firm squeeze was all it took to rip a gasp from her.

"Fuck," he whispered as though tortured.

She trembled and lifted her gaze to find his hot and hungry on her.

One song turned into two, and before she knew it, they'd been dancing, swaying, and grinding for long minutes. She'd given up trying to ignore the rock-hard press of his erection against her stomach. Instead, she moved against it, reveling in every flare of his pupils and hitch in his breath.

He kept his hand on her ass, aiding her movement in her mission to drive him crazy. In return, he made her just as mindless with need.

What the hell was happening to her? She'd felt desire. She'd had sex. Sure, it'd been years ago, but she wasn't unfamiliar with orgasms. It'd just been her providing them to herself for the past seven years. But this sensation was something different. Her desire for him was powerful, raw, and frankly, terrifying. She ached to touch every part of him and have him touch her with a ferocity she didn't understand.

She wanted to spend hours memorizing every tattoo on his body and study the dips and rises of each hard-earned muscle. She yearned to know what he'd feel like inside her, filling her. Hell, she even wanted him to be rough with her. To put all that strength to good use and toss her around the fucking bed like he owned her.

Insane thoughts.

She wanted him to make up for the loneliness of the past seven years. To show her what she'd been missing. To prove she didn't need to guard her heart, mind, and body so closely.

But that would never happen. Harper lived in the real world where people did shitty things, and the only way to avoid becoming collateral damage was to protect herself twenty-four-seven.

She stiffened as though she'd been slapped in the face by her thoughts. Thankfully, Jinx didn't seem to have noticed.

He leaned down and spoke in her ear. "You're driving me fucking crazy, Harper. Let's get out of here. Find somewhere private."

Everything she'd been fantasizing about dangled right in front of her face. All she had to do was reach out, and she could spend the night just as she'd dreamed.

But what would happen after? How long would it be before he hurt her? Humiliated her? Destroyed her life?

He must have felt the change in her because he loosened his grip enough for her to step back. She bumped into someone but didn't bother to apologize.

"I'm sorry," she whispered, shaking her head. "I can't do that."

And like the scared little girl she pretended she wasn't, she fled.

She managed to avoid him for the rest of the night, dancing and talking with the girls for the majority of the time. They'd seen her slinking her way through the crowd after dancing with Jinx and refused to let her run home to bury herself under a pile of blankets.

About an hour later, she could admit she was having a fun time.

Until she made the unfortunate error of glancing toward the back of the clubhouse, where she'd run into Jinx.

There he stood with the woman she'd seen talking to him earlier. The woman hung off him like she was a coat and him a tall rack. She giggled, and Jinx laughed hard at whatever had been said. Her heart sank, and her stomach dropped. A sick feeling washed over her.

"That's Jess," Liv said next to her. "She's been after him for a while." She raised an eyebrow in a what-are-you-gonna-do-about-it way.

Nothing.

Harper planned to do nothing. Jinx wasn't hers, and she didn't want him to be.

"Pretty sure they already hooked up," Rachel said as she joined them.

Liv gave her a wide-eyed glare as she shook her head.

"Uh... I mean. I don't know anything." Rachel winced.

"Smooth," Liv said with a snort. She tossed back the last sip of her drink and turned to Harper. "There's still time to grab him. I promise you, he'd leave with you instead of her if you gave him the option."

Harper peeked Jinx's way again. He had his head bent low, still laughing. Jess couldn't stop touching him in ways that made Harper see red.

She cleared her throat. "I have no claim on him. so he can do whatever he wants. I'm not looking for anything from him or any man."

The pitying look she received from Liv let her know her friend wasn't buying her shit. Didn't matter. If she stuck to her guns long enough, it would become easier.

It'd become her truth.

A final glance Jinx's way showed him guiding Jess out the back door with his arm around her shoulders.

That was it. Harper had turned him down, and he'd found someone else, as he had every right to do.

It's what she wanted.

She should go home anyway. She felt sick to her stomach and might be coming down with something.

Chapter Fourteen

No one could deny Jinx had an easily excitable dick.

It liked pussies, it liked mouths, it liked hands, and it liked to be busy as often as possible.

Most of the time, Jinx loved that his dick was ready to go anytime, day or night, but sometimes, it fucking sucked. Like tonight, Harper had gotten him so hard he forgot how damn skittish she was and pushed too hard, sending her running like a scared foal.

Months ago, he'd been horny and had gone against his better judgment and fucked Jess. She had a reputation as a stage-five clinger, which was why he'd steered clear of her for ages despite her aggressive campaign to fuck him. But a night of too many tequila shots spent watching all his coupled-up brothers drool over their women had him throwing an epic pity party. One that ended with Jess in his bed.

Ever since, she'd been angling for a repeat, one he was not interested in. Once was bad enough. Fuck her twice, and she'd start looking at engagement rings. Not to mention he'd developed a problem over the past few weeks where his idiotic dick didn't want to play with anyone but Harper. And that was a huge problem because his prickly Harper didn't appear to be morphing from a porcupine to a teddy bear any time soon.

"C'mon, Jess, this way. I got you an Uber. It'll be here in six minutes."

She giggled a high-pitched tipsy sound and stumbled into him. "Whoops." There went her hands again, all the fuck over him.

He rolled his eyes as he steered her toward the back exit with an arm across her shoulders. "Try to stay on your feet, hon. You'll be feeling it tomorrow if you roll an ankle in those monster heels."

"Monster." She giggled again. "Know what else is a monster?" She turned into him and tried to slide her arms around his neck, but he managed to slip from her grasp at the last second.

He snickered. *Gotta love a loose-lipped drunk.* "I do know. Been living with that guy my whole life." What could he say? He'd been blessed with a big dick. Though now the damn thing seemed to be causing all sorts of trouble. "Right here. Through the door."

He held the door for her, she took two steps and stumbled again. He caught her under her right arm while rolling his eyes. For fuck's sake, why did he have to get stuck babysitting the sloppy drunk?

"We going to find a bed? I don't need one. You could fuck me right here against this building."

He wasn't tempted in the least. "Sorry, hon, not tonight." Or ever again. "You need to get home and sleep it off. I got you an Uber, remember?"

She pouted. "You're no fun tonight. You were fun the last time we hung out. Remember?" Her unfocused eyes stared up at him. "I remember."

"Yeah, well, you won't remember a damn thing in the morning. Let's walk."

He took her arm and guided her to the front of the clubhouse just as a black Toyota Scion pulled up.

Thank fuck this chore was almost over. As soon as he got rid of Jess, he planned to grab a bottle of tequila and drink until he forgot how Harper felt, squirming all over his erection.

Maybe he'd swipe two bottles. Alcohol poisoning might be the only way to erase that memory.

"Here you go." He pulled the door open and helped ease her onto the back seat.

She sat with her feet on the ground outside the car, staring up at him. Jess made one final attempt, spreading her legs and giving him a look that would have been sexier if she wasn't drunk off her ass.

"Enough, Jess," he said. "Not happening tonight." Or any night, but he'd spare her that indignity. "Get your feet in the car."

"You know what? Fuck you, Jinx! You wouldn't know good pussy if it sat on your face." She jerked her feet in the car so hard she toppled down on the seat.

"Charming," he muttered.

"She's not gonna puke, is she?" the driver asked.

"Nope." He slammed the door. At least, he hoped not. She was still ranting while he gave the poor Uber driver a cheerful wave. The frowning driver did not seem thrilled with his passenger.

"How much you wanna bet she ends up fucking him?"

Jinx turned to find Spec standing behind him with a joint at his lips.

"The driver?" He snorted. "Think he'll send me a thank you note?"

Spec chuckled and held out his bud.

"Thanks." Jinx took a hit and then passed the weed back to his brother. "You seen Lock at all? Been wondering if he made it tonight."

"Nope. Don't think he's here."

"Fuck." Jinx rubbed his chin. "Was planning on drinking myself into oblivion, but maybe I should go check on him."

"Got a third option for you." Smoke billowed between them as Spec passed the joint again.

"Yeah? What's that?" Jinx inhaled before handing it over again.

"I asked Pulse to check on Lock since he lives closest, and you head on over to the apartments."

Frowning, he stared at his brother. "How much of this shit have you smoked tonight? Why the fuck would I go to the apartment when I have a perfectly good house?"

Spec smirked. "Because I have it on good authority a certain thorny little hottie is crashing there tonight so she doesn't have to drive home."

His gaze automatically zeroed in on the apartment building, where a lone light shined from the window of an unused studio.

What was Harper doing? Had she fallen asleep? Was she lying on the couch, watching television?

Was she lonely?

How would she react if he paid her a surprise visit?

Probably not well.

"She turned me down, brother."

Spec lowered the joint from his lips. "That may be, but you didn't see her face when you walked off with Jess. Harper one hundred percent thought you were off to fuck some other woman, and she did not like it."

He perked up. "Really?"

"No lies, man. I worried for a moment that she was going to go all cat-fight on Jess, but your girl's too controlled for that shit. She just put on that everything's-fine bullshit mask she always wears." Spec chuckled. "Tell you what, it's gonna be epic when she finally lets her wild out of its cage. Question is, you smart enough to be there when it happens, or you gonna let some other fool reap those rewards?"

Displeasure at that idea rumbled in his chest.

Spec clapped him on the back. "Have a good night, brother." He snuffed out the stub, then made his way inside.

Once again, Jinx allowed his gaze to drift toward the apartments.

Was he going to do this?

"Fuck it," he whispered. If Harper tossed him out on his ass, at least he'd know for sure. Then he could stop obsessing over a woman who didn't want him and find one who did.

He jogged a hundred feet from the clubhouse to the renovated barn. Curly had it turned into four studio apartments for visitors, prospects, or members needing a place for a while.

Or, apparently, beautiful women who didn't want to drive home after parties.

As he bounded up the stairs to the second level, his dick stiffened to the point of agony. If Harper slammed the door in his face, he might have to jack himself off right in front of her door to avoid suffering a world-record case of blue balls. Unfortunately, chances were high that was exactly what would happen.

When he reached the door corresponding with the light he'd seen, he pounded like a SWAT team, ready to bust the thing in.

"Coming." Harper's frantic response had him trying to calm his shit, but, fuck, he wanted her so badly he could hardly think. The sound of her soft footsteps hurrying toward the door had him smiling.

He heard her disengaging the locks, but then she called out, "Uh... who is it?"

Smart girl.

"It's Jinx." Christ, he sounded strained, like he was holding back from kicking the door in and taking her right there.

Which he pretty much was.

"Jinx?" The locks clicked, and she yanked the door open. "Is everything okay?"

One look at her had him swallowing his fucking tongue.

She stood there with a frown on those pretty lips and a wrinkle at the top of her nose. Her feet were bare, with pale-pink toenail polish. Never had he given a shit about a woman's feet, but he had the urge to run his tongue up an arch to watch her squirm.

"Jinx?" she said again. "Why are you here? Is everything okay?"

"What the fuck are you wearing?" he croaked as he found his gravel-ridden voice.

Her cheeks turned pink as she glanced down at herself. "Oh, shit. Sorry, I was hot, and I wasn't expecting anyone." She folded her arms across her chest to cover the prominent nipples beneath the flimsy camisole that had been designed with the sole purpose of torturing slobbering men like him. It showed her cleavage, a strip of her stomach, and had straps so thin he could rip them off with one.

"Don't," he barked, making her freeze.

"Wh-what?" Her eyes widened, but she let her arms fall to her sides. Along with the sinful top, she wore matching baby-blue shorts that he'd kill to see from behind. "What are you doing here, Jinx?" she whispered.

"I'm here because you got my dick so damn hard, I can't think of anything else but getting my hands on you." She gaped but didn't slam the door or tell him to get the hell out. He took a step into the doorway. "I'm here because I want to taste you." He walked closer.

"Your lips."

Step.

"Your tits."

Step.

"This spot right here," he said as he stroked a finger just below her jaw.

Harper let out a shuddered breath.

He leaned forward until his lips brushed her ear. "Your pussy."

A whimper escaped her, making his dick twitch.

"You gonna invite me in, Harper? Or are you gonna keep ignoring the fire between us?"

The scrape of his lips over her ear had her shivering. After a second, she turned her face toward his. Their lips lined up, a breath away, and it was his turn to experience a ripple of sensation.

"D-do you want to come in, Jinx?"

Those words went straight to his needy dick.

"Fuck yes, I do."

SHE WAS DOING this.

She'd lost her mind, and she was doing it.

Nothing had changed. Jinx was still a man, and she couldn't let herself get overly involved while protecting herself.

But it had been so long since she'd been touched, and now that she knew what he wanted to do to her, she couldn't deny the need any longer. His smoky voice whispering in her ear made it impossible to remember all the reasons this was a terrible idea.

She wanted pleasure.

She wanted touch.

She wanted him.

And now she was going to have him.

She watched as he shut the door with a forceful bang, hiding them from the rest of the world. Even with her skimpy pajamas, she was hot and already sweating.

He cupped the back of her head in one enormous hand and

kissed her.

This kiss was nothing like their first. It had none of the comfort, sweetness, or tentative curiosity. Instead, this kiss promised sex Harper had never experienced. Sex with a man who knew what he wanted and had no qualms about taking it.

His tongue didn't wait for admission into her mouth. It breached her lips with the same confidence he showed in all his actions. He held her hand in place as he plundered, stealing her breath and weakening her knees.

She stood there in motionless shock for a few seconds, her arms dangling at her sides. The first nip of his teeth on her bottom lip had her jolting into action. She moaned into his mouth as she grabbed onto his biceps. The ache between her legs had her grinding her pelvis against his thigh, searching for release.

"Fuck yes," he panted out against her lips. "Rub that hot pussy all over me."

She'd have been embarrassed if she weren't already crazed with the need to come. Though she'd never be able to physically move him anywhere, she tried to tug him toward the couch. She wanted to feel his heavy weight pressing into her entire body.

"Bed. I'm too fucking big for that tiny couch," he growled against her lips.

Harper giggled as they both spared a fraction of a second to look at the loveseat. "Bed," she agreed. "*Now.*"

His dark chuckle had her rushing to the bed, which could also stand to be bigger. He'd need a king, at least, but the queen in the studio would do for tonight.

When she reached the foot of the bed, Jinx grabbed her shoulder and whirled her around. Before she could react, his hands were on her waist, and he tossed her on the bed. She hit with a soft bounce.

He stood at the end of the bed, staring down at her. Then, way too slowly, he drew his shirt up and over his head.

Harper propped herself on her elbows, watching the show as each inch of skin was revealed. As soon as he chucked the shirt across the room, he spread his arms and smirked. "Take it all in, baby." He flexed, making his pecs bounce and drawing a laugh from her.

She should have known sex with him would be as fun as it was hot. Jinx knew how to bring playfulness to any situation. "Don't mind if I do." She took his suggestion, letting her greedy gaze roam all over his bare chest. If this ever happened again, she'd make a mental catalog of every hill, valley, and inch of ink. But that required patience, and she didn't have it tonight. "I want to touch you."

He groaned. "In a minute. Give me something to look at too. Like those tits, trying to bust out of your top."

She reached for the hem of her shirt, but he shook his head. "Pull it down?"

"Huh?"

He indicated her neckline. "Pull it down."

Her breathing sped up, making her chest rise and fall rapidly. With unsteady fingers, she pulled the scoop neck of her tank top down. Her breasts popped out and squeezed together from the position of her top.

"Fuck yes, you're sexy. Look at you like that. Offering those beauties up to me."

He crawled onto the bed and up her body.

Breathing became difficult. Jinx was so big, dwarfing her just by hovering over her. "So pretty," he murmured as he stroked a circle around her nipple.

Harper bit her lower lip. Her back arched off the bed, pushing her breasts closer to him as though begging for more.

"What has it been? Seven years since you fucked?" He continued to draw maddening circles around her nipple.

If he would just move those fingers a half inch in, he could pinch her nipple and end the torture. "Jinx…"

He smirked. "Answer the question, baby, and I'll give you what you want."

The question. *Oh yes.* How long since she'd had sex? He wasted no time getting straight to the humiliating questions. "A-almost e-eight," she whispered as her face flushed hot.

"That's a long time."

He had no idea.

"And you were so damn young when you went to prison."

"Yes."

"So you basically don't even know what you like? How you like to be fucked?"

She stared at him, face flaming. Why was he making her admit this? "No."

"Hmm…" He stroked a thumb over her nipple in a gentle touch that didn't give her half of what she needed yet still sent a shocking jolt to her core.

She cried out and arched up again.

"Bet you thought about it, though. Bet you've spent hours stuffing your fingers in your pussy as you think about it. Think about me."

No one had ever spoken to her this way, and it set off a riot in her body. It was simultaneously the hottest and most humiliating conversation she'd ever had.

When she didn't immediately answer, he stopped touching her.

She whimpered and said, "Yes."

He circled her other nipple, chuckling as she growled. "Yes, what?"

"Yes, I've thought about it." She swallowed. "About you." *Here goes nothing.* "As I touched myself."

His grin was pure sex. "Tell me this… as you thought about me fucking you, how did you like it? Was I soft and gentle?" His touch mimicked his words, stroking over her breasts with a light, easy caress that left goose bumps in its wake. "Or did you like it harder? Maybe a little rough?" He pinched her nipple.

"Aah." She arched into the touch. Yes, this was what she'd been waiting for.

"A little filthy?"

He twisted, and the pleasure sharpened, riding the edge of pain. Harper squirmed.

She wanted more.

She wanted the same treatment for her other breast.

She wanted those strong hands everywhere.

"You don't have to answer," he said in a dark, dangerous tone. "Think I figured it out for myself." His dark head lowered until he drew her other nipple into his mouth. And he did it just as he'd described—hard, rough, filthy.

Harper shouted. The hot suction of his greedy mouth made her stomach tighten. She clutched at his back to keep him in place in case he had the foolish idea to leave before she'd been satisfied.

A rumble of enjoyment reverberated from his chest. "Fuck, you taste even better than I imagined." He moved to the other breast, sucking with the same vigor as before.

Almost eight years of repressed desire and unfulfilled need rose to the surface with such ferocity she couldn't hold back. "Jinx," she cried out as she pushed her pelvis into him.

As much as she'd initially thought they'd spent hours learning each other, touching, kissing, licking, and bathing each other in pleasure, she couldn't do it tonight. She knew what she wanted, and nothing else would satisfy her.

He grabbed her ass and held her immobile as he ground his dick against her. She had no shame, rubbing herself along his length. But it wasn't even close to enough. "Jinx, please."

He released her breast with a rough chuckle. "You're in a

bad way, aren't you, baby?"

His voice sounded like sin and promise all wrapped up.

Tomorrow, she'd be horrified by her wanton behavior. For the way she didn't just let her mask slip but threw it on the floor and danced all over it. But Jinx was right. She was in a terrible way.

He rolled his hips, making her whimper, the damn tease. "You want this big dick, don't you? Filling you up? It's been so fucking long."

She moaned at the promise in his words, but, God, if he didn't do it soon, she might die.

"Tell me."

"I want it," she whispered.

"More," he growled out. "Tell me more."

Damn him. He was making it impossible for Harper to hide any part of herself and cling to the last thread of self-preservation. She squirmed but couldn't escape the trap of his hypnotic gaze. Maybe that was it. Maybe he'd hypnotized her with some mind-control magic. It was the only thing she could think of. After years of keeping her emotions in check and letting people see only what she wanted them to, this man shattered it all with one touch.

There was only one way she'd get what she wanted, and it was to give him what he demanded.

"Jinx, please, don't tease me. Give me your cock. I want it. I need it."

His grin was entirely sex. "It's yours, baby." After throwing her a wink, he scooted down her body. "Spread these sexy legs for me."

Oh fuck.

She did as he asked, widening her thighs to fit his bulk.

He groaned, long, loud, and hot as hell. "Goddamn, you've soaked through these tiny shorts."

When she was younger and slept with Aaron, he sure as

hell hadn't stared at the wet spot on her shorts. He'd been an over-eager twenty-year-old hurrying to get to the O.

Jinx was all man and too far gone to care.

"Next time, I get to taste this pussy."

She flushed with heat.

"Mm..."

That sound.

"Jinx," she whispered.

"I know. It's coming. Lift that ass for me."

She did, and he slid the sleep shorts down. She hadn't bothered with underwear, not wanting to sleep in the thong she'd worn to the party.

Sitting back on his heels, he pulled the shorts off as she raised one leg at a time. Before she could lower her leg, he kissed her ankle. The move was so tender it sent a tremor through her heart.

Though tender wasn't on the menu, it couldn't be.

She tried to work some of her mask in place again, broken though it was. She could give him her body to scratch this seven-year itch, but that was all she had to offer.

So when he lifted her shorts to his nose and inhaled the scent of her arousal, it ripped a gasp from her. Then she focused on the raunchy act instead of the sweet one.

She had to protect herself, no matter how much she yearned to throw caution to the wind. That road led to heartbreak, pain, and seven years behind bars.

Chapter Fifteen

Her scent made him dizzy. It was a potent drug he wanted to get high on day after day. Fuck, he might just walk out with those shorts and sleep with them under his pillow.

She was fire beneath him, trying so hard to hide while also getting the pleasure she needed and deserved. Christ, if ever a woman needed dick, it was this one.

And he was there to give it to her.

With a mental note to search for them later, he tossed the shorts over his shoulder. Thank fuck he was a hopeful fucker and had stuck a condom in his back pocket before the party. He fished it out, making a point to show Harper he'd never leave her unprotected.

Her eyes flared.

Yeah, she was so far gone she hadn't given the thing a thought.

"I got you," he whispered.

She nodded and mouthed. "Thank you."

His hands went to the button on his jeans. "Ready to have your mind blown?"

An eager smile curled her lips. "Hell yeah."

She stared as he worked the zipper down, then coasted the jeans and his black briefs over his hips. His hard cock sprang free of its denim cage, and he nearly said of prayer of thanks.

He shoved the jeans to his ankles, then straightened back up, spreading his arms so she could look her fill.

Harper propped herself up on her elbows. "God, Jinx, you're..." She shook her head.

"Thank you, baby." He ripped the condom open and dropped the wrapper on the bed before rolling it down his cock.

Harper's eyes followed every move, and he loved it. There was something extra erotic about reintroducing her to fucking after so many years. After he had the condom in place, he fisted his shaft and gave a few strokes. He groaned when she licked her lips in an unconscious expression of want. "Damn, woman, you wanna get that mouth on me sometime?"

She nodded. "I really do."

"It's a date," he said with a wink.

Something flashed in her eyes, something he knew would be a denial or rejection. It was time to distract his prickly little cactus from her negative thoughts. With a wicked smile, he hooked his right arm under her leg and proceeded to lick the inside of her knee.

When she squealed, he took advantage of her momentary distraction to yank her ass up onto his thighs. There she was, all wet and slippery, inches from his cock. He took himself in hand and rubbed the tip of his dick against her opening.

Harper gasped and bit her lower lip. Her eyes were hooded with desire, and those delicious tits rose and fell with the force of her breath. She gave him a single nod, and he pressed forward. The instant she sucked him inside, he gritted his teeth. It was by far the hottest, tightest pussy he'd ever been in.

"Fuck," he said on an exhale. If Harper hadn't told him otherwise, he'd bet his damn bike she was a virgin.

"Oh my God," she whispered. Her eyes slammed shut as he slid himself all the way in with agonizing slowness.

As soon as he bottomed out, he stopped moving. Christ, she was so goddamn tight that he might blow from two fucking pumps. His balls ached with the need for release and tingled like it wasn't far away. He'd love to slam into her but didn't want to embarrass the fuck out of himself. He also didn't want to hurt her.

Next time.

They were racking up quite a list for their repeat performance, something he didn't ordinarily do, but no way in hell would he miss out on all the things he wanted to do to her.

And have her do to him.

"Feels so good," Harper whispered, and he swore he saw a tear leak from the corner of her eye. He'd never call her on it, though. It'd send her right back into her shell like a frightened turtle.

"Fuck yeah, it does. You like being stuffed full of cock, huh? Better than you remember?"

Her eyes remained closed, but she smiled. "A million times better." When she opened her eyes, they were shiny with unshed tears. "And I like being full of *your* cock."

He grunted. What man didn't like hearing his dick ruled them all?

"Fuck me, Jinx. Make everything else go away and just fuck me."

"Anytime, baby. Any-fucking-time."

The talking gave him a second to get himself under control, and he was ready to send her to the stratosphere.

He hiked her leg up to his shoulder, then leaned forward and gave her a searing kiss. Thank Christ, the woman had some flexibility to her. As they made out, he rolled his lips, dragging his cock through her pussy and pushing deep once again.

Harper moaned into his mouth. Her arms came around

him, and the second he felt the prick of her fingernails on his shoulders, he lost his mind.

He planted one hand near her head and grabbed her ass with the other, using it to control the speed of her hips.

She cried out as she moved her hips to his rhythm. He pounded into her the way he'd fantasized about since the day they met. Her pussy gripped him so tight he had to fight off the urge to come the entire time. This couldn't just be *good* for her. it had to be out of this world. He wanted her to come back for more, and it'd take getting her addicted to his cock to make that happen.

This version of Harper blew away anything he'd imagined. She wasn't quiet, timid, or holding back. Her cries and moans drove him insane with need while sweat broke out across his back.

He wanted more. He wanted to see more of her and watch her take every ounce of pleasure he had to offer. He released her leg and flipped them in a move that had her yelping in surprise.

Harper wobbled, then planted her hands on his chest for support. Her hair was wild, a well-fucked mess. Her tits—God, those tits—were wet from his mouth. Each had a pink mark from the abrasive rub of his beard.

In this position, she was fully on display. He could watch every movement and every emotion playing across her features, and he fucking loved it.

But she knew it and wasn't confident.

"Jinx…"

"Just move, baby. Move that gorgeous body any way that feels good."

She did, slowly at first, but within seconds, she was riding him like a rodeo buckle was in her sights. Her nails raked down his chest as she threw her head back and worked her hips on his cock.

He loved that feeling—the painful scratch. Fuck, he hoped he'd be gouged to shit in the morning.

"Jinx," she said on a moan.

He didn't need more. It was an unspoken plea for help, and he'd make sure she had the climax of her life. Jinx filled his hands with her lush, muscular body and helped rock her over him.

She gasped, then yelled, "Yes, yes, Jinx."

He tried to think of anything to keep himself from coming first—inventory at the tire store, taking a punch to the face, and even crashing his damn bike—but nothing worked. All he could see was the beauty using his body to find pleasure for the first time in ages, and it was the sexiest sight he'd ever seen. Combined with the hot squeeze of her pussy, he was using every ounce of strength to keep from blowing.

"Kiss me," she yelled as she threw herself forward onto him. The second before their lips met, she whispered, "I'm gonna come."

Their mouths met in a kiss so unrestrained it bordered on violence. Harper shuddered and writhed in his arms as she came, and he fucking loved how she wanted the connection of a kiss during that time.

Her pussy squeezed him so hard his eyes crossed. Before she'd even stopped trembling, he flipped them again. Three hard thrusts were all it took to have him explode into the condom. He shouted his release and buried his face in her neck.

It was more powerful than any orgasm he'd had in a long time.

He dwarfed her with his large body. Beneath him, little tremors ran through her every few seconds. They lay quiet, catching their breath, until he felt her slowly begin to stiffen. The reality was setting in, and he wasn't ready.

Jinx lifted his head and clasped her face between his hands.

She tried to look anywhere but him, but he took up her entire field of vision and wouldn't allow anything but her full attention.

"Jinx," she whispered with a near sob in her voice.

"Shh." He kissed her once. Then again. Then a third time until she went pliant beneath him again. No walls would be erected between them. Not tonight. "Let me stay."

"No, Jinx, I—"

"Let me stay. Sleep beside me. We don't need to talk about anything."

She stared at him with all the naked vulnerability she refused to acknowledge.

"O-okay."

He resisted the urge to cheer out loud. Every tiny victory felt like an Olympic win.

He scooted off her and hopped out of bed to take care of the condom. When he returned, he found her on her side, facing away from him.

No problem.

Jinx climbed in, laid down on his side, then pulled her against him. Her ass nestled against his softened cock. Then he draped an arm over her body, nestling it between her breasts.

She was tense and unrelaxed but didn't protest.

He kissed her neck, then whispered, "Good night, Harper."

"Good night, Jinx." She curled her arm over his, and second by second, the tension left her body until she melted into him.

He said no talking, and he meant it. He didn't need words to know she'd enjoyed herself. The fact that she agreed to let him sleep next to her said it all, but he couldn't allow himself to drift off without one whispered confession. Harper deserved to know how amazing she was.

"Thank you for trusting me," he murmured against her ear.

"This has been one of the best nights of my life."

Her breath caught, letting him know she hadn't fallen asleep and heard him. She didn't respond, but he didn't want or need it.

Her warm, sated body plastered to his was all he needed. Within seconds, he'd fallen into a deep sleep and didn't stir until well into the morning hours.

When he finally cracked open an eye, the sun was shining, a dog was barking outside, and he felt more relaxed than he had in a long time.

Until he realized he was alone in the bed.

His first instinct was to jackknife up and search for Harper, especially when he heard her soft footsteps near the door. There weren't many places to hide in the shoebox apartment. He'd bet his left nut she'd woken up, panicked, and he was hearing her attempted escape.

He wanted to go to her, wrap his arms around her, and kiss her until she forgot her reasons for leaving, and they'd end up back under the covers. But he resisted. She wouldn't react well if he interrupted her getaway. Her thorns would emerge, and he was too blissed from the previous night to be punctured by her barbs.

So he'd give her today, but that was it.

Tomorrow he'd come for her.

They'd made a list of future sexual games to play, and he refused to miss out on any of them.

Chapter Sixteen

Harper spent her Saturday doing laundry and cleaning her already tidy apartment while battling last night's memories. They popped into her head randomly throughout the day with unsettling frequency—Jinx's hands on her, his mouth, his cock inside her, and how he'd given her exactly what she'd needed physically and mentally to soothe her rampant anxiety about him being the first man in so damn long.

For crying out loud, the man pretended to be asleep and let her scurry out like the coward she was. She owed him for that and could think of more than a few ways to repay the favor. Well, if she hadn't vowed to leave last night in the past and forbade herself a repeat.

Going back for seconds would be a gigantic mistake. All it had taken was one passionate night with him to screw with her head.

As she'd mopped her tiny kitchen floor, she'd imagined him walking into her apartment, coming up behind her, and kissing her neck. She'd turn around, drop the mop, and lose herself in his intoxicating arms. They'd be so hot for each other that he'd take her right there on the floor, unable to wait long enough to drag her to the bed twenty feet away.

The combination of domesticity and eroticism drove her insane.

What the hell is wrong with me?

She knew nothing of domestic bliss and hadn't ever craved it.

It made perfect sense if she delved deep into her emotions as she'd been trained as a counselor. By spending seven years in prison, she'd been robbed not only of freedom and a physical relationship with a man but of a home she could call her own to feel safe and comfortable.

The eroticism part of her fantasy needed no further analysis. Hell, Jinx had awoken something she'd kept a lid on for years, and after last night, she might need to invest stock in a vibrator company to keep her newly awakened sexual appetite under control. Combining those two needs into one fantasy revolving around a particular sexy man made perfect sense from the therapist's side of her brain.

But she didn't want to think about it clinically. She didn't want to use her training to examine her reactions. That road led to a deep well of buried feelings of betrayal, anger, and loss. At some point, she'd have to confront those emotions to move past them and live a happy, fulfilled life, but the thought paralyzed her with fear. Who wanted to reopen their wounds and bleed all over the floor voluntarily?

Not me.

Some counselor she'd be.

Do as I say, not as I do.

"This needs to stop," she announced as she shoved the mop into the sudsy bucket. Pity parties weren't her thing. She was a master who compartmentalized and hid her feelings.

A knock at her door had her freezing in place.

Could it be Jinx?

She wasn't ready to see him yet. As highly as she liked to think of her stoicism, she hadn't had enough time to get her shields in place again. He'd see straight to the needy, vulnerable core he'd unearthed.

She reached for the door handle before remembering the asshole who'd accosted her in the parking lot. "Uh… who is it?"

"It's your besties," came a sing-song voice through the door.

She blew out a breath while chuckling and pulled open the door.

There stood Liv, Brooke, Jo, and Rachel, dressed to the nines.

"We're here to kidnap you," Liv proclaimed as she ran into the apartment, arms in the air as though she'd scored a touchdown. "And we brought presents." She thrust an overflowing shopping bag into Harper's arms.

"What?"

The ladies spilled into her small space, making it feel even tinier.

Jo glanced around. "Hmm, Tracker has an apartment above the tattoo shop, and this is the exact mirror image."

"Makes sense." Brooke walked over and hugged Harper. Then she tapped the shopping bag. "That is a dress, shoes, and some accessories. We're hitting up happy hour at a bar on the beach about a half-hour ride from here. You'll love it."

They all looked stunning in their dresses and heels. "Your men are cool with this? Considering what happened the other night? I thought they were worried about you guys going out alone."

Looks were exchanged back and forth until Brooke finally rolled her eyes. "As the oldest of the group, I take no responsibility for this. I was coerced."

Liv giggled. "Oh yeah, you fought really hard."

"Okay, I'm lost." Had they managed to sneak away from the watchful eyes of their ol' men? And was that smart?

"Shut up." Brooke swatted at a laughing Liv, who dodged the swipe with ease. "They know we're out. We're not alone.

We have a prospect following us around."

"Yep," Jo added. "They just think we're off to a nice dinner, not happy hour at a popular spring break bar."

"Spring break?" Harper laughed. "Aren't we all a little old for that crowd?"

"Maybe, but the vibe will be fun, and that's all we need. I could use some dancing and girl time. Couldn't you?" Rachel, the youngest and most likely to fit in with a college crowd, arched an eyebrow.

Harper considered their offer. Stay home and clean more of the already clean things or go out and grab another experience she'd missed out on.

Easy choice.

"Okay, give me ten minutes to get dressed and slap on some makeup." All her makeup was brand new. Some of it she'd yet to open, but she sucked at applying all of it.

"Ooh, I'll help." Liv followed her into the bathroom without waiting for an agreement. Harper had no qualms about changing in front of anyone. She'd spent years without so much as a private shower, but she didn't want to make her new friends uncomfortable.

Not that Liv seemed to mind one single bit.

"Okay," Liv said as she shut the door behind them. "I hope this fits you. You're fitter than I am, but we're similarly sized otherwise, so I based the sizes on myself. There should be a sticky bra that'll work with the dress in there as well."

"A sticky bra?" Harper questioned with a frown. What she knew about fashion as well as women's lingerie only included sports bras, granny panties, and jumpsuits.

"Yep. You just sorta stick them on your girls," she said, slapping a hand against her chest. "This way, you don't have to worry about your headlights showing." Liv made herself at home in Harper's bathroom as she spoke, digging through her recently purchased makeup.

Harper blinked. "What the hell are headlights?"

Liv glanced her way. "THO?"

"You're making it worse. I'm lost."

Laughing, Liv straightened from her drawer, rummaging. "Girl, stick with me. I'll catch you up on all that you miss—" She slapped a hand over her mouth, cutting off the words. "Oh, shit! Harper, I'm so sorry. I shouldn't have brought that up. I know about your history because of your background check, but it's entirely inappropriate for me to bring it up before you do. Please forgive me, and I promise it won't happen again."

The second the reference to her jail time left Liv's lips, an invisible hand wrapped itself around Harper's throat and squeezed. But Liv's look of absolute devastation and sorrow released the grip before panic could set in. These girls were her friends, and they were becoming closer friends each day. Pretending her past wasn't a part of her life wouldn't work forever. At some point, she had to be who she was—an ex-convict who'd served time. Maybe opening up to the women was her first step in learning to trust again.

"Liv, it's okay," she said, taking hold of her friend's hands. "Really. It's okay. You're right. I missed out on a lot, including headlights and THO, apparently. But I'm loving all the new experiences I'm having with you ladies. You've never made me feel anything less than normal, and in my position, that's incredible."

Clearing her throat as though Harper's words had affected her deeply, Liv said, "Well, then, I'll fill you in. THO stands for titty hard-on."

Harper snorted a laugh. "What?"

"Headlights mean the same thing." Liv pointed to her chest. "You know, when it's cold, and you're wearing something thin, the nips show. Titty hard-on."

"Oh my God." Laughing, Harper covered her face. "Say no

more. I get it now."

"Good. Now, let's get you ready."

Fifteen minutes later, Liv darted out of the bathroom to announce, "Okay, ladies, let me be the first to present the nightlife version of Harper."

They clapped and whopped until Harper stepped out of the bathroom, then the hollers turned to shrieks and shouts of, "Holy shit, you're hot."

Harper's face heated to a million degrees. "I've never worn anything like this," she said with a nervous giggle as she smoothed the sleek black fabric over her thighs.

"Well, you are smokin' hot. Jinx is gonna los—" Rachel said as Jo's elbow landed in her ribs. "Ow. Uh... I mean, you look smokin' hot. And that's all. I have nothing else to add."

"Subtle, guys," Brooke muttered.

Harper ignored the line about Jinx, instead focusing on how strange it felt to be wearing such a beautiful dress. While simple in its design—fitted, black, short, and two large cutouts on the side, bearing most of her midriff—the dress was beautiful. Two thin straps over her shoulders held the entire thing up. She couldn't bend over without giving anyone a show from behind, but she sure as hell felt pretty, especially with the smoky eyes and pouty lips Liv created. Strappy black heels that made her four inches taller completed the ensemble. It should be a fun night if she didn't break an ankle.

"Okay, let's do this," Liv said as she grabbed her satin clutch off the counter.

Brooke drove them in her SUV. As they got closer to the beach, she cast frequent looks in the rearview mirror. "Do you think he's freaking out?" she asked of the prospect following them on his bike. "He has to have figured out we're not going where we told him."

"I'm sure he's shitting himself," Jo said with a chuckle.

"Probably can't decide if it's better to rat us out and piss off our men and us or let us have our fun and hope the guys never find out."

"Aww, I feel bad for him." Rachel glanced over her shoulder.

"That's just because your man was a prospect until five minutes ago. He'll be fine. It's not like we're going to do anything crazy." Brooke turned left into a crowded parking lot. "We're here."

"Yes! You ladies go get a table, and I'll order drinks," Liv announced as she exited the car.

Harper followed the ladies into the bar and to a high-top table. She took in the crowded place as they all settled into their seats.

People danced and drank everywhere she looked. Some had shots, some beer, and some giant pink drinks with umbrellas and pineapples on a stick. Most patrons were young—early twenties maybe—but some appeared older than she was.

The entire exterior consisted of sliding panels of windows currently open and letting the warm sea air in. Looking to her right, she caught glimpses of the gulf between the moving bodies.

"Like it?" Jo asked from across the table.

"I love it." The open-air concept made her feel free, something she valued above all else. Excitement zinged through her, and finally, she took a breath and promised to enjoy the evening. Hell, she hadn't even thought about Jinx in almost forty-five minutes. That had to be a record since meeting the man with those sexy tattoos, hard muscles, and magic lips.

Damn.

Time to reset the clock.

"Here we go." Liv arrived with a server carrying a tray of

drinks trailing behind her.

Harper's eyes widened. "That's a lot of drinks."

"Yep. A margarita and two tequila shots for all."

"Oh crap," Rachel whispered.

Jo laughed. "So it's gonna be that kind of night. Why do I feel like Tracker is going to have to carry my sloppy ass to bed later?"

"Because that's the goal." Liv instructed the waitstaff to distribute the drinks. Once everyone had theirs, she lifted her first shot glass. "To the Handlers' ol' ladies."

"I'm not an ol' lady," Harper pointed out.

"Give it time, give it time." Liv motioned to Harper's shot glass.

With a roll of her eyes, she grabbed the shot. She'd give this one to Liv even though she wasn't an ol' lady and never would be.

"Bottoms up, ladies!"

They all sucked back the shots. Harper screwed up her face and gasped as the disgusting liquid scorched its way to her stomach. "Oh my God, that's awful."

"Right there with you," Rachel said with a full-body shudder. "Ugh."

"Mm… it's my fave." Live smiled.

"Let's play a game," Jo said.

"Ooh, how about truth or dare?" Liv's eyes lit up.

"That sounds fun." Already, Harper felt her muscles loosening. Whether the shot magically worked that fast or it was all in her head, she didn't care. This was fun, and she planned to make it last as long as possible.

"Okay, then you're first, Harper. Truth or dare?"

"I'll start with a truth to warm myself up."

Liv's smile grew mischievous.

Uh-oh.

"Did you sleep with Jinx last night?"

Well, she'd walked right into that one, hadn't she?

"How about we do our next shot?" she asked, raising her glass. "Yeah?"

A huge grin broke out across every face at the table.

"Oh my God, you did, didn't you?" Rachel asked. She squealed and clapped her hands. "This is the best news ever."

"What? I didn't say anything," Harper exclaimed.

"No, but your face did," Liv called out, laughing.

"And that hickey on your neck," Brooke added with a wink.

"What?" Harper slapped a hand over her neck without even knowing if she had the right spot. How had she missed a hickey? "He didn't give me a hickey, did he?" She gaped at Brooke.

"Nope," Brooke said with an apologetic wince. "But now you just admitted you were with him."

"Oh!" *Well, shit.*

Everyone laughed and cheered.

"Wow, Brooke. That was devious." Liv held her hand up for a high-five.

From there, the game turned hilarious. Brooke dared Liv to trade her five-hundred-dollar shoes for Brooke's twenty-dollar Target ones for the rest of the night. Jo was forced to describe Tracker's *goods* in detail, and Rachel had to crank call the tire shop asking if she could have her tires bedazzled while speaking in a French accent. A confused Ty ended up calling her crazy and hanging up on her, which sent the tipsy ladies into a round of giggles for the hundredth time that night.

"Back to you, Harper. Truth or dare?" Jo asked.

"Oh God, I can't do another dare. I'll go with truth." On her previous turn, she'd had to order a drink called Cum in a Tub. Never in her life had she been more embarrassed than when asking the poor waiter for the nasty drink. Hopefully,

Jo's question would be less painful.

"How are you doing?" Jo asked.

Such a simple question, but Jo didn't mean it in a simple manner. But she left it up to Harper as to how to take it. She could answer with a simple "I'm great," or she could get real. Thank God for tequila, or she'd have taken the chicken-shit way out.

"I'm doing all right." She sipped the margarita. It's funny how she thought the tequila shot was disgusting, but add some lime, crushed ice, and salt, and they were onto something.

She glanced at Rachel's confused expression. Curly's half sister was the only one at the table who didn't have a clue about her past.

"Um... when I was eighteen, I dated a guy who got me in trouble." She went through the whole sorted story, pausing only when another round of drinks was delivered to the table. By the time she finished, the girls had tears in their eyes, and all reached across the table to grab her hands.

"You are strong as hell, Harp," Brooke said as she shook her head. "I knew the basics from the background check, but honey, I'm so sorry that happened to you. I want you to know we are a safe space if you ever need to talk, scream in anger, or break down in tears."

"That goes for all of us. Anything you need to talk about," Liv said with a nod, then a wink. "Including a six-foot-six hulk of a man with a wicked sense of humor and some serious muscles."

"Hell yes," Jo added. "Especially if you want to talk about him."

"I've never been in a situation like yours, but my ol' man has been," Brooke added. "He is also there for you anytime you need it. Having someone who understands what you're going through might be helpful. He's been very open with me about his struggles following his release, so I know it can't be easy for you. One thing he told me that helps him erase the feeling of loss after being locked up for so many years is grabbing every ounce of happiness he can. He doesn't let any opportunity for joy pass him by."

Harper's eyes filled with tears she refused to let fall. How were these women even real? "Thank you. I will take that to heart." The words squeezed past the lump in her throat. After feeling unlucky for many years, she felt truly blessed to have met these ladies.

Thankfully, the conversation didn't linger on her sad story for long. Her friends seemed to understand she wanted to share but not turn the theme of the night into a sob fest.

"Okay, Harp, I think you're asking Liv now."

Over the last hour, they'd all started shortening her name, and she loved it. It felt like an unspoken acknowledgment of her solidified her place in their group.

"Okay, Liv, truth or dare?" she asked as she lifted her gaze from her margarita.

"Dare," Liv said with a tipsy giggle.

"Okay, let's see…" Harper glanced around the crowded room only to have her heart stop dead in her chest. Working their way across the room with some mighty fierce scowls was a pack of biker boyfriends and Jinx.

Busted.

"Um… I dare you to scream out how much you love Spec and why."

"Oh shit," Rachel whispered beside her. She'd caught sight of the unhappy men. "We're dead."

"Well, that's an easy one." Liv stood as the other women noticed their men approaching.

A tension fell over the table, unbeknownst to Olivia. The other women exchanged sheepish glances.

They were in for it now.

"I love Scott with every ounce of my heart," she shouted over the loud pop music. "He is the most sincere, loyal, courageous, and best goddamn man I know. He treats me like a queen and loves me for who I am." She grinned and started to sit before popping back up. "Oh, and his dick is to die for."

"Thanks, baby, but don't think that speech will get you out of the spanking you have coming your way."

Liv yelped and spun around to find her ol' man hovering behind her with his impressive arms folded across his chest. She whipped back around to the table. "Really? No warning? Is there no girl code?" Then she turned to her man again. "Baby! I missed you!"

"Don't give me that shit. You are in serious trouble, Olivia. *Dinner with the girls.* Really, Liv?"

"I ate the fruit in my drink." Liv batted her eyes at Spec.

He snagged her around the waist, pulled her close, and whispered something in her ear that had her kissing him with an intense amount of passion a few seconds later. Harper fanned herself. Hot didn't begin to describe those two.

"I know, right?" a random woman with frosted hair and a plastic flamingo in her drink said from the next table.

Harper was about to respond when a giant form stepped between her and the woman. She looked up, and up, and up to the smirk on Jinx's face. He crossed his arms over his chest and stared down at her.

Whoops.

"Uh... hey," she said, in a stunning display of the English language.

Why does he have to be so good-looking?

If someone had told her she'd be drooling over a man wearing a black wifebeater, jeans, and an MC cut, she'd have laughed in their face. The night before her release from prison, she'd had a dream about meeting a banker. Someone solid, staid, and secure. Also boring as fuck.

Everything Jinx wasn't.

"Hey," he rumbled.

"So, uh… am I in trouble?"

He shook his head. "You're not my ol' lady. You can do whatever the fuck you want."

Oh, well, that was good. Score a point for the single gal.

"No matter how stupid."

Ouch.

"Hey, this wasn't my idea. They showed up at my house and basically kidnapped me."

"Did they force you to wear a dress that should be illegal?"

Glancing down at herself, she frowned. "What's wrong with my dress?"

Jinx rolled his eyes. "For fuck's sake. It's time to go." He slid an arm around her shoulders and steered her toward the exit.

"Wait," she said, trying to peer over her shoulder. "What about the others?"

"Bye, Harp," Liv yelled, waving.

"They're taken care of. You're mine to deal with."

Never in a million years would she admit her brain turned off after the words *you're mine* and her body set on fire.

"Where are we going?" she asked as she practically ran to keep up with his long stride. The crowd parted like he was Moses, letting him pass by without a word.

"Home."

Okay, then.

"How drunk are you?" He cast her a side-eyed glance as he pushed the door open.

"Tipsy," she said with a giggle. "I didn't drink nearly as much as the others."

Jinx grunted his reply.

They stepped out into the muggy evening. The fresh air felt incredible every time she breathed it in. Sure, she'd gone outside almost daily in prison, but always with four high walls around her. It never quite felt like she was truly outside, only in a different cage with slightly less stale air. How could someone fully enjoy the blue skies and puffy clouds when seeing rifled guards if they looked a few feet over?

Even the stifling Florida humidity was a thousand times better.

He held his hand out to her. "C'mon, party animal, my bike is this way."

"Your bike?"

"Yep. Only drive a cage when I absolutely have to."

"I've never been on a motorcycle before."

"Glad to be your first." He winked, waiting with his hand extended.

She hesitated. Hand-holding was a boyfriend activity, wasn't it? She'd held Aaron's hand all those years ago, but no one else's, *ever*.

It's just a hand.

She'd slept with the man for crying out loud. Why was she making such a big deal about holding his hand for a short walk across a parking lot?

Because it felt big—it felt like trust.

Terrifying.

Brooke's words about Curly flashed through her mind.

He doesn't let any opportunity for joy pass him by.

She pasted on a smile and grabbed his hand. "Let's do it."

She could do it. She could snatch happiness and protect herself at the same time.

No problem.

Chapter Seventeen

Jinx believed she wasn't wasted because she clearly hadn't had enough to get out of her own head. He fought for patience at the way she stared at his hand as though it were a hot poker ready to burn her. He wasn't the type to go slow and think through every move. That he didn't just grab her hand and tow her to the bike spoke to a depth of feeling and respect he wasn't accustomed to.

And one he refused to analyze.

Eventually, she settled her smaller hand in his, and he fought back a cheer of victory. Another step toward what? What the hell did he think they were inching toward? A relationship? A life together?

Hell no.

Not now, not ever.

Jinx wanted to loosen her up, give her some fun, and enjoy the hell out of it too.

Sex and fun.

The way he lived his life.

When they reached his bike, he grabbed his dome off the handlebars and plopped it on her head. It wobbled a bit, but he cinched it as tight as possible. It'd do for the ride to his house. Maybe he'd pick one up for her next time he hit the Harley shop.

"What about you?" she asked, pointing to his head.

"I'm good."

Harper frowned. "What if we crash? You need a helmet too. I'll just take an Uber."

He snorted. "First of all, it's a dome, not a helmet. I'm not a ten-year-old riding a six-speed."

Giggling, Harper shrugged. "My bad."

"Second, I ride as well as I fuck. We are not going to crash, okay?"

She hummed. "Well, if you ride like you fuck, I guess it's good that I have the helm… uh… dome since now I gotta worry about falling off the bike while I'm coming."

His jaw dropped, but no words came out. Never would anyone believe it was possible to render him speechless, but Harper had just fucking done it. Shit, maybe she was wasted.

"I'm sorry, but did you just make a raunchy-ass joke, Prickles?"

Her laugh made him so happy. So did the pink blush on her cheeks. "Shut up. I can make jokes."

"Fuck, you're pretty when you're smiling and laughing." He couldn't help himself and wound an arm around her and pulled her close. Her hands went to his chest, resting them on him, but she didn't push or pull. "Gimme those lips."

She rose on her tiptoes, meeting him halfway with a slow and exploratory kiss. She tasted of tequila and lime—tropical and intoxicating—and his cock hardened the second their tongues met.

She trailed her hands down his torso and then under his shirt in a move that shocked him. He hissed at the first contact of those curious fingers on his skin. Now that his dick knew how hot and tight she was, he struggled to keep from yanking her dress up and bending her over his bike right there in the parking lot. But he refused to treat her like an easy-come, easy-go club whore.

"Come home with me," he murmured against her lips.

She stiffened and met his gaze. With his dome on and the uncertainty in her eyes, she was a mix of hot as hell and vulnerable.

"Okay."

"What?" He blinked. As soon as he posed the question, he started making a list of arguments to persuade her, but it wasn't necessary.

"Yeah?"

"Yeah," she murmured. "Take me to your home, Jinx."

"Fuck yes." Riding home with his dick as hard as it was would be the ultimate misery, but it would be well worth it in the end. "Let's go, baby."

He helped her on the back of his bike, then swung his leg over. When was the last time he had a woman on the back of his bike? Fuck, it'd been years, and then it had been a random woman he'd picked up for the night. Now that he was in the MC, having a woman riding with him meant something. Not just anyone deserved to be there.

But Harper wasn't anyone. She was the tough-as-nails, prickly on the outside-vulnerable on the inside beauty he couldn't get out of his mind.

She rested her hands on his hips.

"Fuck that," he mumbled as he grabbed her hands and placed them on his stomach. "Snuggle on in, babe. Press that pussy right into my ass and move with me like you did last night."

She sucked in a breath.

"Ready?"

"I think so."

"Then let's do this, baby," he shouted, drawing a range of looks from people entering and exiting the bar. Not that he gave a shit. Let them look. He had a hot-as-fuck woman clinging to his back. Let them look and let them be jealous.

Life was fucking good.

He revved the engine and let out a loud whoop as he pulled out of the parking lot.

Harper laughed, and he swore he heard a "You're crazy" disappear into the wind.

Having Harper behind him was more incredible than he could have imagined. She relaxed against his broad back like she'd been crafted to fit there. She was a natural, and no one would ever know this was her first ride. Or maybe it was the two of them together that made it so good.

In an unspoken agreement, he took a long way home. Hell, he didn't even steer toward home at first, riding along the coastline to prolong the experience for as long as possible.

His cock stayed hard and needy, but they'd get to that later. This time together was so great he didn't even mind the wait. Never had Jinx delayed fucking for anything, but this ride wasn't a delay.

Her body molded to his.

Her hands, which had slipped under his shirt, softly stroked his abs.

The freedom of the road.

The smell of the salty sea air.

It was its own form of foreplay, intimate and exciting.

After an hour cruising the coast, he routed the bike toward his home. The garage door opened after he hit the button, and he pulled the bike inside. No woman aside from his brothers' ol' ladies had ever been in his house. He didn't fuck there. It was too personal and too deep of a glimpse into who he was.

He killed the engine and sat still as Harper released her arms.

"Don't get up yet," she whispered.

He stilled. What was she up to?

Harper used his shoulders for leverage to climb off the

bike. He got a flash of sexy black panties as she tried to right her dress. "Follow my directions?"

He glanced her way to see her standing beside the bike, still wearing the dome and with glistening eyes. Were those tears?

Shit. His stomach twisted. Had she hated it? Had she been scared, and he'd been too lost in the moment to notice the cues? "Harper—"

"Shh." She pressed a finger to his lips. "Turn toward me and help me get the hel—" She smiled when she realized the mistake. "Uh… the dome off."

It took him a second to comply. The thought that he could have scared or upset her wrecked him.

He lifted his leg over the bike, propping his ass against the seat as he helped unlatch the dome. After hooking it on the handlebar, he turned back to her.

"Harp—"

She launched herself into his arms, kissing him with immense passion.

Christ, it was hot.

He spread his legs and cupped her face, holding her in place so he could tease her with his tongue. Her hands threaded into his hair as she stepped between his legs, deepening the kiss. Just as the kiss started to go from PG-13 to an R rating, he tasted the salt of her tears, and it deflated his lust in an instant.

"Harper, what's wrong?"

She shook her head, then wiped her eyes. "I'm sorry." The smile she gave him lit up the entire garage and made no sense when combined with her tears. "I promise I'm not upset." She cupped his face. "Thank you," she whispered. "I've never…" She swallowed. "I spent so much time as a prisoner. This wasn't just a ride on a motorcycle to me. It was a gift. Even though I'm out now, I haven't felt fully free. I'd forgotten that kind of freedom existed. Tonight, behind you on this bike, I finally felt it. Total freedom."

Christ, this woman would be his downfall.

"Thank you," she murmured again.

He leaned in to kiss her again, but she stepped away. A playful gleam entered her gaze. "Now I have something I want to give you. Lose the pants."

Oh fuck. His dick stiffened once again. "Harper, you don't—"

Her right eyebrow arched high. "Shut the hell up and do what I say."

Well, damn. The claws were out, and he was ready for the kitten to scratch him up.

"Yes, ma'am."

She took another step back to give him room to undress. He unbuckled his belt, unsnapped his jeans, and drew the zipper down slow and steady. Her gaze followed his every move. Was there anything hotter than a gorgeous woman watching him get naked with hunger in her eyes? He shoved the jeans down to his ankles, leaving him in black briefs that barely contained his erection.

Harper swallowed.

Fuck, he hoped she'd be swallowing his load soon. It would feel like he died and gone to heaven.

Next went the briefs. He pulled them down slowly, revealing his dick inch by inch. Harper's breaths came in sharp pants.

"Shirt too?" he asked with a smirk when the briefs met his jeans at his ankles.

"Yes. I want to see all of you," Harper said, though she didn't take her gaze from the long shaft extending toward her.

He removed his cut and set it over the handlebars. As soon as he drew the shirt over his head, Harper yanked it from him and tossed it aside.

Then she dropped to her knees, and he groaned.

This would kill him for sure.

With quick hands, she unknotted his boots and helped him work them off. Once everything was piled on the floor, she rose to a tall kneel, and he spread his legs again.

She placed her hands on his knees and slid them up her thighs.

"You're so powerful," she said with awe in her tone.

He cleared his thickening throat. "And you're so fucking hot I'm already burning up."

"I've been thinking about this," she said, eyes meeting his. "About how you'll feel on my tongue and how I want to watch you lose control because of me and my mouth."

"Harper..."

She was his fantasy come to life.

She wrapped a soft hand around his aching cock and stroked. "Will you let me?'

"Fuck, baby, I don't have a goddamn limit in the world. I'll let you do any-fucking-thing you want to me."

"That almost makes me feel as free as I did on the back of your bike."

"You are free with me, Harper. Free to explore every dark, filthy fantasy you were robbed of experiencing."

She stroked a thumb across the tip of his dick, where a tiny bead of fluid gathered. "I like that," she said before licking her thumb.

His fists curled at his sides. "Jesus." This was going to be an exercise in restraint like he'd never known.

She lifted his shaft, pressing it to his stomach as she cupped his balls. He grunted as she leaned into the sensitive sac. And then she was licking it, and he nearly swallowed his tongue.

"Fuck," he shouted. He gripped the edges of his bike's seat

for dear life. "How the fuck did you know?"

She glanced up. "Know what?"

"That I fucking love having my nuts played with. Best goddamn thing ever."

"I didn't know. I just want to taste you all over." She went back to mouthing his balls, alternating licks and little sucks until he was sweating, and his dick fucking hurt it was so damn hard.

"Harper," he said on a groan. "Your mouth is fucking killing me."

She hummed a happy sound. The woman liked driving him out of his mind.

She played with his balls, and they felt heavy and full as fuck. "Babe," he said between harsh breaths. "If you keep this up for much longer, I'm going to come all over that pretty face instead of in your mouth."

Her head popped up as she chuckled. "We'll save that for another time. Tonight's plans definitely include my mouth." When her silky hand went back to his cock, he groaned.

Torture. Pure, erotic torture.

Harper circled the base of his dick, then angled it toward her mouth. She used that talented tongue all over his dick, running it up and down the sides, tracing the veins, and pressing it to his glans. His dick wept with the need to come, but she kept teasing him.

"Fuck, Harper," he finally said when he couldn't take it anymore. "You gotta put me in your fucking mouth. Please, baby. Stop fucking teasing me."

Her grin was full of sexual victory. A second later, those lips parted, and she inhaled the head of his cock into her mouth. The hot, wet suction had his eyes crossing.

"Jesus, that's fucking good." The only way he could have kept his hands out of her hair was if they'd been cuffed behind him. Even then, he'd try his damndest to break the chains.

At first, Harper blew him with tentative lips, sliding him in and out of her mouth with shallow pulls. But the more vocal he was, the more confident she became. Soon, he was telling her what a hot fucking mouth she had, and she was damn near swallowing his cock.

"Fuck, fuck, fuck," he growled out as he fought to keep from ramming his dick down her throat. It'd been many years, and he didn't want to scare her off.

Harper wasn't shy, though. Once she got fully into it, she held his thighs with a vice grip and bobbed her head on his cock like it was a delicious treat. Every so often, she gagged, and he saw stars.

Her tongue got in on the action, tickling under the head of his cock. It was so damn sensitive, he shouted and gripped her hair with punishing force. Instead of popping off his dick or ending the blow job over the rough treatment, Harper moaned the same sound she'd made when he'd sucked her tits.

The woman liked it rough.

She fucking owned him at this point.

She did the tongue thing again, and he gave another hard yank on her hair. This time, when she hummed her enjoyment, she lifted her gaze to his. The sight of her, lips stretched and shiny, eyes glassy, face flushed, and mouth stuffed full of his big cock, did him in.

"Oh, fuck, coming," he shouted, but it was barely the warning he'd intended to give her. Forceful spurts of jizz shot from his dick into her mouth, where she gulped every drop with rapid swallows.

He hoped to hell he wasn't hurting her, but he'd lost control of his muscles. They clenched and relaxed of their own volition as he unloaded down her throat.

Eventually, he realized he was still holding her hair, so he forced his fingers to relax. She lowered to her heels, which had his soft cock slipping from her lips. Even as drained as his nuts were, his cock tried to rally when she wiped the back of her hand across her swollen lips.

"Christ, you give good head, Prickles," he said as he ran a hand through his hair. "I'm fucking weak now."

A shy smile tilted her lips.

He helped her to her feet, though he might have been even more unsteady than she was.

"Come in so I can repay the favor at least twice."

Before she could answer, his phone rang.

"Well, fuck me sideways. Let me get rid of whoever this is." He checked the screen and then frowned. Lock. *Fuck.* "Hey, brother, what's up?"

"Jinx, you busy, man?"

Was he busy? Fuck yeah, he was busy. He had some pussy to eat. But he was the type never to turn down a brother in need. "What do you need?"

"I got an emergency call. Chick locked herself out of her apartment and can't get ahold of her super."

Harper watched him with a worried gaze. To ease her mind, he kissed her forehead before hugging her to him. "Thought you stopped doing night calls when you got custody of Caleb."

"I did, but this is a friend of Deanna's." Lock's sister. "I had a helluva time getting Caleb to sleep tonight, so I hate to wake him and drag his ass out. Just need someone to be here while I'm out."

He bit off a groan. There went his plans to make Harper come over and over again.

"Of course. Be there in ten minutes."

"Thanks."

He grunted a goodbye, disconnected the call, and stared at the ceiling. "Fuck, I'm sorry, babe. Lock needs help."

"I heard him," she said with a sweet smile.

"You wanna stay here? You can catch some sleep in my bed."

"What if I come with you?"

He raised an eyebrow. "You don't wanna do that. Lock's life is a fucking mess, and so is his house. Stay here and watch Netflix. Relax. My brother's problem is not your responsibility."

She bit her lower lip. The gears in her head cranked so loudly he could practically hear them. "What if I, uh… what if I said I wanted to come with you?" Her gaze shifted to the garage floor when she toed an invisible crack. "That I'd rather come with you," she mumbled.

Because she wanted to be with him or because she felt uncomfortable staying in his home alone?

Even though he was dying to know the answer, the question wouldn't pass his lips. One of those options lit him up, energized him, and made him feel like he stood at the top of a mountain. One of those options would put the same goofy grin on his face he saw on his brothers' faces when they looked at their ol' ladies.

And that was plain ridiculous. Jinx didn't do smitten, and that's what his brothers were. Smitten, whipped, locked down. Pick an answer. They were all the same.

It was D, none of the above for Jinx, and that's how it'd stay.

Regardless of her reasoning, he liked the idea of her joining him for another ride. Of her hanging with him while he helped a brother. He straight-up liked being with her, no matter the task.

"All right. Let's do it." He clamped down on his lower lip to keep that damn smile from forming.

Chapter Eighteen

The ride to Lock's house allowed Harper to bury her face against Jinx's broad back and relive the last hour. A huge part of her wanted to blame her actions on the alcohol, but without it, she'd have never ordered Jinx to lose his pants, drop to her knees, and fall on his cock like it'd sustain her more than water.

But it'd be a whopper of a lie.

She'd imagined that very scenario for days. In the dark of night, in the privacy of her apartment, in the safe cocoon of her bed, she'd let her hands drift down her body, touching herself while she imagined having Jinx in every way she could dream up. Her experience with men might be lacking, but that didn't mean she was ignorant to the idea of every sex act out there. Prison gave her an education she'd never have gotten otherwise. Not a practical education, but she's heard *everything* there was to hear and then some.

For two years, she'd had a sex worker as a cellmate. The woman hadn't been arrested for her craft but for poisoning a john who'd had trouble respecting her limited but firm boundaries. The stories that woman told had opened Harper's eyes to a myriad of filthy delights. And her cellmate had only been one of many women she'd met with wild tales.

Nothing shocked Harper anymore, and instead of that

shock turning to distaste, a great many stories intrigued her more than she'd admit out loud. So, while her experience was limited, her imagination was vast. And Jinx played the starring role in all her fantasies.

The act of dropping to her knees and swallowing his cock didn't have her head mixed up, but the implications sure as hell did. As did her offer to join him on a favor for his brother. What the hell had she been thinking? Sex again was one thing. At least she could rationalize that away with physical needs and wanting to show appreciation for the eye-opening ride along the coast, but offering to spend platonic time with him?

That was stupid.

That was dangerous.

That was relationshipy.

After tonight, she needed to get her head on straight and take a step back. If they kept this up, she would end up handing too much of herself over to the man and think he could be trusted as she had believed Aaron could. And then she'd end up hurt, broken, or, worst-case scenario, blamed for a crime she had nothing to do with.

Jinx navigated a handful of back roads to get to Lock's, which wasn't nearly as fun as riding along the beautiful beach, but it still beat being trapped in a car. Maybe she should learn to ride a motorcycle and get one for herself. Then she could experience incredible freedom whenever she wanted. Though she had a sneaking suspicion that half of her enjoyment came from clinging to a specific man.

The man she'd been hot for since the second he walked into the bar.

Damn Lock and his interrupting phone call. She'd been in for an epic experience, and she knew it.

Maybe Lock calling had been for the best. It gave her some space before she sank even deeper.

A few moments later, Jinx rolled to a stop in front of a small house on a quiet street. He cursed as he killed the engine.

"This is probably a dumb question, but are you sure this is his house? It doesn't look like anyone lives here." Unkempt grass and a few weeks' worth of overflowing trashcans made the house appear abandoned.

"This is it. I don't know what the fuck's going on with him, but I'll get a company out here to take care of the yard tomorrow."

Well, that was sweet.

"Fair warning, the inside's probably worse."

She wrinkled her nose, which drew a chuckle from him.

"All right, let's do this." As though it was the most natural thing in the world and they'd been doing it forever, Jinx slid his palm against hers.

A shiver ran up her arm, and her stomach flipped. Why did the simple act of holding someone's hand mess with her head more than having his cock in her mouth?

She had problems.

When they reached the door, he frowned. "Will the doorbell wake the baby?"

She shrugged. "I have no idea. Not exactly swimming in baby experience over here. Maybe knock lightly, just in case."

"Good thinking." He did just that, rapping his knuckles against the door with a light touch. It flew open almost before he got a second knock in.

"Hey, thanks," the man who must be Lock said.

The poor guy appeared exhausted, stressed, and frazzled. His shaggy hair needed a good cut, or hell, even a brush. He wore a rumpled Harley T-shirt and jeans with his MC cut and boots, much like the rest of the club. Nothing surprising there, but his eyes were bloodshot, and he moved with a jerky impatience as he grabbed his keys and wallet off a small table.

His gaze landed on her. "Who are you?" The smirk didn't do anything to lessen the appearance of exhaustion. The dark circles and red eyes remained. Before she could answer, he shifted his attention to Jinx. "Pretty piece you got here. Let me know if she's worth it when you're done. Might take a crack at her."

He winked, and she sputtered. The dress she'd felt so sexy in all night now felt too revealing, and she wished she'd had sweats to change into.

"Hey," Jinx said with a growl. "Watch your fucking mouth, asshole. This is Harper. She works at the She Shed with the girls. Show some fucking respect."

Lock shrugged, clearly unbothered by the scolding. "I might be a few hours. I'll text."

He didn't move to let them enter, instead pushing straight through them, forcing Jinx to release her hand. He caught his brother's arm as he passed.

"Hey, the fuck's up with you? You on something?"

"What? No, fuck off." Lock tried to yank his arm from Jinx's hold, but it didn't budge.

"You got a fucking kid in there, brother. Don't be stupid." This time, when Lock jerked his arm, Jinx let it go.

The disheveled man got in Jinx's face even though Jinx had a few inches on him. "I know I got a fucking kid. I'm the one who spent two hours rocking him while he screamed so he'd finally fall the fuck asleep." He turned and marched down the walkway to his bike in the driveway. "Better hope he stays asleep so you don't have to deal with that shit."

He revved his engine a few times, making Harper wince. Such a loud racket for the time of night and silent neighborhood.

"Fuck, this is not good." Jinx ran a hand down his face. "That fucker better not wreck his bike out there tonight. I'm pretty sure he took something."

Harper watched the headlight disappear with worry in her gut. From what she'd been told, Lock had been through the wringer lately. The sudden death of a twin sister and becoming guardian to their baby in the NICU would throw anyone for a loop. "I think he needs some professional help."

"Yeah, you and the whole club think that, but Lock isn't receptive. Maybe I can get Curly to convince him."

"Hmm…" Maybe she'd give it a try herself, one damaged person to another.

A loud wail came from inside the house. "Damn him," Jinx muttered. "Just had to rev the fucking pipes. C'mon, I'll grab a bottle and see if I can settle Caleb back down."

She followed Jinx into the foyer, coming up short at the sight of the disaster before her.

"Christ, it's worse than last time." Jinx shook his head. "He's gotta get his fucking act together. There's a couch through there," he said, pointing to the room on the left. "Hopefully, you can find it in all this mess. I'm gonna fix up a bottle for Caleb. Be back in a bit."

He disappeared down the hallway toward what she assumed was a kitchen while the baby's angry screams grew in intensity. Harper made her way into the living room, having to step over pizza boxes, beer cans, empty liquor bottles, and clothes.

With a sigh, she planted her hand on her hips and assessed the mess around her. Lock needed help, and the least she could do was make herself useful while there and do a little cleaning. A moment later, the crying stopped. The little guy must have been happy to have the bottle.

Harper followed the hallway Jinx had taken until she found the kitchen, which was even more disgusting than the living room. Thankfully, Lock had a full stock of unopened cleaning supplies under the sink, even rubber gloves, probably purchased by Brooke at some point.

She'd love to kick off her heels, but who knew what she'd step on, so she left the uncomfortable things on. Then she gloved up, grabbed some rags and cleaner, took out an unopened box of garbage bags, then set to work. Once she had the full sink of dishes cleaned and the trash off the countertops, it looked like a space someone could cook in. After she gave the table and counters a good scrub, they not only looked better but smelled fresh and sanitized.

Lock would have to take care of the floor himself or hire someone since she didn't see a mop. In the zone, she made her way down the hallway, collecting trash as she went. Next was the living room. She started with the couch, gathering up the takeout containers and beer cans until a baggie with a white substance caught her attention. Her stomach bottomed out.

"Shit."

Jinx had wondered if Lock was using anything, and there was the proof. This would crush him, but no way could she hide it. Lock lived alone with a baby. His downward spiral included drugs, and it seemed the club had to know. With a sigh, she set the baggie on the couch and resumed cleaning.

Before she knew it, an hour and a half had passed in the blink of an eye, and the house looked livable.

"Where the hell is Jinx?" she muttered as she wandered down the hall. An open door with dim glowing blue light caught her attention. As she stopped in the doorway, her breath caught.

Was there anything more precious than the sight of a big man with a tiny baby?

No. She could officially verify that it was the most adorable scene in the entire world.

Jinx sat in a rocking chair with his head resting back, eyes closed. His chest rose and fell in the telltale pattern of sleeping, and on that impressive chest slept Caleb. His chubby little cheek rested against Jinx, and his lips made the most precious pout. She pulled her phone out, needing to capture the sweet moment. If the world ever had a negative population crisis, all they'd need to do was show this picture to the remaining women, and they'd be lining up to get pregnant. She pressed a hand over her lower stomach as though she could shield her ovaries from the hormonal surge.

She held up the phone and snapped a pic. The click of the camera had Jinx's eyes slowly opening. After a few blinks, his gaze landed on her.

"Shit," he whispered as he glanced down at the sleeping infant in his arms. "Fell asleep, huh?"

"Yes, you did."

"How long?"

"We've been here about an hour and a half."

"Well, fuck. I'm sorry. Didn't mean to abandon you like that."

With a smile, Harper waved away his concern. "No problem. I kept myself occupied."

Jinx stood with a quiet groan and moved to the crib, where he placed the baby on his back with easy movements. Caleb made a squeak of protest but didn't wake.

"You're good at this."

He shrugged. "Been helping a bit over the last few months. Plus, my mom got knocked up when I was seventeen. Took care of the baby a lot."

"Wow. That's a big age gap."

"My family went through a rough patch when I was a teen. She was looking for comfort and ended up with a baby."

"I'm sorry," she said as her heart ached for the young Jinx and whatever put that look of sadness in his eye.

"For what?"

"Whatever you went through. It must have been painful."

He stiffened. "I don't talk about it."

"Oh," she whispered in deference to the sleeping baby. "I wasn't asking you to. Trust me, I understand wanting to keep things close to your chest."

"But you told me your story."

Their gazes met. "I did."

Tension rose, but not the bad kind. The sexual kind. God, she wanted what he'd promised before Lock interrupted.

"Let's get out of here before we wake him again, and I'm forced to take another nap."

"Good idea. You seemed so miserable."

His low laugh warmed her heart. So did the way he slung his arm around her shoulders as they walked out of the room. She'd let the change of subject slide, but her curiosity would have her asking more about his family at a later time.

"What the fuck?" he said as they entered the living room. He released her and did a slow perusal of the room. "You cleaned?"

"Um… yeah. I didn't have anything else to do, and he obviously needed some help with it, so I did the kitchen and this room."

"Harper." He pulled her close.

The warmth of his body bled into her tired muscles. It'd been a long day, and having someone hold her at the end felt incredible.

"You did not have to do that," he murmured against her hair and kissed her head. Such a simple, chaste kiss, but it went straight to her wounded heart.

She cleared her thickening throat. "I know. But it really wasn't a big deal. Most of the mess was trash, which is in a bunch of bags by the front door, by the way. But once I bagged that all up, it really wasn't bad. Some dishes, a load of laundry, and wiping a lot of counters."

"It might not be a big deal to you, and, unfortunately, Lock probably won't give you the thanks you deserve, but it means something to me, Harp. So thank you."

She peered up into his eyes, but words wouldn't come. His expression said so much more than his words. Gratitude, appreciation, admiration, and desire if she read him correctly.

"You're amazing," he whispered in a husky tone as his mouth moved toward hers. His phone chimed. "Always with the bad fucking timing."

"Everything okay?"

He swiped his phone screen. "Yeah, looks like Lock will be another hour." He shifted his roguish gaze to her. "Hmm… whatever will we do to pass the time?"

"Um…" She suddenly thought she'd just become prey to this wild animal.

He advanced on her, forcing her to back up. "Oh, I have an idea of something to keep us busy."

"What? Oh!" The backs of her legs hit the couch, causing her to lose her balance and plop down.

"Oops," he said with a complete lack of sincerity. "Hold on, let me help you out there." He pulled over a giant ottoman and sat on it in front of her.

"What are you… oh my God."

Jinx grabbed the back of her legs and hauled her halfway onto his lap. Her back hit the couch with a bounce as her borrowed dress hiked up, revealing the very skimpy panties Liv had gifted her.

He had a prime view of the tiny swatch of fabric covering her pussy, which rapidly grew wet.

"Jinx!" She scrambled to pull the dress back down, but he grabbed her hands and anchored them to the couch on either side of her head.

"Hell no. You got a chance to eat earlier when I didn't. Now I'm hungry, and I want my treat."

Holy crap, who talked like that?

He did, and apparently, it did it for her because she left her hands right where he'd placed them when he released her.

"Fuck, look at you. All spread out for me. Wet. Hot. Tight fucking nipples trying to escape that sinful dress."

Her legs dangled over his, unable to reach the ground. It gave her this feeling of being suspended in midair, helpless, his for the taking. He was so much bigger than her, could overpower her in a second, and yet she trusted him, with her body, at least. Even though he could, he'd never take advantage of this moment of her vulnerability.

In the past, trusting the wrong person had destroyed her life. And there she was, letting another man in a month after being released from prison, breaking the one hard and fast rule she'd made for herself.

It's just sex. You don't need to let him in more than that.

She could trust him with sex. She'd already let him walk through that door.

And she wanted him so bad that closing the door again might not be possible.

"Enjoy all those racing thoughts while you still can think."

Of course, he could see into her head.

His wolfish grin chased away the very thoughts he'd been referring to. Screw her rules. She was strong enough to draw the line at getting naked.

"I'm just wondering if you're thinking you can make me come by staring at me. Because even you aren't that good."

His face reflected surprise for a fraction of a second before he laughed. "Damn, you got some sass hiding under all those prickles." He smirked. "Those hands stay there or grab my hair. Got it?"

She nodded. "Whatever you say."

"Ooh, I like that."

In a move so smooth she'd have sworn he'd practiced all day, he gripped her ass, shoved the ottoman back, and sank to his knees all at once.

Harper yelped as her legs landed over his shoulders. He buried his face against her panties and inhaled a long breath.

"Fuck, I could get drunk on that." He turned his head and nipped her inner thigh, making her gasp.

Then there were no more games. Jinx used his nose to push her panties aside and expose her sex to him. He squeezed her ass in those giant pleasure-inducing hands as his tongue went to work. Slow at first, as though he knew ramping her up was the best way to drive her crazy.

He drew figure eights through her folds, making sure to flick her clit on each upstroke. Every time his talented tongue brushed the sensitive nerves, she whimpered. Then, on the fifth stroke, she slid her fingers into the soft strands of his hair.

Maybe when she could speak, she'd ask him what product he used because, damn, that was soft. She lightly scratched his scalp, which he seemed to love because his tongue went up ten notches on the aggressiveness scale.

The swirls stopped, and he sucked her clit, making her cry out, pressing her pelvis into his face. She slammed her eyes closed to keep the rest of the world out. Stars danced behind her lids, and her belly coiled tight.

Jinx went back to licking but alternated it with surprise sucks every few seconds. Harper grew antsy. As much as she loved everything he was doing, her pussy fluttered, empty and wanting.

"Jinx," she whined as she squirmed in his hold.

The man must be a mind reader. He slid two thick fingers into her, instantly crooking them forward.

"Aah, yes." Harper's back bowed off the couch. It was so damn good, especially when he added his tongue back into the mix. How had she gone seven years without this—touching and being touched? She didn't want to go without again now that she had it.

"You taste unreal," he growled out against her skin.

The words vibrated through her at the same time he squeezed her ass, and she nearly came right then.

He must have sensed how she hung on the precipice of a monster orgasm. "You're close."

Not a question.

"Y-yes." Her legs trembled on his shoulders, and her pussy rippled around his fingers. He sucked her clit again and moved his fingers quickly inside her. White light flashed behind her eyes. The tension coiled to nearly unbearable as she burst into a spectacular detonation of pleasure.

Her neck arched, and her hips bucked up while wave after wave of endorphins flowed through her. Jinx coaxed her through the entire thing with soft licks and flicks of his fingers. Eventually, she sagged against the couch in a limp heap of jellied muscles.

Her feet hit the floor as Jinx hauled her up so she was actually sitting on the couch once again. She opened her eyes to find him right there.

"Can I kiss you?"

With her flavor still on his lips? Was it weird that she wanted it?

She nodded.

He kissed her, and her eyes fluttered shut. Sure enough, she tasted herself. There was something so raw and primal about it. All her possessive instincts flared to life.

But she shoved them down with a quick internal mantra.

Just sex. Just sex.

Then he went and whispered next to her ear, "I want to tell you my story. I never talk about it, not even with my brothers. But I want you to know me like you're letting me know you."

Her heart flipped over in her chest. Those words were so more than sex. "Tell me. I'll keep your secrets safe."

He sat next to her and pulled her against him. "It's a short story, but it changed my life forever. I had a girlfriend when I was sixteen. Puppy love, much like you felt about Aaron at the time. We were wild little things from a rough neighborhood with parents who didn't give a shit what we were up to. One night, we went to a party with my older brother. He was eighteen and offered to drive. Promised he wouldn't drink."

"Oh God," she whispered.

He paused, and she stayed quiet, allowing him time to prepare to talk about something painful. "I didn't see him much at the party, so I believed he didn't drink. Tanya, my girlfriend, did, though. So did I, but she was blasted." He blew out a breath and squeezed her close. "Fuck, this is hard."

"Take your time. I'm not going anywhere."

He kissed the top of her head. "I let her sit in the front on the way home, thinking I was a gentleman. My brother drove. He and Tanya got in a stupid argument about a fucking television show. That stupid fucking show," he whispered.

She didn't need him to finish. This story had an obvious and heartbreaking ending.

"She grabbed the wheel."

It felt as though her heart had stopped. "Oh, Jinx…"

"I fucked up my shoulder, and they lost their lives."

She lifted her gaze to meet his. So many emotions swirled in his eyes. "Don't downplay the effect on you. Way more than your shoulder got hurt."

He nodded. "Yes. I was fucked up for a long time. Fell down a dark hole, caused trouble, and got kicked out of school. Riding was my therapy and probably the one thing that saved me. Only time I felt good was when I was on a motorcycle. I'm okay now, but I don't let myself think about it. And I don't talk about it. I'm sure, as a counselor, you'd tell me that's not healthy, but it's what works to keep me moving forward."

She kissed the underside of his chin. "I don't judge you or anyone for how they cope. There isn't a right or wrong answer. You pulled through something awful and became an incredible man."

"Yeah. Well, I pulled through, anyway. Don't know about the great part." He rested his cheek on her head.

"I do." She closed her eyes and soaked up the intimacy. They'd shared their pain, and she felt so close to him right then.

"Thank you for coming with me tonight, for helping my brother. Outside the club, no one has ever had my back like that. I think you're beautiful, incredible, and perfect. And you make me happy."

Her eyes flew open.

Icy terror raced through her as she realized something horrifying.

This was so much deeper than sex, and she loved every word out of his mouth.

Chapter Nineteen

Jinx strode through the clubhouse with heavy steps and what had to be a fierce scowl because he got more than one side-eyed glance. Hell, some chick Pulse had hooked up with the night before practically hid behind him as Jinx passed by.

He was fucking pissed, and they'd all have to deal with it.

He stormed into Curly's office without bothering to knock and tossed the drugs Harper found at Lock's onto the president's desk.

Curly glanced up from his phone with a raised eyebrow. "You bring me a snack?"

Jinx snorted. "You know what the fuck that is."

As he set his phone face down on the desk, he gestured for Jinx to sit. "Meth if I had to make an educated guess, but what I'm stuck on is why you're bringing it to me. This little gift from one of Lobo's guys?"

Christ, the thought of it turned Jinx's stomach. To think Lock might have purchased it from the same dealer responsible for his twin sister's death showed how low he'd sunk. "Don't know. Don't wanna know. Found it at Lock's."

That had the unflappable president's jaw dropping. "You're shitting me."

"I wish I fucking was. He called me last night to ask if I could sit with the baby while he ran out on an emergency call. Harper was with me, so she came along. While I was tending to Caleb, she did some cleaning. You have no idea what a shithole that house had become. Anyway, she found this in the couch."

"Well, fuck."

One of Curly's rules for the club was no hard drugs. Alcohol, of course. That shit flowed freely. Weed, hell yeah, but nothing that would fuck them up. Curly had seen too many lives destroyed by the shit in his previous club, so it'd been a no-brainer for him.

Jinx never cared for the stuff, not since the accident. The potential loss of control freaked him out.

"Fuck," Curly said again. He laced his fingers behind his head and pressed his lips together for a moment, thinking. Then he asked, "He home today?"

Nodding, Jinx said, "Pretty sure. Harper offered to watch the baby if he needed to go out, but he told her he had a quiet day at home."

"All right. I'll pay him a visit."

"You want backup?"

Curly stared at the ceiling. "I'll bring Pulse. I don't want him lashing out at you once he realizes you were the one to find his stash."

"You're not gonna strip his patch, are you? I'm not here to narc on him. He needs help, and I want him to get it, not be the reason he's kicked out of the club."

"No. I won't. But he's gonna quit that shit, or eventually, I will take his patch. None of that's on you. We all know he's been tumbling downhill at a rapid pace. Just didn't realize it'd gone this far. Fuck." Curly dropped his arms and shook his head. "What the fuck is he thinking? His goddamn sister just went out from this shit."

"Don't figure he's thinking much at all."

An agreeable hum came from Curly. "Yeah. His life's been

flipped upside down ten times over in the past few months, hasn't it?"

"Sure has." Jinx took a moment to put himself in Lock's shoes—grieving the loss of a sibling, followed by the surprise news that he'd be a parent to a child in the NICU, and a few months of court battles and hospital visits while trying to keep a business afloat. And then, bam, he had a baby in his house, dependent on him for everything. There was no nine-month lead-up period or partner to share the heavy tasks of raising a baby.

Who wouldn't turn to mind-numbing drugs?

"Thanks for bringing this to my attention," Curly said. He reached into his desk and pulled out a pad of paper with notes scrawled across it. "Got something for you too, brother."

Jinx raised an eyebrow.

"Shut the door."

Interesting.

"This isn't club business."

Even more interesting. Jinx closed the door and returned to his seat.

Thankfully, Curly didn't make him wait. His stomach had already twisted into a knot.

"I have a contact at the prison in North Carolina. Guy I served a few years with. He was in an MC there and serving time for weapons trafficking. Goes by Blade. He's got a handful of years left and owes me a favor."

Jinx's heart kicked into overdrive. *Fuck yes.* This could be the 'in' he'd been hoping for. "What kind of favor?"

"The kind that will ensure your girl never gets contacted again by the fucker who ruined her life. Blade'll be having a little chat with Aaron today to impress upon him the importance of ending communication with Harper. Then he's got a guy in the mailroom who'll keep a lookout for any letters and make sure they get destroyed just in case the boy is stupid enough to try again. Once he's released, we'll pay him a final visit to remind him you're under our protection."

Fuck yes. This was more than he'd hoped for but exactly what Harper needed. "Thanks, Prez." He held his hand out. "I owe you one."

"Get out of here with that shit," Curly said, but he shook Jinx's hand. "We're fucking family. Not keeping a tally."

"Mind if I go tell Harper the good news?"

"Be my guest. While you're out at the shed, let Brooke know I'll swing by there at noon to take her to lunch." When the option presented itself, Curly always avoided texting. It made sense since he missed out on thirteen years of technology growth while in jail, but it still cracked Jinx up. He could have told Brooke about lunch at any time but chose a human messenger over a text.

"Will do, Prez."

Armed with news that should make Harper's week, Jinx grabbed an ATV for the trip across the farm. Ray, who was outside playing as usual, ran alongside him, happily yipping as though they were playing a game.

"You coming in, bud?" he asked the dog as he hopped over the rickety steps onto the platform leading to the trailer. The ladies would be beyond thrilled to have construction on the shelter finished so they could move their office. Unfortunately for them, they still had a few months of building left to endure.

Ray followed him, also skipping the steps.

Jinx knocked on the door with a heavy fist.

"Ooh, think that's the stripper we ordered?" Liv called out from inside.

"I'll check." The door opened, revealing Jo. She put on an exaggerated pout and huffed. "No luck. It's just Jinx."

"Ouch." He clutched a hand to his chest. "You ladies are

brutal."

All laughed except Harper, who sat at her desk with her spine so straight he'd have sworn it was a lead pipe. Her eyes were wide, and she wore a slightly panicked expression as though she knew he'd come for her and wasn't sure how to react.

Always wary, his prickly cactus.

"We're just messing with you, Jinx," Brooke said from behind her laptop.

"Yeah, feel free to take your clothes off and dance around. Promise we won't mind a bit."

He snorted and pointed to Liv. "I'm telling Spec you said that."

With a smirk, she waggled her eyebrows. "Please do. That man delivers the best punishments."

"Gah. TMI, woman," he said, chuckling.

Coming as no surprise, Harper watched the exchange with a mixture of horror and intrigue. She'd get used to their banter with time.

Or she'd run screaming from them all, which would probably be the smarter decision.

"Hey, you ladies mind if I steal Harper for an early lunch? Got something I need to talk about with her."

Brooke glanced between Harper's look of shock and him before raising an eyebrow. "Long as it's okay with Harper."

All gazes shifted to her.

"What?" She blinked as her face turned pink. "Oh, yeah, sure. That's fine." She popped up as though ejected from the chair. "Let me grab my bag."

As he watched her scramble around with nervous energy, he couldn't help but smile. Maybe it made him an asshole, but he loved how he could rile her up just by being present. "This what you're looking for?" He lifted a purse from a small table to his right.

Harper froze. "Oh, yes, thank you."

As she headed his way, Jo called out, "Have fun, you two," with a healthy dose of innuendo in her voice.

Harper groaned, and he flipped a laughing Jo off.

"Ignore them," he said as he opened the door for her. "They're jealous, all of 'em."

"Remember, Harper, you can always kick him in the nuts if he gets too handsy," Liv called out.

"Oh my God," Harper muttered as she practically dove outside.

"You ladies suck," Jinx yelled as the door swung shut behind him. He swore he heard Liv mutter, "I do, and often." Damn, Spec had been a terrible influence on her.

"Sorry, they're out of control sometimes." He slung an arm around her shoulders, making her stiffen, but she didn't pull away or shove him off, so he left it.

After a moment, she relaxed into the touch. "No, they're fun. And good for me. It's been a long time since I had healthy friendships like they have."

That had him laughing. "God, I love that you call the crazy ol' ladies in an MC healthy."

Harper glanced up at him with sincerity. "They are healthy. You all are. Conventional? No. Always on the right side of the law?" She shrugged. "Probably not. But trust me, I know unhealthy. I lived with it for seven years. I don't see that here." Then she frowned. "Well, maybe Lock."

Jinx sighed at the reminder of that mess. "Yeah. Club's working on that."

"So, uh... what'd you need me for?"

"Got some news to share. Figured I'd do that over lunch."

Uncertainty crossed her face, making him roll his eyes.

"Promise you'll like it, Prickles. You can keep those thorns tucked away."

She gave him a dirty look which had him laughing his

head off. God, he couldn't wait for the day she acted like that around him all the time. Once in a while, she dropped her shields and let the sass fly, but it never lasted long. Hopefully, it wouldn't take seven years to undo the trauma her psyche had sustained from that motherfucker, Aaron, and the aftermath.

Speaking of that shit stain, they needed to get this show on the road.

Jinx guided her to his bike, and after another memorable ride with her behind him, he pulled into his favorite Tex-Mex restaurant. They were seated with lemony waters and a giant basket of chips a few minutes later.

Harper scooped up some guacamole, then shoved an entire chip in her mouth. Her moan rivaled the ones she made while naked and did nothing to help Jinx remain decent in public.

"I don't know how you knew, or it's a lucky coincidence, but chips and guac is my favorite snack in the entire world. Well, my favorite crunchy snack. I'm still loyal to ice cream. God, I missed this stuff. It's even more delicious than I remember from years ago." She blinked. "What? Why are you smiling like that?"

He hadn't realized he'd been grinning at her like a psycho. "I like that you're getting comfortable enough with me to make offhand comments about your time in prison like that. I hope it means we're moving forward."

Her expression changed as quickly as if someone had snapped their fingers. Gone was the open woman he'd been admiring, and out came Prickles.

Me and my fat fucking mouth.

It felt like a massive two steps back.

Harper cleared her throat as she dipped another chip. "So, uh… what did you need to tell me."

As much as he wanted to press, he followed her lead to let her know it was okay for her to get comfortable with him, even trust him.

"Curly called in a favor. You won't get any more letters."

She paused with the chip halfway to her mouth. "From Aaron?" she whispered, eyes darting around as if spies could be anywhere.

He nodded. "Yes."

Her mouth opened and closed a few times. "I, uh… wow. Give me a second to, uh… process this."

"Take your time."

An adorable wrinkle formed between her eyes. "Is something going to happen to him? Can I ask that?"

Jinx held her gaze. "Do you really want to know?"

She considered the question with a quiet moment of reflection. Knowing she wasn't rash or impulsive was a great thing. Sure, she hated the man, but she didn't have a vindictive need to see him harmed, or she'd have asked to know the dirty details of the *message* Aaron received.

"You know what, I don't." She bit her lower lip. "Wait, just let me know one thing. He's not… I mean, you didn't have him…" She winced.

"Killed?"

She leaned in again. "Yeah, that," she whispered.

Chuckling, he shook his head. "No, babe. We didn't have him knocked off, but I can promise you he won't be writing to you again."

"Good. That's good." She gulped water from her cup, then looked at him with glassy eyes. "Thank you." Her throat rose and fell as she swallowed back the tears. "I don't understand why you'd do that for me, but thank you so much. I can't tell you wh-what a relief that is."

The hitch in her voice told him more than her words how great her happiness was at not having to wonder if and when a letter would show up from the man who put her behind bars. But one part of her statement tore at his insides. "Breaks my fucking heart that you don't understand."

"What?"

"Why I'd step up for you. It's so fucking simple, Harper." He stared straight into her eyes, trying to convey with the strength of his gaze how much he meant every fucking word. "You deserve it. You deserve someone in your corner. Hell, you deserve a hundred people in your corner. You might not believe it or trust in it today, but hear me now... you are not alone anymore, babe. You have people who care about you, and in our family, we go to fucking bat for those we care about."

A single tear rolled down her cheek. She huffed a sad little laugh and swiped at it as though trying to smack it into submission. "I've been alone a long time. Not physically..." she tapped her heart, "... but in here. You guys, you especially, seem too good to be true sometimes. It scares me."

"What scares you? Trusting us? Me?"

She nodded. "Yes."

"Is it because of the club? Are you worried we'll do something that lands you back in jail?"

Thankfully, they were early for the lunch crowd, so the restaurant barely had any customers. Combine that with the high-back booth, and no one could overhear this conversation.

Harper chuckled. "You'd think so. I probably should be, but that's not it. I'm terrified of betrayal, of someone I lo—" She stopped before she said the word. "Uh... someone I trust turning on me. I don't think I could survive that kind of pain a second time."

"Can I tell you what I've seen over the past few weeks?"

She nodded.

"I've seen you fight trusting us. The girls, the club, and me most of all, but I've also seen signs that little by little, you are coming to trust us anyway. It's in the way you talk to us. In the way you share, have allowed us into your world, and how you've come into ours."

Her half smile gave him hope. "Thank you," she whispered. "I'm so tired of fighting with myself."

"So don't." He held up a hand when she went to say something else. "I'm not telling you to put your blind trust in me, but maybe, stop fighting so hard." He'd dropped the 'us,' referring only to himself. When it came down to it, it was all he wanted. She didn't need to trust the club or the girls, but fuck, he wanted her trust in him.

"Stop fighting, huh?" She fiddled with the cocktail napkin under her drink, a dead giveaway to her anxiety.

"Yep." He gave her his most disarming grin.

"Damn you," she said as she huffed out a laugh. "Do you have any idea how hard it is to say no to you when you look at me like that?"

"Why do you think I do it?" He winked.

Once again serious, she nodded. "Okay. I'll try. That's all I can give right now, and I'm sorry if it's not enough, but it's more than I ever thought I'd give anyone again."

Fuck. Yes.

"I'll take it." He'd take it, run with it, and make damn sure she never regretted it.

Chapter Twenty

"How was your lunch?" Liv asked with blatant curiosity the second Harper walked into the shed an hour and a half after she'd left.

The others weren't around, probably at lunch, so only Liv and she occupied the trailer.

"It was good." Harper sat at her desk and opened the laptop they'd given her.

"Pfft. Good? That's all I get?" Liv flounced over and perched herself on the edge of the desk. "C'mon, I'm nosy as fuck. Good isn't gonna cut it. Give me details. *All* the details."

Harper worried her lower lip between her teeth. Details. She wasn't ready to talk about the favor Jinx and Curly had done for her. That was too raw. It'd be a hot minute before she processed it herself, let alone be ready to share it. Besides, it seemed like the kind of information where the fewer who knew it, the better.

"I think I might have agreed to be with him. Or date him."

"You think?" One of Liv's perfectly shaped eyebrows arched up.

"I don't know." Harper dropped her head into her hands. "I'm a mess."

"Babe, mess is the standard around here, so you fit right in. Tell me what he said."

"He told me he understood how hard it was for me to trust after what happened in my past. He said he didn't expect me to trust him at this point, but he asked me to try not to fight it if it starts to happen." She rolled her eyes. "Which, let's face it, I think it is, and I have been fighting it like a champion boxer."

Clapping her hands, Liv squealed. "Oh, this makes me so happy. You two are great for each other. You give him some purpose, and he brings much-needed fun and lightness into your life."

Well, that was sweet. The idea of her and Jinx providing something the other needed sounded really good. No one wanted a one-sided relationship.

Not that this was a relationship.

Oh God. It might be heading for a relationship.

"What do you mean when you say I give him purpose?"

Liv sighed. "I love Jinx dearly, but the man skates through life without giving a crap about anything beyond the club. You give him something, someone to care about, and it's taking him from a joking fuckboy… excuse the comparison… to a man who thinks and puts someone before himself. This version of Jinx is fantastic, and that's because of you."

"You think he wants more from me than sex?" Her face felt hot and was probably red as a tomato. In prison, sex talk happened all the damn time, but she'd never had anything to add to the conversation, being she'd only slept with one guy before getting locked up, and she had less than zero interest in discussing him.

"Absolutely." Liv flicked her hair behind her shoulders. "I'll be honest with you. Jinx has never had a problem getting women to sleep with him. I mean, look at the man. I don't have to tell you how sexy he is. Women flock to him."

Harper frowned. This conversation wasn't exactly boosting her confidence.

Swatting her shoulder, Liv laughed. "None of that face, girl. What I'm trying to tell you, and apparently doing a shit job at, is that the man can get sex from any girl, anytime. He does not need to spend weeks getting to know someone as locked up as you if he wants to get laid. He wants more. Trust me."

The irony of those last two words weren't lost on Liv. She gave Harper a sheepish grin and shrugged.

"Can I say one more thing? Then I'll get my ass out of your business."

That drew a laugh from Harper. "Sure."

"Jinx is a good man. Perfect? Hell no. Will he fuck up, probably often? Yeah, they all do. But he's a good man. You have no reason to believe me, but he would never betray you. I can't imagine how hard it is for you to believe those words after what you've been through. You had so much stolen from you because of an untrustworthy man, but I promise you with everything in me…" Liv pressed her hands over her heart, "… he is a good man who would blow up the world before betraying you."

The words were spoken with such sincerity and heart that Harper had no choice but to believe Liv truly meant them. "Thank you. That really helps settle my mind."

"Good." Liv slapped her hands on her thighs. "My work here is done, and I'm famished, so I'll leave you to your thoughts and go find my man so we can grab some lunch."

"Have fun."

After Liv left, Harper dove into her long list of tasks, pushing all thoughts of Jinx and relationships aside. She'd have plenty of time after work to obsess, and her to-do list was a mile long. Half an hour or so passed when her phone rang, making her jump out of her skin.

Jinx's number flashed on the screen, and her stupid heart immediately fluttered with happiness like a smitten teenager.

Ugh, I have it bad.

"Hey," she said, trying not to sound as excited to hear from him as she was. For crying out loud, it'd barely been an hour since she left him. "Thought you had to work."

"Hey, beautiful. Someone sounds happy to hear from me."

So much for playing it cool.

"And yes, I'm at work, but I need a ridiculously big favor that will be repaid with dinner and orgasms."

Well, shit. Jinx had her attention now.

"Anything," she replied, then rolled her eyes. She'd been going for helpful, but it came out desperate for the rewards he'd promised.

Jinx laughed but thankfully didn't press the issue. "Any chance you can head over to Lock's for an hour or so? Curly was there earlier, but he couldn't stick around. Plus, I think he had some harsh words for Lock, which meant Lock probably didn't want him to help out today. Anyway, Lock ended up with a last-minute appointment, and the sitter can't make it."

Watch the baby? What the hell did she know about babies? "Um… I really want to help out, but you remember I've spent the last seven years in prison?"

The sound through the phone could have passed for a snort or a laugh. "What does that have to do with anything?"

"I know I told him I'd help whenever he needed it, but I've never even held a baby. I don't know what to do with them. And you think Lock wants to leave his child with an ex-convict?"

Now he was full-on belly laughing.

"I'm hanging up now."

"No, don't," he said, doing a terrible job of controlling his laughter.

Harper rolled her eyes. She'd never really hang up on him, but making him sweat a bit was fun. Being playful with him was fun. Liv might have been dead-on in her assessment of

Jinx bringing much-needed lightness into her life.

"Okay, babe, first off, I'm fucking jazzed that you're talking about your past so freely. Secondly, you do realize everyone in the club has been arrested at least once? Well, maybe not Pulse, but he's a goodie-goodie. The rest of us? We're all fucking ex-cons to some degree. And, believe me when I tell you, not one of us, Lock included, has any fucking idea what the hell we're doing with a baby. They're a lot harder to kill than you'd think."

"Oh my God. You did not just say that," she said, chuckling.

"So, you in?"

She didn't give herself time to think or talk herself out of it. "Yeah. I'll head there now."

"Thanks, babe. You're the best, and you have one helluva night coming your way."

Her grin grew so big she was glad to be alone. The ladies would rib her to no end if they saw the dopey-as-hell smile. "That's a pretty good deal," she said. "Drink lots of water. Maybe eat a protein bar. I have high expectations."

"Oh, fuck yes. Love it when you show me some sass, baby. Wait there until I get a prospect to ride over with you."

"Jinx. It's broad daylight, and I'm going straight to one of your brother's houses. No stops. I don't need anyone with me."

He hesitated, then sighed. "Fuck. Customer just came in. Okay, text me to let me know you got there. Okay?"

"Promise."

"Bye, Prickles."

The line went dead as she rolled her eyes. That silly nickname seemed to be around to stay, unfortunately. She gathered everything she needed and headed to her car, trying to ignore the flurry of nerves in her stomach.

You got this.

You are strong.
You are capable.
You are good.

Affirmations were something she'd be recommending to the women she counseled in the shelter. Time to start practicing what she preached.

Fifteen minutes later, she parked beside Lock's bike in his driveway.

As she jogged up to the door, a crash from inside had her moving faster. Another followed shortly after.

Shit. Is he okay?

"Lock?" she called as she pounded on the door.

After ten seconds of no response, she knocked again, shouting his name louder. Hopefully, he didn't have any nosy neighbors who'd be popping out to investigate the noise.

A third crash sounded, this time accompanied by shattering glass.

She gasped. Something was very wrong. "Lock?" She tried the door knob and, finding it open, let herself inside. "Lock," she called again.

Noise came from the living room, so she rushed there. All she could see were visions of Lock, wasted and crashing into his television.

What she found was ten times worse.

Lock lay on the floor, face down, with a puddle of blood oozing from his head. Her vision tunneled to him and how to help. She rushed forward on instinct without even glancing at her surroundings. Four steps in, movement in her periphery had her freezing dead in her tracks.

Blood rushed in her ears as a feeling of dread washed over her. A man in a black hoodie and black jeans charged straight at her.

She didn't have a second to react. No time to flee. No time to absorb details about him beyond the fact he was a light-skinned man with light facial hair and a four-leaf clover tattooed on his hand. The rest of his features were hidden beneath the dark hood.

He crashed into her shoulder, sending her flying into a bookshelf. Her head whacked against the wood. "Aah," she cried as stars exploded across her vision. The worst part was the way her shoulder blade and spine dug into the bookshelf. There'd be bruises tomorrow, for sure.

The front door slammed, and Harper blew out a breath of relief.

He was gone. *Thank God.*

Her eyes floated shut, and she sank to the floor. As her butt hit it, her head cleared. "Lock!" Her eyes flew open. He hadn't so much as moved an inch. "Lock, wake up."

She scrambled across the floor on all fours, stopping just short of touching him.

"Oh God, please wake up." A tentative shake to his shoulder did nothing to rouse him. She breathed through her nose to try and keep from hyperventilating as she stuck two fingers under his body against his neck. God knew what she'd do if he didn't have a pulse. She'd probably pass right out and be of no use to anyone.

Thankfully, after a few seconds, she felt a light flutter against her fingers.

"Oh, thank God," she said as she blew out a breath. With shaking hands, she withdrew her phone and dialed emergency services. They instructed her not to try to move him while promising help was on the way and asked her to stay on the line until the ambulance arrived. As she sat there trembling next to his unconscious body, her entire reason for being there slammed into her harder than the assailant.

"Caleb," she whispered.

"Ma'am?" the dispatcher asked in her ear, but Harper ignored it.

Where the hell is the baby? Is he here? Is he hurt?

She shot to her feet, groaning as her newly acquired bruises protested. The discomfort would have to wait. She ran through the house and into Caleb's room, where she found him sound asleep in his crib, making the most adorable snuffling sounds.

Relief hit so hard she doubled over panting, but only had a second to process before the sounds of sirens had her running to the front door.

EMTs rushed through the door and straight to Lock. Dispatch hung up, and Harper was asked a million questions about Lock and his situation, none of which she knew the answers to. As the team went to work assessing Lock's condition, Harper made another phone call, this one for herself as much as Lock.

"Hey, baby," Jinx said by way of greeting. "I was getting worried. Took the scenic route, huh?"

"Jinx?" she said, her voice wobbling.

The teasing immediately stopped. "What's wrong? Where are you?"

"At Lock's house. He's hurt. I need you."

Chapter Twenty-One

"Hey, I'm okay. I promise. You can stop hovering."

Jinx glanced across his small, rarely used kitchen to Harper, sitting at his table, seeming small, uncomfortable, and shaken.

Yet still fucking gorgeous.

Her phone call had brought equal amounts of stark terror and animalistic male pleasure. How he could experience two such opposing emotions simultaneously would remain a mystery. Still, as the fear and sadness in her voice had penetrated his brain, the panic won out over being overjoyed she called him in her time of need.

What the fuck had Lock gotten himself involved in?

Whatever it was, it earned him a hospital say for a grade four concussion and a three-inch scalp laceration. The idiot was lucky he didn't have bleeding in his brain, according to the emergency room doctor. Curly and Brooke had taken Caleb to their home while Pulse and Tracker followed the ambulance to the hospital, leaving Jinx to tend to the bruised and traumatized Harper.

Damn, when he'd walked—okay, ran like the hounds of Hell were on his heels—into Lock's house to find her sitting on the floor against the wall with her legs drawn up and her head resting on her knees, he nearly lost his shit. A woman like Harper, who'd already suffered so much, shouldn't experience another day of sadness, fear, or worry for the rest of her life. Unfortunately, the world didn't fucking work that way.

"Jinx?" She observed him over the mug of tea with two shots of whiskey he'd given her when they arrived a few moments ago.

"Sorry. Just thinking." He pushed away from the counter and went to her, placing a kiss on the top of her head.

"Well, I said I'm okay. The mother hen routine is sweet but not necessary."

Sweet? The woman gave him far too much credit. He snorted as he dragged a chair next to her and sat. He placed his hand on her thigh, needing to touch her to settle his soul. "Maybe not necessary to you. But it is for me. I'm still salty you refused to go to the hospital."

She rolled her eyes but laid her head on his shoulder. The move seemed unconscious and natural, as though she hadn't thought it through or spent time analyzing her moves. Knowing her as he did by now, if she'd been in tip-top shape, she'd have put her mask on and shut him out. But she was sore and shaken from what happened at Lock's. As much as he hated that for her, he loved having her react to him without dissecting every word, thought, and action as she often did.

"The paramedic checked me out after you threw that epic tantrum." She did a horrible job of concealing her smirk behind the mug.

He scoffed, giving her thigh a playful squeeze.

Tantrum, my ass.

"Seriously, I have a lump on my head and some bruises on my back. That's it. Nothing to be concerned about. The paramedic didn't even blink when I said I didn't want to go to the hospital."

So, they were going there, huh? "First off, the only reason that shitty-ass EMT didn't push it is because he was hoping giving you what you wanted would get him your damn number."

"What?" The complete shock in her voice made him snort. "You can't be serious?" She lifted off his shoulder to gape at him.

He grabbed the side of her neck and drew her head—the goose-egg-free side—down to his shoulder.

"He was just doing his job, and he was totally professional the entire time."

"Please. That dickweed was just disappointed the bruises were on your back and not your tits so he could cop a good fucking feel during his *'examination.'* " He crooked his fingers in a quote motion.

Harper was full-on laughing now. "You're insane."

"Separate issue." Damn, he loved making her laugh. Whether it was a small snicker or a full-body roar, the sound was music to his ears. But her flirty giggles were his favorite. They were the hardest to pull from her and the most rewarding. He planned to keep her laughing long enough to make up for the last seven somber years. "Which brings me to my next point. I do not throw fucking tantrums."

"Ha. Are you trying to tell me you reacted well when I told you the robber, or thief, or whatever you want to call him, slammed me into the bookshelf?"

He grunted. "Fuck no, I didn't react well. I was pissed as hell, but it wasn't a damn tantrum. I dare you to find any man who'd react well when his most favorite woman in the world is hurt."

She stiffened.

Too much?

If only he could see her eyes. Then he'd know if his Prickles' shields were back in place.

She lifted off his shoulder again, and even though his heart sank, he allowed her to retreat.

But then she questioned, "I'm your favorite woman?"

He met her serious gaze. "Fuck yes. Hell, I think you're my favorite person. I think I even said *most* favorite. That's an important distinction."

She didn't take the bait and banter back. Her long swallow and the way she clenched her hands in her lap revealed her nerves. Lately, he got more from her without having to chip through the tough outer shell. Whether she let him in consciously or plain forgot to shield herself didn't matter. It was the end result, the slow building of trust and connection he cared about.

She gave him a shaky smile and whispered, "I think you're my favorite person as well."

Goddamn, did those words twist him up inside. If it wouldn't have scared her away, he'd have ripped off his shirt, pounded his chest, and wailed like Tarzan. Instead, he leaned in until he was close enough to kiss her, sliding his hand along her cheek. "You have no idea how fucking happy that makes me. Same with you calling me today when you needed help. Damn, Harper." He patted his hand over his heart twice. "I was so fucking glad to be the one you reached for."

She nuzzled into his palm. "I didn't consider anyone else. I just wanted you there. I knew you would come, no questions."

An eyebrow arched. "Maybe you trusted me a little?"

"I think I do," she whispered with a single nod. Her eyes shone with vulnerability matching her words.

He'd never take this moment for granted. It was, hands down, the most precious gift he'd ever received. Winning the Super Bowl couldn't have felt better. He kissed her. What other choice was there? It was meant to be a gentle, comforting kiss to soothe her frazzled nerves, but his woman was hungry. She let out a little frustrated growl and scrambled into his lap without breaking their connection.

He managed to retain enough brain power to shove his chair away from the table so she wouldn't smack her injured back.

Then it was game on.

Harper devoured him, flinging her arms around his neck and pouring everything she had into the kiss. His dick hardened instantly, and when she rolled her hips into him, he grabbed her ass and ground up into her.

Her moan made him want to slam her to the floor and fuck her until she screamed, but he refrained. Hurting her was the last thing he wanted to do. Plus, Harper was taking the lead, and he damn well wouldn't fuck that up for her. So he endured the torture of the hottest kiss he'd ever experienced with his sexy woman squirming all over his lap.

And she was his. She might not admit it yet, but he'd claimed her.

If he came in his pants like a fucking newbie, so be it.

It'd be her fault, anyway.

After she'd driven him to near madness with her soft moans and eager lips, she rested her forehead against his, panting. "Take me to your bed, Jinx. Take me to your bed and make me yours."

Fuck. Yes.

Her words alone might make him come. His breath caught in his lungs. "Yeah? Mine?"

She smiled, and it was so damn bright it lit the room. "Yes. I want to be yours."

"You already are." He stood, lifting her under her ass.

She yelped, but it quickly turned to a laugh as she wound her arms and legs around him. He ran to his room with her in his arms just to hear her squeal and laugh again.

"Don't drop me," she squealed.

"Never."

They reached his room in seconds. His king-size bed beckoned like a neon flashing light. Any other time he'd toss her on it, but he'd rather leave the club than hurt her back further, so he set her down with ease.

Words weren't necessary for the next few moments. They scrambled to remove their clothing as though waiting for the other to do it for them would be a waste of time. Harper ended up naked before him because he was distracted each time she peeled off an item.

Once she was naked, and he still wore boxer briefs, he gave up the task of disrobing in favor of taking in every sexy inch of her. Harper had put on some weight over the past few weeks, filling out in all the ways prison had slimmed her. He liked her a little fuller and healthier-looking. This way, he wasn't so worried about breaking her if they got a little vigorous.

"You're studying me pretty hard," she said as she leaned on her elbows.

The move thrust her tits outward and had his boxers stretched to their limit.

"Well, I'm not stupid," he said with a wink. "You're so pretty and in my bed. Of course, I'm going to study you. What if there's a test later?"

"No test. Just me." She spread her legs, and his knees nearly gave out. Where had this confident vixen come from?

He palmed his cock over his boxer briefs. "There's no just about it. You are everything."

Harper blinked quickly as though battling tears. He'd kick himself in the dick if he made her cry, even if they were happy tears. He didn't like to see it on her.

He hooked his thumbs in his boxers, then paused. "Let me know if your back starts hurting at any time. Okay?"

She tilted her head, then nodded. "I'll be fine. I want you

so badly, Jinx. Not gonna lie, but tonight scared me. You make me feel good, and I want more of that. I want all of it. So please don't hold back on me."

Well, fuck. Who was he to deny such a sweet request?

He planted his hands on the bed on either side of her. "You said you wanted me to make you mine."

Nerves flickered across her face, but her whispered "Yes" chased them away.

"Do you know what that means? Being mine?"

"Tell me."

"It means you sleep in my bed." He kissed the side of her neck, drawing a breathy sigh from her.

"Yes." It was said with a sigh.

"It means you're on the back of my bike." He nibbled up to her jaw.

"O-okay."

"It means you trust me. Fully." He kissed her lips once, then again, before looking into her troubled eyes. "Maybe not this second, but someday. And I trust you just as deeply."

She gripped his biceps. "Yes. I will get there, Jinx. I want to get there and never thought I would be willing to put in the effort. But I am for you. Please be patient with me."

He smiled. "That's more than enough for me." If the desire were there, she'd make it happen. She was one tough lady.

And for his part, he'd never give her a reason to doubt him.

A thought hit from nowhere. "What if being my woman meant getting a Handlers' tattoo one day?"

Her grin grew sly. "I'd do that if we were long-term."

Fuck, she'd look so damn hot with Handlers' ink on her skin. His dick ached at the thought of it. If the day came when she got a Handlers' tattoo, he sure hoped she'd let him come all over it as soon as it healed.

"What if I wanted to mark you another way?" He gently

bit her shoulder before sucking the skin into his mouth.

"Y-yes," she said on a shaky breath.

"All over?"

"Oh God."

He moved to her neck, sucking hard enough to leave a mark. Harper moaned.

"You like that? You like the idea of me leaving love bites all the fuck over you, knowing under your clothes is evidence of how much I wanted you? How much I want you all the time?"

She trembled against him. "Yes, Jinx. It's so hot, do it. I want to see it. I want to look in the mirror and count the spots you leave."

"Jesus Christ." She was goddamn perfect for him. He sucked right below her collarbone, then the side of her tit, until she moaned. The gentle swell of her stomach was his favorite spot. When he drew the skin between his lips, she giggled and squirmed before it turned into a moan and she yanked his hair.

"Jinx," she said as she panted.

"Hmm?" He moved to her inner thigh, sucking hard and making her squeal.

After that, he straightened to admire his handy work. She lay sprawled on his bed, legs spread, one arm over her head and one at her side. Six pink hickeys practically glowed against her tan skin. Her eyes were heavy-lidded and full of wanton desire.

"Beautiful." His dick leaked, soaking through the gray boxer briefs. Harper's gaze went straight to the spot.

She licked her lips, and his dick released another drop of precum.

No matter what happened in the rest of his life, he didn't think he'd find a moment more perfect than this, and he needed to capture it. Preserve it.

"Don't move a fucking muscle." He hopped off the bed and rummaged through the pile of clothes for his phone.

"What are you... oh!"

He opened the camera and snapped a series of photos he'd jerk off to for the rest of his life.

"I knew you'd be gorgeous with my marks all over you. But I need to leave one more."

"Whe... *Jinx*!"

He flipped her onto her stomach, making her yelp in surprise. The round globes of her perfect ass called to him. Before she could ask what the hell he intended, he nipped her ass and sucked until she shouted. When he released the skin, he gave her other cheek a playful smack.

She buried her face in her hands and made a noise of frustration. He froze. Fuck, had he gone too far?

"Harper?"

"Why the hell is that so fucking hot?" The words were muffled by her hands, but he still heard every one.

She liked it—his lips and his palm on her ass. He smacked her cheek again, drawing a porn-worthy groan from deep within her before she mumbled something.

"What was that?"

"Do it again." The words were spoken as though she felt shame for what she wanted. That would change. He was a dirty fucker, and he planned to introduce her to every sinful delight out there. Soon, she'd be openly begging him to smack her ass without a second thought.

He smacked her ass again. When she moaned into her hands, the sound almost did him in. He squeezed his dick through his boxers and bit his lip to stave off the rogue orgasm. His breaths came in heavy pants, and sweat rolled down his skin from the effort of holding it off.

Harper rolled to her back. "You look like you're in a bad way," she crooned. "Maybe it's time to stop playing and fuck me."

Chapter Twenty-Two

Harper felt sexy.

She felt powerful.

It was in the way Jinx looked at her. The way he put his mouth all over her skin. The wet spot on his boxer briefs over his enormous erection.

How could she not feel like a goddess when he made his desire so evident?

He'd introduced her to things she'd only heard about, and though it initially embarrassed her, she wanted more.

She wanted everything.

"Ride me." He flopped onto his back next to her, making her mouth drop open.

His boxer briefs disappeared before she could process what he wanted from her. The thick cock jutting from between his legs drew her attention. It was long, wide, veiny, and nearly purple at the tip.

He wanted her to ride it. She was so hot on full display, open and vulnerable before him.

"You're studying me pretty hard," he quipped with a snarky smirk.

She laughed. "Did you just throw my words back in my face?"

"Sure did. Now, hop on, baby. I can't promise how long

this guy will last with you sitting there all sexy and marked up. You don't want me to be humiliated for the rest of my life if I come all over myself just from looking at you, do you?"

God, this man knew exactly how to cut through her nerves and make her happy. Fuck feeling nervous. She sat up, twisted around, and threw one leg over his wide body.

"That's it. Fuck yes, you look good up there." His big hands went to her hips, warm and possessive.

She shoved away the last of the apprehension and grinned down at him. A sense of power washed over her. Jinx was big, strong, commanding, and a force to be reckoned with.

And he wanted her.

Only her.

And now he was spread out beneath her for her to do with as she pleased. What a tempting offering. She ran her hands over his rippled abs, tracing his ink and muscles. Jinx sucked in a breath, and his stomach quivered beneath her touch.

She thumbed his nipples, drawing a hiss, then sank her fingernails into his hard pecs.

She got drunk on the thrill of pulling such visceral reactions out of him.

"Jesus, Harper, I can't fucking take it. Get on my dick before I die." The hard set of his jaw and the darkening of his eyes was positively feral. He gripped her hips so hard there'd be bruises along with the hickeys he'd left.

She'd be a mess later, and she loved it.

Jinx shoved a hand under his pillow. When it reappeared, it was to toss a condom her way.

She arched an eyebrow his way. *Always prepared or basic fuckboy behavior?*

"Don't look at me like that. I stuck that there last night in a fit of hope that I could convince you to come back here again."

Every word from his mouth rang so true she didn't even

question it.

God, she really was growing to trust him.

With unsteady hands, she tore the condom wrapper open and pulled out the latex ring. As long as she didn't fumble too badly, she could keep him from noticing that she'd never done this part before.

The second she touched his dick, he bit out a savage curse. Instead of pulling back, Harper kept going. She'd never grow tired of seeing him lose his mind over her.

"Christ," he muttered as she unrolled the condom down his length. His hands fisted the simple blue comforter, and sweat poured off him. Once done, Harper danced her fingers along the length of his cock. "Fucking kill me now. Please, woman, put me out of my goddamn misery."

She rose on her knees and scooted up his body until she was positioned over his cock. Jinx pushed onto his elbows, and his gaze went straight between her legs to where she wrapped a hand around him and began to lower it.

"Sexiest fucking thing," he whispered. The deep gravel to his voice made her shiver.

She sank down on him slowly, taking in each delicious inch. He stretched her and had her eyes wanting to float closed so she could only focus on the soul-changing sensation, but she didn't dare miss a second of the way he watched her body accept him.

"You feel so good." Her throat thickened. "I've never felt anything so good. I don't ever want it to end."

When she could lower no further, they both sighed. Their gazes met, and Harper's heart exploded at what she saw in his eyes. If she didn't know better, she'd swear he loved her. But it'd been too soon. And she was too messed up.

Maybe someday.

But not yet. Certainly not yet. And that feeling in Harper's chest wasn't love either.

It wasn't possible.

"Fuck, you feel good, too, baby. Tightest, hottest pussy imaginable."

Not words of love. Words of desire.

Perfect.

She was quickly learning she excelled at fulfilling his desires and fled from the notion of love.

"I need to move." Now she understood why he'd called it riding him because it's exactly what she wanted to do—plant her hands on his chest and ride him to the stratosphere.

"Let me help with that." He lifted his hips off the bed, thrusting up into her.

The sharp thrust pushed his cock deeper than it had ever been, and Harper swore her head popped off her shoulders. She did exactly as she'd imagined and slapped her hands onto his chest to keep from flying off.

Jinx wasn't a passive partner. He didn't lie there and watch her move above him but used his hands to help her ride while thrusting his hips up and down. Gone was the playful pace they'd started with. Now, they grunted and fucked like two animals becoming one.

Every time she slammed down on him, a sharp zing of pleasure shot from her pussy through the rest of her body. She never wanted the physical pleasure and squishy feeling in her heart she was afraid to analyze to end.

"Fuck, fuck, fuck." Jinx powered up into her over and over. "Wanna see you come apart. Work your tits for me."

A shiver ripped through her at his raunchy command. She did as asked, pinching her nipples and rolling them between her fingers. The added sensation was almost too much to endure. Her head fell back, and her eyes closed.

Jinx lifted his knees, giving her something to rest her back against. Their fucking changed from furious and frenzied to a slow roll and grinding hips.

"What are you doing to me?" she whispered into the universe. She could feel herself falling with each passing minute they spent together.

"Told you," he said as one hand left her hips. "Making you mine." He stroked a thumb over her clit.

Harper cried out.

He did it over and over until she couldn't think anymore. She trembled over him, still playing with her nipples as he drove her insane with his talented fingers and thick cock.

"Ready to come, baby?" His voice had deepened to a spine-tingling rasp.

"Yes. Yes. Please."

He chuckled as he increased the speed of his finger on her clit.

Harper worked her hips against his hand and rode the wave of ecstasy as it washed over her. "Jinx," she shouted as she lost control of her movements. Her muscles twitched, her pussy pulsed, and she swore she flew to the clouds.

"Oh fuck." Beneath her, Jinx's back arched off the bed. "So fucking tight," he said on a groan. "Goddamn." He roared out his pleasure. The muscles in his neck corded, and the veins in his arms bulged as he held their pelvises tightly together.

Watching Jinx come was almost as good as her own orgasm, knowing she was the one who'd brought him such pleasure. She was wanted, appreciated, and was given as much as she gave. More, even.

Those were some powerful realizations.

Eventually, Jinx went slack beneath her. "Holy fuck," he said, huffing and puffing. "I'm gonna need to crank up my cardio to keep up with you, woman."

He pulled her down to his chest, making his softening cock slip from her. They both groaned, but the warmth of his body and his arms encircling her made up for the loss.

Her mind spun when she should have been more relaxed than ever, but she couldn't stop the intrusive thoughts from hacking their way into her brain.

She was his now.

As hard as she'd fought herself, she'd given him the power to hurt and destroy her. The feelings she'd had for Aaron were those of a teenager—puppy love. Nothing that would have lasted in the long run, and that betrayal ruined her life.

What would happen to her if Jinx did the same?

She wouldn't survive it. Maybe there was still time to reerect the wall he'd blasted through.

"If you're still able to think this much, I didn't do my job," he said as he ran his fingers along her spine. "Do I need to fuck you again?"

She let out a tired laugh. "Not sure you could right now, big guy."

He snorted. "I'm going to pretend I didn't hear that. Now, stop thinking and sleep."

"Want me to move? I have to be crushing you." As she tried to lift off him, he anchored her in place.

"Don't fucking think about it. Love feeling you on me like this."

Well, when he put it like that.

Harper rested her cheek on his chest and listened to the soothing, steady beat of his heart. Then, after a few minutes, he shifted and pulled a blanket up, covering them.

Harper had never been more comfortable, more sated in her entire life. If she could spend the rest of her days right at that moment, she'd be the happiest woman alive.

Fear and uncertainty tried to worm their way back into her head, but she managed to keep them out for the moment.

Mostly.

"Don't hurt me," she whispered into the quiet room long after Jinx's breathing had steadied.

Chapter Twenty-Three

"Ready to roll?" Spec strode into the clubhouse armed to the teeth. He tossed a pistol to Tracker, then one to Jinx. A military-grade knife hung from his belt alongside another pistol. Without having to ask, Jinx also knew the backpack slung over Spec's shoulder held a few more guns, brass knuckles, a retractable baton, and probably a few surprise party gifts.

"Good to go." Jinx shoved the gun in the small of his back and nodded at his brother.

"Let's do it." Tracker slapped Spec on the back. "Ladies are working on getting tipsy at the prez's house. Curly's there with 'em, and Ty will join in a bit. He got stuck at the tire shop."

"Good." Spec pulled open the door, and the they walked out into the muggy evening.

"Your ol' ladies know what we're doing?" Jinx asked as they approached the bikes. They'd received a tip from one of Spec's contacts about where the asshole who'd attacked Lock could be found. In the three weeks since Lock's two-night stay in the hospital, they'd not seen much of their brother, but according to Curly, he wasn't managing his life any better than before he'd earned himself a hefty hospital bill.

The ladies had seen him the most, helping out with Caleb

as often as they could and making it known the club was here for him when Lock was ready to crawl out from the bottom of the pit he was currently living in. Even Harper saw him more than Jinx did these days. She'd fallen in love with the baby and never turned down a chance to sit for him.

"Liv knows the basics. I don't like to keep her in the dark, but I also hate to make her worry."

Tracker snorted. "I live with a former cop. She knows. There ain't much she doesn't know."

Laughing, Spec swung a leg over his bike. "I hear that, brother." He turned toward Jinx. "You tell Harp?"

He frowned as he shook his head. "No. Wasn't sure how she'd take it. Didn't want to stress her the fuck out." The past few weeks had been good. Amazing, really. Not perfect, but amazing. He and Harper spent nearly every free moment together—meals, motorcycle rides, walks on the beach, and many, many hours in bed. For the most part, Harper's walls stayed down. Every once in a while, her prickles returned, usually if they had a miscommunication or she got too caught up in her head, but they'd worked through it together. And once they sorted the issue, she kept her walls down, which he figured was a damn important victory.

"You might wanna clue her in next time. We're pretty open with our ol' ladies," Tracker said. "Curly doesn't mind them knowing shit within reason, and Jo appreciates being kept in the fucking loop. I'll tell you that."

"Liv too. She's like a bloodhound when she senses something is off. Don't know how men in other clubs keep their women in the dark about shit. She's relentless until she gets what she wants, and she'd never go for that shit."

Jinx laughed. "Man, you two sound pussy whipped."

Tracker revved his engine. "Look in the mirror, brother."

"Woohoo, how the mighty have fallen," Spec yelled. "*Oh, Harper, you look so pretty today,*" he said in a horrendous imitation of Jinx's voice. *"Harper, wanna go steady? Harper, will you have my babies?"*

Not even close.

"I don't fucking say that shit." Jinx flipped them off.

"What? Can't hear you." Laughing, Spec cupped his ear as Tracker shot out of the parking lot.

Assholes.

But he was chuckling as he rode off after them.

The ride to the address Spec's contact gave them took about forty-five minutes. "Jesus," Jinx said as he pulled up to a dilapidated house with a chain-link fence surrounding the entire property. The gate leading to a walkway was halfway open with a twisted latch that wouldn't allow it to remain closed. A dim flood light above the garage lit the area enough to assess their surroundings.

The house, or crack den, was made up of light-colored shingles. A handful were missing, revealing the insulation beneath. All the windows had been boarded up long ago, and someone graffitied various gang symbols all over the plywood. Anyone walking by would assume the house was abandoned.

"Nice place," he said as Spec strode toward him.

"Yeah, well, I don't think tweakers are known for their design skills."

A ferocious bark ripped through the quiet air.

"Holy fuck," Tracker shouted.

The three of them jumped at least a foot back as a snarling pit bull lunged straight for them off the crumbling front porch steps. Thankfully, a three-foot chain kept the growling beast from tearing them to bits. The sound of the links clanking together as the beast tested their strength sent a wave of unease down Jinx's spine. So much for the element of surprise. Anyone inside would know they were coming long before they figured out a way in that wouldn't end up with their bones gnawed by an angry beast.

"Shoulda brought Brooke," Tracker muttered. "She's crazy enough to walk right up to that fucker and hand him a damn sausage."

Jinx chuckled. "You know he'd be cuddling up to her within five seconds, too, even while baring his teeth at us. She's a goddamn dog whisperer."

"Hey, pup, any chance you wanna take a nap while we walk past you into the house?"

The dog's answer was another round of ball-shrinking growls.

"Nice try, brother," Jinx said with a snort. "The chain's short, so we can walk around back without becoming his dinner. I'm sure there's an entrance back there."

"But is it nailed shut?" Spec grumbled.

"Why hasn't anyone come out to see what's upset the dog?" Tracker asked. He was as much of an animal lover as Brooke, so his concern for the animal came as no surprise.

"It's nine o'clock. Anyone in there is already passed out or too fucking blasted to give a shit." Spec stepped through the gate onto the property. He plastered himself against the fence and side-stepped along even though twelve or so feet separated him from the dog. The barking and growling increased tenfold. "Fuck, this guy wants to rip my throat out."

"Too bad you didn't think to pack hotdogs with your guns." Jinx followed Spec through the gate with Tracker on his tail. "Let's get this fucking over with."

"Impatient now that you've got better shit to do, huh? Rather be in bed with your ol' lady?"

Jinx grunted. "Obviously. Wouldn't you?"

Tracker laughed. "Fuck yes. I'd live there if we wouldn't die of starvation."

Thank fuck Tracker refrained from commenting on how

Jinx didn't refute the ol' lady comment. Harper wasn't his ol' lady. The one time he brought it up, about a week ago, she'd gone into full-on prickles mode, snipping and erecting a steel barrier between them for the day. That was a topic he wouldn't be revisiting anytime soon.

She wasn't ready, and he had to respect that, even if it sucked.

They rounded the house to the pitch-black backyard, which was even nicer than the front. And by nice, he meant a complete shithole. The lawn hadn't been mowed in a century, and a foot-tall fire ant hill by the back door served as a nightmare-inducing boobytrap.

"Jesus fuck, imagine stepping in that fucker?" Tracker said with a full-body shudder. "I'd rather face the dog."

"Aww, you afraid of a little buggy?" Jinx asked with a laugh.

"I'll give you a thousand bucks if you stick your hand on that hill right now, asshole. Cold hard cash."

Still laughing, Jinx shook his head. "Fuck no. I ain't that stupid."

"Then keep your fucking comments to yourself, dickhead." Tracker shoved his shoulder.

"Can't believe I'm the one fucking saying this shit, but you think you could stop acting like children and get your heads in the game?"

"Ooh, Daddy Spec means business. We better be good boys," Jinx mocked.

"Fuck off," Spec retorted, but his shoulders shook with suppressed laughter. He reached the sliding back door, which was covered inside by a dark curtain. "Ready?" he asked as he grabbed the handle.

Tracker nodded, as did Jinx when he met Spec's gaze. "Do it."

They had no idea if the man they wanted would be inside

or what the asshole even looked like. Harper hadn't gotten a good look at his face, but they knew he was average-sized, pale-skinned with facial hair, and known to hang out in this shithole. At the very least, they hoped to come out with a name and a better description.

Spec tugged on the door. It opened with ease, screeching as it slid along the unoiled track.

None of them were surprised the door wasn't locked. Crack houses weren't known for their security. Ironic, considering the thousands of dollars in illicit drugs they probably had within these walls.

"Fuck me," Jinx said as he stepped inside and was assaulted with the acrid stench of smoke and sweat. He waved a hand in front of his face. The thick, gray haze filling the room made it impossible to see more than five feet in front of his face, especially since only one dim table lamp shone from the far corner of the room.

Whispers bounced off the wall along with the slap of skin on skin, in the classic sound of fucking.

Two seconds in and Jinx craved a shower.

He buried his nose in the crook of his elbow and coughed as his eyes stung. "We're gonna get fucking lung cancer if we're here for more than five minutes," he mumbled. The walls were streaked with brownish-yellow stains from day after day of smoke and filth.

"Seriously. This place is fucking nasty." Tracker waved a hand in front of his face, but the smoke was so thick it barely swirled away. "Burns my damn eyes too."

As he followed Spec down a hallway, his eyes adjusted to the dark. They entered a common area with two futons and a small sofa. Two rail-thin women were passed out on the couch, half on top of each other. Four others—three men and a woman—sat on the futon to his left, smoking and staring at nothing. Two more women and a dude occupied the final dingy futon, fucking each other like they weren't in a disgusting dump surrounded by other people.

Not one of the occupants reacted to seeing three large bikers tromping through the room. They were probably used to junkies coming and going at all hours of the night.

"Christ," Jinx muttered. "What a shitshow."

"Listen up," Spec shouted. A few glassy eyes shifted his way. "Looking for someone. White dude, average size. Hangs here a lot. Got a four-leaf clover tatted on his hand."

One of the women involved in the sleazy threesome untangled herself from the pile of limbs. Fully naked, she strode over with her ribs protruding, her small tits sagging, and the saddest fucking eyes. "Well, aren't you a big boy," she said as she approached Jinx with an interested gleam in her otherwise flat expression. "Looking for a place to party?" She lifted a hand toward his chest.

"Don't you fucking dare," he ground out before she could get her bony fingers on him.

She pouted, but it wasn't sexy, only pitiful, like this entire place. "Promise I'm better than whoever you're currently fucking," she crooned.

Dissing Harper wouldn't earn her any favors. Even before Harper, he'd have passed on this one without a second glance. She didn't need another man to fuck her. She needed a damn rehab facility.

She tried to touch him again, and this time, he barked out, "Answer the man's question."

"Hmph, you're no fun." She huffed and spun away, walking back toward the bed where she'd left her two partners mid-sixty-nine. Jinx could count the bones of her spine.

"Check the first bedroom on the left down the hall." She sounded bored as hell as she waved a lazy hand toward the hallway before picking a pipe off the bed and taking a long hit.

Jinx followed his brothers down the foggy hallway before having to watch the woman join the others back on the futon. Witnessing them fuck wasn't even close to sexy. Greasy hair, dirty fingernails, and fumbling half-baked movements didn't do shit for him besides make him grateful as hell to have Harper.

Spec reached the room first and pounded a fist on the door.

"The fuck you want?" they heard from the other side of the closed door. It had a crooked sign that read *Leave Me The Fuck Alone*.

Sorry, buddy, not today.

"Information," Spec said.

"What kind of information?"

Enough was enough. He didn't want to spend one more minute than necessary in this godforsaken dump. "Open the damn door," Jinx shouted, smacking the side of his fist against it.

"Not until you tell me who the fuck you are and what the fuck you want." The reply came instantly, but the tone was tinged with nerves.

Spec put a hand on Jinx's chest. "We're looking for someone. Guy with a four-leaf clover tat on his hand."

Silence, then rustling, sounded behind the door. After a moment, it opened a crack. Neon blue shone into the hallway from the room. "Haven't seen him lately," the guy said.

"Can't fucking see you. Open it up." Spec nudged the door.

It opened a smidge more. "Said I haven't seen him." Whoever this joker was, he wore a gray sweatshirt with the hood pulled up and over his face. Baggy jeans and threadbare Converse completed the outfit.

Spec grunted, shoved the door open the rest of the way, and got in the guy's face.

He backed up a few steps. "What the fuck? Said I haven't

seen him. Get the fuck out."

"Get his hood off," Spec ordered.

Jinx towered over the loser, having at least eight inches on him. He wasn't scrawny, but certainly not an impressive specimen. As he reached up to yank the hood back, the guy reacted with startling speed.

A knife appeared from nowhere, slashing through the air with deadly intent. A tattooed four-leaf clover caught Jinx's attention a second before searing pain burned through his arm as the blade made contact. "Fuck!"

The guy threw an elbow into an unsuspecting Tracker's face, then darted between him and Jinx. Another slice of pain, this time in his side, had Jinx unable to make chase.

"He fucking stabbed me." The knife still protruded from his side.

"Don't pull it," Tracker shouted one second before Jinx planned to do exactly that.

Tracker rushed over. Blood streamed from his nose, but he ignored it. As a volunteer for search and rescue, he had a fair amount of first-aid knowledge, so Jinx would do whatever he said.

"He okay?" Spec called out.

"I got Jinx. Go after him," Tracker called back. "Sit." He pointed to the bed behind Jinx.

Spec pulled out his gun and rushed out of the room after the man who'd sent Lock to the hospital and put bruises on Harper.

Blood poured down his arm from the clean slice, but it was the knife in his side that had him worried.

"Lemme see," Tracker said as he crouched next to Jinx.

"You know you're fucking bleeding?" Jinx asked.

"I know, but a stab wound beats a broken nose, so let me see."

Any amount of movement shifted the knife and made it

hurt like a son of a bitch. Together, they lifted the edge of Jinx's shirt so Tracker could assess the wound. Blood had already soaked into his white T-shirt, and the knife held it pinned to his body, making it nearly impossible to get a good look. "Fuck." He hissed when Tracker prodded the area around the knife. "I'm gonna end up in the fucking hospital, aren't I?"

" 'Fraid so, brother." Tracker wiped under his nose, leaving a streak of blood on the back of his hand. "But first, we gotta manage to get the fuck outta here."

Spec reappeared. "Lost him. Fucker is fast as shit. Think he hopped the back fence, and it's too goddamn dark to see shit." He glanced from Jinx to Tracker. "Called Curly. He's sending Ty with a prospect and a cage. Ty will take you to the ER, and the prospect will ride your bike back."

Jinx's head fell back on his shoulders. *What a fucking mess.*

"Want me to call Harper?" Tracker asked.

Fuck. She was going to lose her shit.

"No. I don't want her to see me like this. Wait until I'm patched up and they tell me I'm not dying. Then I'll go see her."

Tracker and Spec exchanged a look, but Jinx was in too much damn pain to try and decipher it.

"Whatever you want, man. Let's get you out of here," Tracker said.

This was not how the night was supposed to go. All he could do now was hope Harper didn't run screaming from the dangers associated with his club.

Chapter Twenty-Four

The whispering was what finally did her in.

The night had been fun—drinks with the girls and a delicious salmon meal barbecued by Curly. She'd also been grilled by the pack of nosy women wanting every detail of how her relationship was progressing with their friend. But she found she didn't mind because it was done with love and excitement for her and Jinx.

Then Curly got a phone call, and everything changed.

The energy in the air shifted from a pleasant buzz to a heavy rigidity. He'd grown tense, and that tension set Ty on edge. Next came the looks. Worried glances between the women set her on edge. But when Curly and Ty held a whispered conversation complete with frowns and violent hand gestures, everyone picked up on the fact something was wrong.

Very wrong.

Harper assumed it was club business and tried her damndest to keep from obsessing, but once Curly whispered to Brooke, the news, whatever it was, seemed to travel through the entire house in a poorly disguised game of telephone everyone was in on.

Everyone except for her.

Why the secrecy?

Why was she the only one out of the loop? Because she wasn't officially an ol' lady and therefore not a permanent part of the club? Should she leave so they could discuss without having to hide information from her?

Ugh. The exclusion made Harper feel sick.

She pushed her dessert bowl away, unable to take another bite no matter how delicious the peach cobbler tasted.

Concerned glances were still being exchanged when Tracker walked in without knocking. This group never bothered to knock and busted into each other's homes as though they all lived together.

Tracker went straight to Jo, who stood from the table to wrap her arms around him. They whispered to each other as he rubbed her back. Why did she need soothing?

What the hell was going on?

And that's when Harper's stomach really took a nosedive. Where was Jinx? He'd been with Tracker tonight. Spec as well. Where were the other two men?

Had something happened? Were they injured? Everyone knew something she didn't, and she was done waiting in the dark.

She shoved her chair back and stood. All gazes shifted to her. "I can't take this anymore. You're all shit at keeping secrets. Never play poker. Now, someone please tell me what the hell is going on."

Shame crossed Brooke's face while Liv cringed.

"Shit, sorry, Harp," Brooke said. "We're not trying to keep secrets from you. We just didn't want you to worry."

Oh God. She pressed a hand to her stomach. "W-worry about what?" No one spoke. "Jinx?" she whispered. "Is he okay?"

Tracker walked over and cupped her elbow. "Why don't you grab your stuff? Jo and I will take you home. Jinx said he'd meet you there later tonight."

Tears practically choked her. She faced Tracker. "Please. Is he okay?"

With a nod, Tracker pulled her in for a hug. "He'll be fine, hon."

He'll be fine. Not he was fine or he would be fine. As in not fine now but will be in the future.

"He's hurt?" She pulled away so she could watch Tracker's face and assess the truth of his words.

He cleared his throat. "Nothing major. He's getting some stitches and will be done soon."

Stitches? So he was hurt bad enough to need medical care. She might pass out. "Take me to him." Not a question. A demand.

"Hon—"

"Take. Me. To. Him."

Jo walked over as Tracker sighed. She put her arm around Harper's shoulders.

"I promised him I would take you home and not to the hospital." Tracker made an 'X' over his heart with his fingers. "He'll come to you the second he's finished. Swear it."

"Finished getting sewn back together, you mean?"

"Uh…" He looked everywhere but at her.

Fucking men.

"Fine. Let's go. I'm done here anyway. Watching you all whisper and give me the side-eye all evening destroyed my appetite."

Tomorrow, she'd be mortified by the way she stomped from the table like a child, shaking off Jo's arm and failing to thank Curly for the delicious meal. But she was sick with worry for Jinx and had no idea how to handle the emotional storm rising inside her. She hadn't had anyone to worry over in years, and being out of practice made those feelings even more distressing.

As she sat in the back of Jo's car, staring out the window

and bouncing her knee, she realized this was so much more than worry. She'd have been worried if any of the men in the club got hurt. Now she was petrified. Good thing she hadn't finished her dinner—less for her to throw up all over the back of Jo's car.

How had she let this happen? How had she gotten here again, being confused, in the dark, and not knowing what the hell was happening because of a man? But this was different. She sat there fearing *for* the man, not fearing him or what he'd done.

Sitting there, feeling like she could crawl out of her skin with worry for Jinx, set off a lightbulb in her head. The intensity of her internal reaction, the way she wanted to jump out of the car and run home just to feel like she had control, was something she'd never experienced.

She wanted to see Jinx alive and unharmed more than she wanted her next breath.

She wanted to arrive at her apartment and find him waiting for her with the wide smile she loved so much and his arms open for her.

And that said it all, didn't it?

She loved his smile. Loved his presence in her life. Loved the way he made her feel each and every day. Loved waking up to him. Loved going to bed with him.

She just loved him.

Plain and simple, and yet the most complicated emotion in the world. This was the exact position Harper had promised herself she'd never end up in—emotionally shackled to a man. Jinx had the power to destroy her heart and life, and she'd given that power to him.

What the hell had she been thinking, allowing herself to get close to him?

You were thinking of how wonderful it felt.
Well, it doesn't feel good now, does it?

She let her head thunk against the window as a few rogue tears leaked from the corners of her eyes. Her chest ached with a hollow sadness.

"Harper?" Jo said from the seat in front of her a few moments later. "We're here."

She straightened off the door, wiped her eyes, and gazed up at her dark, lonely apartment. "Thanks for the ride." God, she sounded miserable even to her own ears.

Jo turned. "I'll come wait with you. Tracker can stay down here."

"No. I got it. Thanks."

Frowning, Jo and Tracker exchanged a glance. "Harp..." Jo said.

She lifted a hand. "Look, I'm sorry if I'm being bitchy, but I want to be alone right now. Okay?"

Jo stared at her as though trying to see inside her head.

"Please, Jo."

"Babe..." Tracker ran a hand down his ol' lady's arm.

With a heavy sigh, Jo finally ceded, "Fine."

"Thank you." She started to open the door as Jo spoke again.

"But we're waiting right down here until Jinx shows up. Deal with it."

Tracker chuckled, shaking his head. "I wouldn't argue with her, Harper. She's damn fierce when she wants to be."

More tears filled Harper's eyes. Why the hell was Jo being so nice to her after she'd been such a shrew the entire ride. "Thank you," she whispered.

"None necessary, hon. It's what family does." Tracker winked while Jo gave her a nodding grin.

"I'm not—"

"Now you're gonna piss me off," Jo said, holding up a finger. "You *are* family. Deal with that too."

Afraid if she spoke, her voice would wobble and she'd cry

more, Harper reached out and squeezed Jo's hand.

"Go on up. We'll talk tomorrow," Jo reassured.

As she trudged up the stairs toward her studio apartment, Harper had to admit that knowing they were sitting down there in support helped her keep her shit together.

She stepped in, turned on the light, and gazed around the room.

What now?

Reading a book wouldn't work. She'd never be able to concentrate. Same with watching television or trying to listen to music.

"Fuck it all," she muttered as she walked to her small couch. She sat down and stared at the door, willing herself to remain calm and not think the worst.

And that's all she did for the next hour until the door opened and the most beautiful sight walked into her apartment. Jinx, on two legs, tall and handsome as ever. A large bandage covered his forearm, but aside from that, she didn't see any other visible injuries. Relief hit with such ferocity she couldn't hold back a sob.

"Jinx!" She shot off the couch, flew to him, and threw herself into his arms.

He caught her as she'd expected but with a pained grunt and a stagger backward.

Immediately, she released him. "What's wrong? Did I hurt you?" She frowned.

"Nah, baby, I'm okay." He cupped her face. "Damn, it's good to see you."

"No," she said, shaking her head. "Something's not right. You hurt more than your arm." She reached for the hem of his shirt, and he sighed.

"I promise you it's not that bad."

"What's not that bad?" she asked as she gently lifted the T-shirt. A gasp ripped from her as she saw the bandage taped to his side. "Oh my God. I slammed into you. I'm so sorry."

"It's okay, baby. They numbed it all up to stitch it, so I barely feel anything now."

An obvious lie, but she let him have it. "What happened?" she asked, still staring at the bandage as she held his shirt up.

Jinx sighed. "Let's sit, and I'll tell you everything. They gave me a pain pill, and I'm dead on my feet."

"Oh, yes, sorry. Of course. Would you rather lie down?"

He shook his head. "No, baby, sitting's good. But first." He cupped her face and leaned down, placing a sweet, lingering kiss on her lips. She closed her eyes and sank into it until her brain kicked in, and she stepped away.

"Are you supposed to be bending like that? Sit."

"Those lips are worth any amount of pain," he said with a wink.

Do not swoon.

She followed him to the couch and sat with about a foot separating them to keep from hurting him. He rolled his eyes and hauled her closer as though he didn't have a fresh wound on his side.

"Jinx, you're hurt."

"It's just one stab wound. Didn't even hit anything vital, and they stitched me all up. I'll be good as new in a day or two."

She froze, a complete block of ice. "Stabbed?" she whispered as cold waves washed over her.

"Shit. You just got fucking pale as fucking powder. You're not gonna pass out on me, are you?"

As he reached for her, she batted his hands away. "Stabbed?" she asked again.

Jinx sighed, long and with a hefty dose of regret. "All right, here's the story. We got a tip about the guy who hurt Lock. The address of a place he hangs out. Tracker, Spec, and I went to check it out. He was there, but shit went sideways, and he sliced my arm and nicked my side."

She blinked at him. "You said the three of you were picking up money someone owed you, and it would be a quick in and out. You said there was nothing to worry about."

He had a wary glint to his gaze. "I did say that."

"So you lied?"

Jinx swallowed. "I didn't want you to worry."

Was he for real? "Didn't want me to worry?" she parroted.

"Yes. You're new to the club. I didn't want you to think I could be in danger."

She scoffed. "But you *were* in danger. And I was the one who found Lock at his house. Don't you think I deserved to know you found the guy?"

"I—"

"Oh my God." She covered her mouth with her hand. "Did the other ladies know where you were?" Had she been the only fool in the dark?

"I don't know exactly what their ol' men said to them, but they knew at least some of it."

Harper groaned. No wonder they'd been all quiet whispers and covert glances. They were probably having a good laugh on her behalf—the naïve little idiot who had no idea what was going on behind her back.

"Nicked your side?"

His mouth flattened, and he rolled his eyes. "He stuck the knife in my side. Tracker had to wrap it up and drive me to the hospital with the fucking handle sticking out. He couldn't pull it because he didn't know what was hit or if I'd hemorrhage. Is that what you want to hear?"

Harper gagged, then jumped off the couch. "Yes! That's what I wanted to hear, but I wanted to hear it hours ago! And I wanted to know where you really were and what you were really doing like the other ol' ladies. You lied to me, Jinx. You lied to me after you told me I could trust you."

"The other ol' ladies?" He stared at her hard.

She stopped pacing and planted her hand on her hips. "What?"

"You said you wanted to know like the other ol' ladies. But you're not my ol' lady, are you?"

"That's not fair..." How dare he throw that in her face when she'd already given him so much.

"Maybe not, but it's true, isn't it?" Anger crept across his features.

Her shoulder's sagged. Jinx didn't get it.

"I'd have made you my ol' lady in a heartbeat. I'll do it right fucking now. We can head to the clubhouse, and I'll claim you in front of all my brothers. In front of the whole fucking world. But every time it comes up, your thorns come out, and you put a wall between us."

She threw her hands in the air. "What does it matter? I said I was yours. I say it all the time. Why can't that be enough?"

"Because of this," he said, waving a hand between them. "Because it's your way of keeping distance between us. So when shit gets real, you can fall back on how grateful you are you didn't give all of yourself to me."

"Well, can you blame me?" she shouted. "You lied. Kept a secret. For crying out loud, you didn't tell me you were stabbed! I held myself back because this is what happens when you give someone power over you. You get hurt. I get hurt. The last man I was with messed me up, and I didn't even love him. I love you. Do you have any idea how you could destroy me?" Her eyes widened as words she never meant to utter flew from her mouth.

They stared at each other across the room, chests heaving and eyes shooting sparks.

God, why had she said that? Now that the words were out there, she felt nothing but pain and despair.

"Say it again," he whispered.

She shook her head. "I think you should go."

"No." He rose and then walked toward her.

Turning away to look at anything but him, she said, "Jinx, please. I shouldn't have said it. I didn't mean to say it. Please go." Her voice sounded as though she hung on the edge of desperation, exactly how she felt. "Please."

He reached her, stopping right in front of her. "Say it again."

"No." Harper banged her forehead against his chest. "Go."

He cupped her face between his hands, forcing her to meet his gaze. "So fucking prickly. Say it."

"I didn't mean it." She reached for the lie as a lifeline. The final straw to grasp and save her heart.

"Now who's lying? I love you, Harper. So fucking much."

She closed her eyes as pain lanced her heart. "No."

He kissed her, soft, slow, and intoxicating. His calloused thumbs brushed her cheeks as his sweet breath mixed with hers. For one second, she let herself sink into it and soak up the comfort and excitement only he could provide in equal measure. She swore she could taste the love on his tongue, but her brain had gone into full-body armor mode, trying to protect her heart. "No," she whispered, pulling his hands from her face. "I can't do this, Jinx. You have to go."

He stepped away, sadness crossing his features. "Running away from me doesn't make it any less true, but if you need to flee, go ahead. I'll be right here waiting to say it again when you're ready to hear it."

"What if I never am?" she whispered as the cracks in her heart became deep fissures.

"You will be. You got this." He hauled her in for one more kiss, then released her and walked out the door without a backward glance.

Harper followed as though attached to him by a chain connecting their hearts. When she reached the door, she flattened her palms on it and rested her forehead against the cool wood. The first sob came seconds later, followed by another and another. Before she knew it, her knees gave out, and she sank to the floor, crying harder than ever.

How was it possible for this pain to be worse than when she received a prison sentence?

Jinx said he'd wait, but for how long? How long until he got tired of her issues and moved on to another woman? The thought of him touching someone else made the tears flow harder. She'd die if he abandoned her for someone else.

So why the hell are you shoving him away so hard?

Had she made a mistake? Was this an overreaction? How was she supposed to know? She had no experience with men beyond one life-altering betrayal that had clearly fucked her up for any other man.

What the hell was she going to do? Jinx didn't want half a commitment anymore. She asked what it mattered if she became his ol' lady, but in truth, she knew. The girls had explained the significance as far as the club. It was the highest level of commitment, valued even above marriage.

It represented complete trust and devotion.

After tonight, she wasn't sure she was capable of it.

"You will be. You got this."

Those were some of her favorite words, but as she sat on the floor sobbing her heart out, she wondered if that was true.

And for the first time, she feared she might not ever have it.

Chapter Twenty-Five

"You okay, brother?" Curly asked as he sat next to Jinx at the bar.

Jinx grunted and turned his attention from his drink to his president. "Don't I look okay?"

"You look like day-old shit." As he spoke, Curly signaled to a hang-around behind the bar to grab him a drink. The new kid wanted to prospect but needed to get to know everyone before someone would sponsor his prospecting.

"Gee, thanks." He lifted his glass in a toast. "Appreciate the support."

"You get any sleep last night?" Curly asked, nodding his thanks as the hang-around delivered his drink. The kid was so damn eager he nearly knocked over the glass, sputtering under the president's attention.

Any other time Jinx would have jumped on the opportunity to bust on the kid, but the heaviness sitting on his chest wouldn't allow him to joke around.

"It's two in the afternoon, and I'm on my third drink. So, no, I did not get any sleep last night."

"You know, when I got out of prison, I spent some time up in Tennessee?" Curly asked.

"Yeah. With Copper and the club up there. It's what gave you the idea to come down here and open your own chapter, right?" After being framed by a local MC-hating detective, Curly spent thirteen years behind bars for a crime he didn't commit—the heinous murder of a child.

"That's right. I took a few months to myself, even before going to Tennessee. My head was..." He huffed a half laugh. "Christ, it was fucked up. Still is sometimes. When you experience a betrayal like I did, it changes something in you on a cellular level." As horrible as it had been for him to be set up by the cops, Curly eventually found out some members of his former MC were complicit in the framing. Talk about betrayal.

"In prison, you always need to protect yourself," Curly went on. "Physically, mentally, emotionally. At some level, you're on guard one hundred percent of the time, no matter how many years you're in. I imagine it's no different in the women's prison. You can't trust anyone. Not fully. And when you combine that with a betrayal like Harp experienced... well, some people can't move past that."

"You did," Jinx pointed out and took a long drink. "What helped you?"

"I'm flattered I have you so fooled, but I still struggle, Jinx." He blew out a breath. "Probably always will to some extent. But, fuck if I know where I'd be without Brooke. She..."

Jinx watched as Curly gazed at nothing for a moment. He might not be the most effusive, romantic, or mushy man, but there wasn't a person in the world who could doubt his immense love for his ol' lady. She was his world, and he'd fight the fiercest dragon to keep his woman from one second of unhappiness.

Curly turned his gaze on Jinx. "She's fucking everything, brother."

A suffocating sense of loss watched over him. "I think I fucked up, Curly. I wasn't honest, and then I pushed too hard." He ran a hand down his face. "Fuck, I think I pushed her away. How the hell do you guys get it right all the time?"

He frowned as his president burst out laughing.

"Jinx, I said Brooke was everything. I didn't say she was perfect. And I'm sure as fuck not perfect. I'm a hard-headed biker with issues coming out my ass. Hell, we both have mountains of issues. We fuck up all the damn time."

"But you're the strongest couple I know."

Curly shrugged as though the answer was simple. "We come back to each other every time."

If only the solution were that easy. "She told me to go."

"You think Brooke ain't ever kicked my sorry ass out of the house?" He snorted. "You'd be dead wrong. But we came back to each other. Emotions settle, the heat of anger cools off." He winked. "Or turns into another type of heat."

"So, you telling me all I have to do is return to her?"

"Fuck no. That's just step one." He rose from his barstool, drink in hand. "Then you put in the work to learn how to give each other what you need. You'll both fuck up. It's inevitable. But what you can't do is give up. That girl has been through so much, Jinx. Give her some grace. Give yourself some too. Promise you it's worth it. It's so fucking worth it. And I know Brooke would say the same." He slapped Jinx on the back, then strode off toward his office.

They had church in a few hours. Jinx planned to spend the rest of the afternoon right there on that barstool, mulling over Curly's words and planning his next steps. Because one thing was for sure, he wasn't willing to let Harper shove him out of her life.

"THERE WILL BE a guard station before you can enter, right?" Harper asked as she, Brooke, and Liv met with their contractor. The crew had begun work on the service road leading directly to their shelter from the main road so residents of their shelter wouldn't have to traipse across the entire farm or past the clubhouse to get there.

"Yes, ma'am," Bob, their contractor, said. If she had to guess, he was a fit guy in his early fifties. After years of working out in the sun, his skin had leathered and had a deep tan that probably never faded. "That'll be built next week."

Knowing whoever came onto the property this way would have to pass a guard would make the women they served feel a million times safer.

"This makes it feel so real," Liv said with a wide grin.

Laughing, Brooke said, "More real than siding going on the actual shelter?"

"Yes. The shelter can have all the siding it wants, but if no one can get there, it's not real."

"She has a point," Bob said with a chuckle. Curly had handpicked him and his entire crew. Anyone working on or near Handlers' property had been thoroughly vetted. The company didn't mess around with their safety or the safety of their women.

They were so protective.

And now she was thinking of Jinx again. Well, she'd made it five whole minutes that time.

Progress.

Her stomach cramped. Maybe she should put something in it besides coffee, but the thought of food made her want to hurl. She hadn't wanted the coffee, but it'd been a necessity after staring at her ceiling the entire night, so she'd choked down multiple cups.

"What do you think, Harp?" Liv asked. The poor ladies had been trying to engage her all day. They wouldn't take the hint and leave her the hell alone to brood in silence.

Probably why she loved them so much.

At least she'd managed to apologize to Jo earlier in the day. Of course, Jo had waved off the apology and made her promise never to think of it again.

They were too nice and more than she deserved.

"I think it's perfect. Will you be hiring a guard or using someone from the club?"

"Since we'll need someone round the clock, we'll hire an agency." She rolled her eyes. "Should be a fun process finding one the guys are willing to use."

"Seriously," Liv muttered.

A group of sweaty men walked past, about fifty feet away. They wore hard hats and carried gallon jugs of water. One of them caught her eye. Wearing cargo shorts, a white wifebeater, and steel-toed boots, something rang familiar about how he moved.

"Thanks, Bob. We appreciate you taking the time to update us. I know how busy you are," Brooke said.

He tipped his hard hat. "Never a problem to chat with three beautiful ladies. You gals behave now."

"We make no promises," Liv said as she hooked an arm through Brooke's, then Harper's. "Make sure you stay hydrated. It's hot as hell out here."

Bob nodded and turned back toward his crew. He followed the group that had recently passed by.

Harper allowed Liv to tow her along toward the shed.

She shook off the feeling of familiarity. Most likely, she'd seen the guy working around, and that's why he ticked in her brain.

"Okay," Liv said once they were back in the shed. She went to the mini refrigerator and pulled out a bottle of white wine. "We've given you all day to mope. Now it's time to chat, and I have wine to loosen your lips."

Despite her shit mood, Harper smiled. "It's only four o'clock."

"That's right," she said as she twisted a corkscrew into the bottle. "See what you're driving us to?" She pulled the cork out with a *pop*. "I forgot glasses, so just take a swing."

Brooke laughed but took the first sip the passed the bottle to Harper. "Have at it, sister."

Rolling her eyes, she snatched the bottle from Brooke's grip and took a long sip. The wine was cold, crisp, and had a zing to it that set her taste buds dancing. "That's good."

"Of course it is," Liv said with a pretentious sniff. "Now start talking."

Looked like there was no getting out of it. Maybe it would help. She was a proponent of talking about feelings, being a counselor and all. Too bad it was so hard to follow her own advice. "I'm pretty sure I overreacted last night."

"You think?" Liv asked with a snort.

Brooke whacked her with the back of her hand.

"Ow! What was that for?" Liv asked, rubbing her upper arm.

"A little tact, please. You can't pretend you've never overreacted before."

"No, she's right. It was too much." Harper motioned for the bottle. "Gimme that thing." After another long sip, she wiped her mouth with the back of her hand and made a noise of frustration. "I don't know how to keep myself from assuming the worst."

"From Jinx?" Liv asked as she held her hand out of the wine bottle.

Harper nodded. "Yes. Even after listening to him explain why he didn't tell me what he was up to last night, I couldn't get my mind off the idea he was purposely holding back to trick me."

"Last night was intense for multiple reasons, Harper. Jinx was injured. Of course, you reacted strongly... any of us would have. You can't tell me you feel the same way today as you did when your emotions were running high last night."

"No. Today I feel embarrassed that I threw Jinx out of my

apartment. But I'm still annoyed that everyone knew what was going on except me. And I'm annoyed he didn't call me right away when he got hurt."

"So tell him that," Brooke said.

"What?"

"Just tell him. Harp, if you want something with him, and I think you do, you have to give the man an opportunity to correct it if he screws up. And he should do the same for you. You know your circumstances are not ordinary, and you have more baggage than most." Brooke reached over and squeezed Harper's hand. "I don't say it to be mean, but it's the truth."

Harper accepted the bottle from Liv without even looking. "No. You're right. I know you're right. I just so badly want to be normal, be past my crap, and…" she swallowed as tears threatened to fall, "… I want to be happy. And now I'm afraid he's written me off because I'm too much."

She hadn't heard a peep from him since the night before. Though, to be fair, she'd been the one to make him leave.

"Oh, sweetie." Liv rushed over and gave her a side hug. "There is no normal, especially not here within this club."

"She's right," Brooke added. "Unless you want to say that our normal is fucked up." Her expression held understanding and compassion. "Everyone of us was brought here under different but no less extreme circumstances. I think it's why our family fits together so well. There's no judgment, no expectations beyond loyalty and love."

Liv rested her head on Harper's shoulder. "We're all broken toys, Harp."

That had the three of them chuckling.

"He told me he'd be there when I was ready," she shared after they'd silently passed the bottle a few times.

"See?" Liv bumped her shoulder. "Trust me, that man isn't going anywhere. Just talk to him. It'll be fine. You two are meant for each other… I can feel it. Besides, we aren't letting you go from our ladies' group, so you two have no choice but to work it out."

"What she said," Brooke added with a smile.

If only she had their confidence. But they were right. After what she'd been through, she might always have trust issues. But the only way to handle them would be to deal with it head-on and talk it out with Jinx. If she was going to be his, and this distance showed her she really wanted that, she needed to put in the effort. With the reward being nights in Jinx's bed, days on the back of his bike, and the rest of her life enjoying him, whatever she had to do would be well worth it.

Now that she wasn't so worried Jinx was lying dead on a gurney in the ER, she could think more rationally. Still, a small voice whispered a relationship would never work, she'd never be able to give him her trust, and he'd be guaranteed to hurt her. But today, with a fresh perspective and help from her friends, she could close her eyes and imagine boxing that intrusive voice straight out of her head. A visualization technique she'd learned while getting her degree and one that had worked in prison whenever dark thoughts crept in.

A peace settled over her as a game plan formed in her mind. In some ways, she felt decades older than her twenty-five years since she'd seen and heard so much while behind bars. It was enough to feel as though she'd lived three lifetimes. But then there were some basic experiences she'd completely missed out on, including learning to communicate in a healthy relationship.

"Thank you, ladies," she said, shooing away tears with rapid blinks. "I wish I could express with words how important you've all become to me, but I don't think anything I say will be enough."

"Oh, Harp." Liv sniffed and wiped away a tear. "You're making me cry. You don't have to say anything. We all know because we feel it too."

Brooke looked a little misty as well. She fanned her hand by her eyes and stared at the ceiling. "Don't you dare make me cry."

"Group hug," Liv called out and spread her arms wide.

Chuckling, Harper joined her and Brooke in a crushing girls' hug.

They stayed there for another half hour or so, polishing off the bottle of wine and moving on to lighter topics. Around five, Brooke stood. "Okay, girls, that's enough for one day. I'm heading home, but I'll be back at the clubhouse in a few hours. I think Curly said something about a bonfire."

"Yeah. Spec mentioned it. I'm meeting him at the gym when they're done with church, then we're grabbing dinner, but we'll be there. What about you, Harp? You're going to talk to Jinx, right?"

Both women stared at her.

She glanced at the time on her phone. The men should only be another fifteen or twenty minutes. "Yes. I'll hang here until they're done in church, then I'll wander over to the clubhouse and grab him for a chat.

"A '*chat*,'" Liv said, crooking her fingers in air quotes. "We all know how these boys like to chat."

The three of them giggled.

Brooke grabbed the empty wine bottle and brought it to the trash before gathering her belongings. "I'll see you troublemakers later. Careful at the gym, Liv. We're all a little tipsy."

"Hmm…" She tapped her lips. "Maybe I can convince Spec to burn off some calories with a *chat* of our own instead." Her face lit up. "Yeah, that's a fantastic idea. Catch you later." She snatched her purse off her desk, then practically ran out of the trailer.

"Bye," Harper called after her.

Brooke waved, then followed a bouncy Liv out the door.

Once alone, Harper took a breath and tried to concentrate on work, but with each passing minute, she grew more anxious to talk to Jinx. Nerves popped and fizzled under her skin, and her stomach fluttered, making it impossible to focus.

The clock on the wall revealed fifteen minutes had passed since the girls left. She closed her laptop. Trying to work anymore was useless. Time to head to the clubhouse. She sent up a quick prayer to whoever was listening that Jinx would be receptive to talking with her.

After a quick tidying of the office, she shut the lights off and headed outside. The early evening sun still shone strong with burning rays, and the humidity immediately dampened her skin. Harper didn't mind, though. All it did was remind her of the freedom she'd never take for granted.

Using care, she walked down the three steps to the ground and stretched her arms over her head like a cat in a sunbeam. As she lowered her arms, movement to her left caught her attention.

A lone man rounded the side of the shed and came to a stop the moment he saw her. She frowned. The crew typically left at five, which passed about a half hour ago. Maybe this guy had forgotten something and returned to retrieve it.

She started to lift a hand in greeting when recognition slammed into her. This was the man who'd seemed too familiar earlier, and now she knew in her bones who he was.

Even from a distance, the clover tattoo glowed like a beacon on the hand he had shielding his eyes from the bright sun.

This was the man who'd attacked Lock and sent her crashing into the bookcase. This was the man who stabbed Jinx last night.

They both froze, apparently stunned by the sight of each

other. Harper's heart rate shot up like an eager stallion out of the gate.

He reacted first, seeming to levitate off the ground as he sprinted toward her.

Run. Run. Run!

Her mind screamed at her, but her body remained immobile, feet rooted to the ground as she watched him rush closer in utter shock. His feet seemed to move to the hammering beat of her pulse.

"You fucking bitch," he shouted.

It was the kick she needed to get her ass in gear. Harper dropped her bag, spun, and ran toward the clubhouse like her life depended on it, which it very well might.

"Help," she screamed as she pumped her arms and legs with more speed than she ever had before. Feet pounded on the dirt behind her, driving her to push harder and run faster. "Help *me!*"

Please, please, somebody help me.

Her lungs burned, and her muscles ached.

Why the fuck didn't the clubhouse seem to be getting closer?

A loud bark had a drop of relief washing over her until a heavy weight slammed into her back.

She crashed to the ground on her stomach with the man on top of her.

Every ounce of breath whooshed out of her. Her diaphragm spasmed, then seemed to stop working. She couldn't breathe beneath him.

Dirt crammed beneath her nails as she clawed at the ground in a desperate attempt to escape.

He snarled as he pinned her between her shoulder blades, keeping her immobile and breathless.

Was this it? Was this the end of the line? Had she survived seven years in prison and finally met the man of her dreams only to have it ripped away?

    She hadn't even had the chance to tell him she was sorry.

Chapter Twenty-Six

Jinx bounced his leg under the table as the meeting dragged on. No one had ever described patience as one of his strong qualities, and never had that been truer than sitting there in church while he wanted to be clearing the air with Harper.

She'd had enough space as far as he was concerned. As soon as Curly ended the meeting, he'd be out the door and searching her out. They weren't over, and he planned to prove it to her.

Wincing, he shifted. His side ached like a son of a bitch. It might have had something to do with his refusal to take any more pain meds. They made him a little fuzzy-headed, and the last thing he needed was to stick his foot in his mouth while talking to Harper because he'd had one too many pain pills.

Once they'd worked their shit out and made up with a few hot fucks, he'd down a few pills. He could stand a bit of pain until then.

"You all right?" Tracker whispered from his left.

He nodded. "I'm good. Just fucking aching." He shifted again, this time unable to hold back a soft grunt of discomfort.

Curly's gaze landed on him. "Last bit of business," the prez said. He paused, then sighed. "I don't know how to say this, but it's time to take some action with Lock." He slumped in his seat, looking more defeated than Jinx had ever seen him. "I've given him time to clean his shit up."

"A lot of time," Ty said in support. They all knew this decision had been killing Curly. He truly thought of them as family—they all did—and as head of the family, he felt a sense of responsibility for all of them. Lock's downward spiral hit him hard and left him feeling guilty.

Nodding, Curly continued. "I'd hoped the incident a few weeks ago would have been the catalyst he needed to get himself straight, so I backed off the pressure from my side. For fuck's sake, Caleb could have lost another parent. Or fuck…" He ran a hand down his face. "What the hell would have happened if Harper hadn't interrupted? Would the baby have been taken? Makes me fucking sick. But nothing's changed. He's not living up to his club responsibilities, he's barely working, he drinks from sunup to sundown, and Brooke takes care of the baby more than he does."

"What do you want to do?" Jinx asked, fully invested now.

"I'll give him a choice. One last chance. He can dry his ass out in rehab, or he's out of the club."

"We really gonna boot his ass out when he's at his lowest?" Spec asked. Not long ago, he'd been close to the edge himself. If it weren't for Liv, who knew where he'd be? Possibly dead in a ditch after starting shit with the wrong person.

Pain crossed Curly's face. "Fuck, I hope not. I hope to hell he makes the right decision."

"And if he doesn't?" Spec asked.

"We'll cross that bridge when we come to it." Ty gave Spec a sharp look. "Sometimes tough love is necessary."

Jinx got it. He really did, and it just sucked. "What's the plan for Caleb if Lock goes to rehab?"

"Brooke and I'll take him."

The sound of Ray barking drew their attention. The

German Shepherd wasn't much of a barker unless it was to alert his master, Brooke.

"He out there playing with Betty White?" Jinx asked Tracker.

"No, she's at the groomer. I'm picking her up as soon as we're done here."

"Huh."

Ray barked again. And again. The sound grew from alert to furious.

An icy trickle worked its way down Jinx's spine.

He met Curly's gaze. "Something's wrong." As he spoke the words, Ray's bark turned into a ferocious snarl, and the bottom dropped out of Jinx's stomach.

The men all reacted at once, leaping from their chairs and charging out of the room.

Jinx reached the outside door first. He couldn't say why, but something in his gut drove him to respond faster than he ever had before. Dread deep in his bones pushed him toward the door. Whatever was happening would affect him greatly.

He felt it.

He yanked open the door, then dashed outside and jumped over the porch steps without assessing the threat. If someone was waiting there to beat his ass, so be it. His brothers would be out in a hot second, and they'd always have his back. No one survived Spec's wrath.

"Christ, hold up, Jinx," Tracker shouted from behind him.

He didn't stop. Couldn't stop. Ray's distressed barks gave him a direction to turn, and as soon as he did, he nearly crumbled to his knees. The sight of a man on top of a woman about seventy yards away had him stopping dead in his tracks as though he'd hit a brick wall.

He wasn't still for long, only a fraction of a second before he burst forward as though he'd been hit with a cattle prod.

"Jinx," Spec yelled.

He wasn't armed, had stitches, and hadn't slept a wink the night before, far from top form. It didn't matter. Even though he could only see the hair of the woman being attacked, he knew it was Harper. Neither injury, exhaustion, nor lack of a weapon would keep him from rescuing his woman. He'd tear her assailant apart with his bare hands. He could be cuffed, blindfolded, and bleeding, and the man wouldn't stand a chance.

With a primal roar that rivaled Ray's howl, he chased the dog across the farm toward his woman. Pain lanced through his side in a fiery, agonizing burn as stitches popped and the freshly healing wound tore open. Fuck the pain. Nothing short of his guts spilling out would keep him from getting to Harper. Even then, he'd shove them back in and keep running.

Hold the fuck on, baby. I'm coming.

And if he ended up with a murder charge at the end of the day?

So be it.

THE WEIGHT ON top of her lifted, and for one glorious second, Harper had hope of escape. Finally, air rushed in, and she tried to push up on all fours, but rough, careless hands grabbed her shoulders and flipped her over.

"No," she cried.

Hair and dirt stuck to the perspiration on her face. He straddled her, sitting hard on her hip bones. It felt as though her pelvis would crack in half. A rock drilled into her spine, and the toe of her attacker's work boot dug into the thin skin of her shin with so much force she'd have a monster bruise for weeks. Those intense discomforts combined had nothing on the fear of what she was sure he planned to do with her.

To do *to* her.

"Get the fuck off me," she shouted.

Barking sounded in the distance, but she could barely hear it over the jackhammering of her pulse.

"You fucking bitch," he snarled. Sweat dropped off him, and spittle flew from his furious mouth. "Do you have any idea what you've cost me?"

"Get off me! You're on Handlers' property. Do *you* have any idea what they'll do to y—" He grabbed her throat and squeezed, stealing her words. Her eyes bugged, and her mouth flapped like a fish. A high-pitched whistle was the only sound she made.

She kicked her legs and flailed her arms, desperate to get him off her, but with each passing second, her energy fled, and she grew weaker from lack of air.

"I owe people money," he shouted. His other hand joined the first, wrapping around her throat. The shift allowed her to suck in the air, but it vanished just as quickly. "People who make your fucking bikers look like kittens." He shook her. Her head bounced on the ground. Her brain rattled, and her eyes felt like too loose orbs jiggling around in their sockets.

She tried to talk, beg him to release her, but she couldn't make a sound.

The barking sounded closer, and she almost thought she heard someone shout her name, but there seemed to be so much wind. A hurricane sounded in her ears.

"Lock has my money," he shouted, still shaking her.

She flopped like a rag doll. His enraged face grew hazy, then gray.

Blackness crept in from all corners of her vision. She flexed her fingers against the dirt, unable to muster the energy for a more vigorous fight.

"Harper!"

Jinx? Is that him?

Everything was wavy and gray, melding together. She couldn't think, tell up from down, or what day it was.

God, she wished that was Jinx's voice. It'd be so nice to see him before she fell asleep, but she was so tired, and he sounded far away. Maybe this was all a dream. Maybe when she woke up, she'd be lying on an uncomfortable bunk in the prison she'd called home for so many years.

What a lovely fantasy Jinx had been.

A vicious growl split the air as a black and brown cloud streaked across her field of vision.

She blinked as the pressure around her throat disappeared, and the air she'd once thought thick and humid flowed into her lungs like the most precious gift.

"Ray, leave it," someone ordered as strong arms came around her in the gentlest hold, cradling her to a massive chest.

The sound of flesh hitting flesh would have frightened her if it wasn't for the immediate feeling of safety these arms provided.

"Save him for me," someone growled.

Jinx?

"He's mine."

"Abso-fucking-lutely."

Harper blinked. As she gulped in air, her vision cleared, and the most beautiful sight came into view. "Jinx?" she croaked.

He winced. "Yeah, baby, it's me."

He was there.

He saved her.

He didn't hate her.

"I'm so sor—"

"Shh… God, baby, not now. Save your voice until we get you checked out at the hospital."

"But I—"

"Shh. Baby, please. Your voice is shot… don't talk." He kissed her forehead, and her eyes floated closed as a warm sensation traveled over her.

Was it only yesterday they'd fought?

That one night apart might as well have been a lifetime for how awful it felt. God, she'd missed this.

He kissed her head again, her cheek, and her lips a few times. She sighed, content even as her throat and neck throbbed.

"I'm tired," she rasped.

Damn, her voice really did sound as though someone had taken a meat grinder to her vocal cords.

"Then sleep, baby. You're safe, and I won't let you go for a second."

She blinked a few times as exhaustion became too heavy to ignore. A man sat on the ground, bloodied, with an obvious German Shepherd bite on his arm. Spec stood over him, rattling off orders on his phone. Ray sat beside Curly, teeth bared as though ready to go again.

"Good doggie," she whispered, then her eyes fluttered closed.

"The fucking best," Jinx replied. He rocked her gently from side to side, and the calming motion had her near sleep within seconds. "He's getting a steak dinner tonight."

"No," she whispered. "You're the best. The best for me. I love you."

She never heard a response because sleep claimed her, but she felt his lips on her forehead once again. Maybe she'd only said the words in her head.

She'd tell him again when she woke.

If she woke.

Maybe he'd only been so sweet to her because he knew the prognosis wouldn't be good.

Chapter Twenty-Seven

How long did it take one fucking woman to wake up?

"Sir? Sir, visiting hours are almost over. We're going to need you to go home soon. I promise we'll take good care of your fiancée."

He was a damn cliché, telling the hospital he and Harper were engaged so he could be at her bedside.

This perky little nurse who barely looked a day older than graduation could fuck right off if she thought she had a chance of kicking him out. He stood from the shitty bedside chair to his full six foot six and scowled down at her.

She couldn't be much over five-foot-two and swallowed as she visibly trembled. "Uh… well, um… maybe you could have a few more min—"

"Jesus, Jinx, quit it. You're scaring her to death." Pulse walked in dressed in royal-blue scrubs, the same hospital issue Harper's nurse wore.

"Hey, Kels, he's a friend of mine. I'll take care of him." Pulse gave her a charming smile and patted her shoulder. "Promise he's not as scary as he looks."

"I'm fucking scarier," Jinx mumbled.

The nurse, Kels, gave him a wary look but shifted her gaze away when he glared again. "Okay, but if he causes trouble, it's on you."

Pulse lifted his hands in surrender. "I'll take full responsibility for him. Promise."

"Fine." She pulled off her gloves, tossed them in the trash, and practically ran from the room.

Good riddance.

"Why the fuck is she still sleeping, Pulse? Does she have a fucking brain injury?"

He shook his head. "No. They did brain scans, and she's all good. They gave her some muscle relaxers to help with the neck and pain medicine. She's just exhausted, brother. Nothing to worry about."

"Well, it's fucking bullshit." He ran a hand through his hair. If she didn't wake up soon so he could satisfy himself that she was truly okay, he was going to start flipping tables.

Pulse chuckled. "Would you rather her be awake and in miserable pain?" Pulse asked, taking on a professional tone.

Jinx reared back. "What? Fuck no, I don't want her to be in pain."

"Then chill the fuck out and let us do our jobs. We're taking good care of her. I promise."

Fuck, maybe he was acting like an overbearing psycho. He dropped back in the chair, cringing as the vinyl crinkled. "Fine. I'll back off."

"Hold her hand. Talk to her. Be here when she wakes up. And she will wake up, brother. Swear to you on my life."

They didn't need anyone else risking their lives today, but he appreciated the sentiment. "Thanks, man."

Pulse nodded. "After she wakes up and you're satisfied she's okay, you take your ass down to the ER to get that wound in your side evaluated. You bled through your damn shirt. I can only imagine how much you fucked up the doc's work." He held his knuckles out for a bump.

With a sigh and a muttered "Fine," Jinx tapped his against Pulse's, then found himself alone, staring at the woman who'd mumbled she loved him right before passing out.

Had she meant it, or was it pre-loss-of-consciousness rambling? This afternoon would live rent-free in his head for the rest of his days. He'd replay the heart-stopping moment of terror when he realized Harper was on the ground every night in his nightmares. Seeing that piece of shit's hands around his woman's throat sent a murderous desire through him that nothing but the fucker's death would slake.

The club had him on ice, and as soon as Harper was settled, Jinx would take his pound of flesh. He wasn't the enforcer for a reason. Jinx was a lover, not a fighter. Though he could hold his own if need be, his preferred method of violence was a sharp tongue and a wicked sense of sarcasm, but tonight, he'd gladly peel the skin off that asshole one strip at a time.

He lifted Harper's hand and kissed the knuckles. Had she always seemed so small and frail? Had he not noticed how breakable she appeared? How easy it was for someone to hurt her.

No. That was shock and anger talking. Harper was the strongest damn woman he knew. Still, her hand felt tiny and cold in his. He bowed his head, resting it on the side of her bed.

"Christ, I'd never been so scared," he whispered. "It was bad enough when I thought I lost you yesterday because of my stupidity. But today was a level of agony I never imagined. Please wake up, baby. Wake up so I can tell you how fucking sorry I am. I love you, Harper."

A soft hand landed on his head, sifting once through his hair before he connected the dots. He straightened so fast his back cracked. "Harp!"

She watched him with tears in her eyes. "I love you too, Jinx. And I'm just as sorry." Her ravaged voice sounded as though she'd smoked three packs a day for longer than she'd been alive. Horrifying purple bruises ringed her neck as well, but she was alive.

And awake.

And smiling through her tears.

The most beautiful sight he'd ever seen.

"I freaked out the other night." She frowned. "Last night? What day is it?"

"Last night," he said. "But none of that matters, baby. I'm the one who fucked up. Not you. Never you."

She chuckled, but it sounded more like a witch's cackle. "Love that you think that way, but it's not true."

He stood and leaned over her, pressing a kiss to her head. "I don't care. I don't care if you fuck up every single day of your life. I want to be with you."

"Same," she whispered, looking up at him with adoration. "Kiss me?"

"Every chance I get for the rest of my life, baby." He kissed her softly, taking care not to wrench her neck in any way.

She sighed into his mouth. "Much better."

He didn't argue, but he wouldn't feel better until she was out of the hospital and no longer looking like an extra in a slasher film. "Love you," he whispered instead.

"Love you," she said back.

He'd love to climb in the bed with her, but they didn't make the damn things for his size. Instead, he sat back in the chair and took her hand.

"When can I go home?" she asked, then cringed. "My voice sounds terrible."

"It'll heal, baby."

"I sure hope so. Otherwise, you're stuck with an ol' lady who sounds like an old dude who's smoked his whole life."

He laughed, and it felt so damn good after all the day's tension. Fuck, he loved this woman. Able to crack jokes less than five minutes after waking up from a horrible attack. If that wasn't strength, he didn't know what the hell was. "I'll take you any way I can get you, baby."

"Good answer," she croaked. A few seconds later, her eyes began to droop again.

"Sleep. I'll be right here when you wake up again."

"Mm...kay," she mumbled. Her hand went slack in his almost before she finished speaking.

Jinx exhaled a thousand pounds of pressure from his chest and rubbed a hand over his heart. That woman owned the heart lying beneath his palm. No matter what happened in the future, he'd never get it back. It was hers, and he wasn't the least bit upset about it. In fact, it felt fucking incredible.

Unlike the pain in his side, which grew more intense by the second.

Brooke and Curly showed up a few minutes later, allowing Jinx time to get the wound checked out. No surprise, he busted the hell out of his stitches. Unfortunately for him, the same ER doctor who'd sewn him up the night before was working. The sadist seemed to take an immense amount of pleasure in jamming the needle into Jinx's skin again and again. He'd never make an accusation, but Jinx swore the doctor went light on the numbing injection just for shits and giggles as a punishment for Jinx fucking up his original handiwork.

The next time Harper woke, she could swallow some ice chips and a bit of Jell-O. It'd hurt, but her doctor seemed pleased. They released her the next morning with a pile of instructions, follow-up appointments, medications, and a promise to have someone stay with her.

That wouldn't be a problem since Jinx planned to settle her in his house and stick to her like glue. The fact that she didn't put up even an ounce of fight against that suggestion showed how off her game she was.

When they arrived at his house, the ladies were already

there, waiting with a freezer full of ice cream, a bunch of crappy movies sure to make them all cry, and about ten bottles of wine, which he vetoed. The rest of them could get as sloshed as they liked, but he wasn't taking any chances combining Harper's meds with alcohol.

"C'mon, Jinx," Liv pressed as she rolled her eyes. "Since when do you follow the rules?"

"Yeah, where's your outlaw spirit?" Jo chimed in.

"Since the woman I love more than anything else in the world was almost killed. No mixing booze and meds. I'm not taking a chance she gets anything worse than a paper cut. Even that's too much. Those things hurt like a bitch."

"Oh, well, that's actually very sweet," Jo grumbled as she yanked the cork from a bottle of wine. "But I'm having some."

"Knock yourself out." He rolled his eyes, then leaned in toward his woman. Harper sat on his couch wearing a cute light blue lounge tank and shorts Brooke had brought. A light blanket covered her lap, and she held a pint of her favorite ice cream in one hand with the spoon in the other. This could look like any weeknight if it weren't for the gruesome bruises and destroyed voice. But as he was about to go and exact some serious revenge on the man who attacked his ol' lady, this was anything but normal.

"Behave," he whispered against her lips. "Don't talk too much, no booze, and no getting up unless you need the bathroom. Oh, and eat every last bite of that ice cream."

Harper nodded and gave him a sweet smile and a nod while Liv snorted. "Oh my God, *Dad*, just go. Do your pissed-off biker thing. We'll take good care of your girl."

He gave Harper a sweet lingering kiss. "I mean, if you wanna call me Daddy later, I won't say no."

Her soft chuckle reassured him more than anything else that she'd be okay.

"Go," she whispered, giving him a gentle shove. As he pulled away, she grabbed the collar of his T-shirt and tugged him close again. "Wait." She kissed him. "I love you," she whispered.

Fuck, those were the best goddamn words in the English language. His heart did a happy dance in his chest like some mushy hero in a romantic movie. "Love you, baby," he said back, then gave her one more quick kiss before she released him.

"Make good choices, ladies," he called out as he slipped out the door.

"We should be saying that to you," Jo yelled back.

He grunted. He'd be making good choices all right. Good for him, good for Harper, and good for the universe, but not good at all for the fucker who'd hurt his woman.

Twenty minutes later, he stood over the piece of shit who'd stabbed him and attacked Harper. The guy didn't look nearly as cocky now, bruised and bloodied.

"Looks like you had some fun without me," he said to Spec, who was wiping blood off his knuckles.

"Yeah, sorry, brother. I wanted to wait, but Donny here is a mouthy fuck who wouldn't shut the hell up, so I had to help him out."

Donny was a stupid fuck. Pissing Spec off never worked out well.

Jinx grinned. "Not a problem."

"So whatcha wanna start with? You wanna slice his arm? Stab him? Personally, I'd strangle the fuck outta him. Make sure he knows exactly what your ol' lady was feeling." Spec held a knife out in case Jinx chose that route, but he wasn't here to get revenge for himself. This was one hundred percent about Harper.

"Hmm... I'll decide in a second." He crouched down.

At some point, Spec clearly broke the guy's jaw. Probably

when he'd mouthed off a few too many times. His left cheek had turned an ugly dark purple, and his mouth hung partially open at an unnatural angle.

"Not so chatty now, are you?" Jinx patted his cheek. Okay, it was more of a light slap.

A medium slap.

Donny's head flopped to the side, and he moaned pitifully.

"Fuck you," he slurred. A string of bloody drool dangled from the corner of his mouth. "She was begging for it. Fucking slut wanted my—"

Jinx saw red. Quick as a snake strike, he had his hands around the fucker's throat. Jinx squeezed. Within seconds, Donny's face turned eggplant purple. His eyes bugged, and he fought like a wet cat, clawing at Jinx's arms. But Jinx was big and damn strong, so Donny didn't stand a chance.

"Feel good? Just listen to you begging me for it." He squeezed until Donny's eyes rolled back, and he lost consciousness. "Oops," Jinx said with a laugh as he released his victim. "Got a little overzealous."

Spec snickered. "He'll be back in a minute. Then we'll have a nice chat about the rest of his shitty life."

As Jinx stood, his knee popped, and his back twinged. "Damn, I'm getting too old for this shit."

"Tell me about it. I'm in my thirties, but my body feels like it's eighty most days." Spec nudged Donny with his foot but didn't get a reaction. Still out cold.

"I hear you. Guess that's what happens when you live hard and party harder."

Donny groaned. He blinked a few times before his eyes stayed open. The second the fog seemed to clear, he tried to scramble away, but Spec stopped him with a heavy boot on his sternum.

"Welcome back, baby. Hoped you're enjoying your time with us because we own your ass now, Donny boy." Spec reached over to a cart where he kept an assortment of *supplies* for such situations and grabbed a syringe with a nasty needle.

Jinx didn't know what hell the shit was, but he never wanted to be on the wrong end of a single one of those items.

"Whoever you were loyal to before us, that's over. You see, my club wants Lobo." Spec leaned over Donny. "And you're gonna help us get him."

Donny's eyes went to the needle and grew wide as saucers. He shook his head. "No. Don't! I'll do whatever you want."

"Oh, I know you will." Spec waggled the syringe. "This is just a little insurance. Our way of making sure we can find you at all times."

"W-what is it?"

"Well, it's a microchip, Donny."

Jinx barked out a laugh. "We're chipping our new pet?"

"You bet your ass we are. You know how awful it is to lose a pet?" Spec grunted. "Can't have that happening. Hold 'im still for me, brother."

Jinx gripped Donny's shoulders as Spec readied the syringe. Donny fought the hold, but as before, he was no match for Jinx. Without any warning or countdown, Spec shoved the needle in the space between Donny's shoulder and neck. Donny moaned, but the pain of it didn't last nearly long enough to satisfy Jinx.

"Here's how this is gonna go," Spec said once finished. "You answer to Jinx now. He calls, you come running. You do whatever he asks whenever he asks to keep my club happy. If we're not happy, your sad life will end. It's all very simple." He placed the syringe back on his cart. "Got it?"

"Y-yeah." Donny nodded fast, then flinched as his neck moved.

Good. Hope it hurts like hell.

"Great. You tell anyone about this, what's gonna happen?"

"Y-you'll kill me."

"No, Donny. I'm not gonna kill you." Spec jerked his thumb in Jinx's direction. "He will."

Jinx gave him a feral grin and rubbed his hands together. This shit was fun.

"W-what happens when it's over? Am I free?"

"Well, now, that is a good question, Donny boy." Spec stroked his chin as though deep in thought. "I think I'll leave that up to my man, Jinx, here." He slapped Jinx's shoulder. "Guess it'll depend on how pissed he still is that you almost killed his woman."

Jinx's grin went from feral to straight-up evil. He'd never forget. Donny was screwed.

"I can take it from here if you wanna head home, brother."

"You sure?" Jinx asked.

Spec nodded. "Go be with your woman."

"Thanks." Jinx hugged Spec, slapping him on the back. If Harper wasn't at home waiting for him, he'd stick around, but he was anxious to return to her.

After leaving Spec's little torture playhouse, he hopped on an ATV and rode across the farm.

Time to get back to his ol' lady.

Chapter Twenty-Eight

Harper loved her friends like the family she'd always yearned for, but she really wanted them to leave. They'd done a fantastic job of trying to take her mind off everything, including what Jinx was doing right then, but she hurt and could use a fifteen-hour nap.

Besides, nothing could stop her from worrying about the man she'd recently professed her love to. What was he doing?

Something that could land him in jail?

Something that could get him injured?

Something that would haunt his nightmares?

After yesterday, she'd have enough of those to last them a long while.

"You look exhausted, hon. Do you want to go lie down?" Brooke sat next to her on the couch, concern all over her face.

Tired as she was, lying down didn't appeal to her. She wanted Jinx to return, and she might start whining if this dragged out much longer. "Nah, I'm okay. Just worried about Jinx."

"If he's with Spec, as I'm guessing he is..." Liv said, "...then he's fine. Pretty sure there's not a force in this world that could take my man out."

Her worry extended far beyond something taking Jinx out, but she didn't mention it. "Thanks, Liv. My head's still a little scrambled from the pain meds and... well, everything, so if I failed to say it yet, thank you to all of you. I appreciate your friendships so much."

"We love you too, Harp," Liv chirped.

"Even if we can tell you'd like to kick us the hell outta here," Jo added.

"What? No." Could she sound any less sincere?

Thankfully, her friends didn't have wafer-thin skin and only laughed at her weak attempt to reassure them their presence was desired. "I'm sorry." She flopped back against the couch, wincing when the careless movement jostled her sore body. "I'm just overstimulated. I kinda want to sit alone in the dark until my brain settles."

"I get that." Brooke walked in from Jinx's kitchen with a fresh glass of icy water.

Swallowing sucked right now, but the cold did feel wonderful on her throat.

"Thanks." She accepted the glass from Brooke with a grateful smile. "I really do appreciate you guys, even if it doesn't seem like it."

"We know. Trust me. You're a whole lot less cranky than I'd be." Jo shuddered. "I do not like being babied."

Liv snorted. "Believe her. She's the shittiest patient imaginable."

"Hey!"

"Am I lying?" Liv asked with an arched eyebrow.

"No," Jo grumbled.

Ever the voice of reason, Brooke patted her hand. "I'm sure Jinx will return soon, and we'll get out of your hair. You two need some quiet time to yourselves. Seems like you worked out your issues, though."

For the first time in what felt like days, Harper smiled. "Yeah. I think we did."

"Good." Brooke beamed. "Without a doubt, you are the

best thing that's happened to that man."

Damn, that was nice to hear. Before she had a chance to thank Brooke for the sweet compliment, the door opened, and in walked her six-foot-six, rough, gruff, sweet, and very sexy ol' man.

He looked fantastic. Settled in a way he hadn't appeared since before getting stabbed. "Ladies," he announced. "I love you all, but get the fuck outta my house."

"Not even a thank you? Or a travel mug with coffee for the road?" Jo pouted. "Geez, where's the appreciation?"

Jinx grunted. "Bet your ol' man will appreciate the hell outta you if you get your ass home."

"Hmm… you make a compelling point. He does like my ass." With a wink, Jo shook her ass in Jinx's direction.

He rolled his eyes as the girls laughed, including Harper. It felt good to enjoy their silly banter.

"Bye, sweetie," she said as she walked past Harper, dropping a kiss on her cheek. "Call if you two need anything. I'll keep my phone close."

"Same." Brooke also came over for a kiss goodbye. "Or if this big brute starts to get on your nerves." She winked Jinx's way.

Liv gave her a quick hug. "So, what, should we expect to hear from you in about ten minutes?"

"*So, I guess we'll hear from you in ten minutes,*" Jinx said in a mocking tone. "Good one, Liv. Get the hell out."

"So rude." Instead of hugging him as the others had, Liv swatted his arm. But she was smiling. "Bye, you two." She blew them a kiss and slipped out the door after her club sisters.

Harper drank in the sight of him standing there, watching her as well. Nothing appeared to be out of order with him. No visible blood, no new bruises, and clean knuckles. "Everything okay?"

"You first. How are you feeling?"

Rotating her neck from side to side, she grimaced. "Sore. Tired. All peopled out."

He strode over. "Sorry, baby, I should have been faster."

"No, that wasn't it. I think I'm just processing." She tilted her head up to take in all of him as he stood before the couch. "Your turn."

"I'm good. So fucking relieved you're here."

That wasn't what she meant, and he knew it. Should she push? Would he tell her what he'd been doing? Did she want to know?

"Wanna lie down? Nap? Rest? Just be horizontal for a while?"

Oh, that sounded heavenly. "Yes, please." She started to stand, but Jinx stopped her by scooping her up as though she were a damsel in distress. "I can walk, you know."

"I do know. But I'm gonna need to touch you a lot over the next few days to remind myself you're okay."

"That sounds nice." She rested her head against his chest.

He barely seemed to notice her weight in his arms, not straining or becoming winded in the least. With so much care, he set her down on his bed. She kept her gaze on him as he kicked his boots off and stripped down to his boxer briefs.

Her lower belly clenched with need, and she grew wet. The man did it for her, even as tired and sore as she was. God, he was stunning.

She couldn't imagine how hideous she looked at the moment—bruises, messy hair, sloppy clothes. She'd forced herself to avoid mirrors but would have to look at herself eventually.

"Get out of there," he whispered, tapping gently on her forehead.

She blinked, having missed the moment he laid down beside her. "Sorry. I'm trying, but there's a lot to process right now."

"There is." He pulled her into his arms. Warmth surrounded her, chasing away the chill of the air-conditioning. The man liked his house to mimic an icebox.

Beneath her ear, his steady heart lulled her to a peaceful calm. It was quickly becoming her favorite sound. Within seconds, she was floating on a cloud of comfort for the first time all day. But there were things they still had to say, and she didn't want the opportunity to pass her by.

"Is he dead?"

Jinx stiffened but didn't play dumb. "He is not."

She sagged as relief washed over her. Carrying the burden of the man's death on her soul would have sucked, even if she wouldn't have blamed Jinx for it. "What did you do to him?"

He drew back enough to see her face. "Do you really want to know?"

It was a question she'd been thinking about since he left earlier, and she'd decided with little internal debate. "Yes. I want to be as much a part of this as the other ladies. I want to trust that you won't do anything to put me at risk. I *do* trust you'll protect me and won't do anything to put me at risk or land me back in prison."

"Fuck, never." He kissed her, and she melted into a pile of goo. "Spec had already worked him over pretty good by the time I got there. But I was able to send my own message." He stroked a gentle finger over the bruises on her neck.

The soft touch made her shiver. "Did, uh… did you guys let him go after?" Maybe he'd turned the air-conditioning off because the room was getting uncomfortably warm.

"Not yet." He kissed her neck with no more pressure than a butterfly landing on her skin.

Her eyes floated closed as desire ramped up, making her needy and achy.

"But we will. Sorta. Spec told him we own him now. He does our bidding and will get us any information we need about his bosses. The club needs to cut the head off this snake."

"Yeah." Wait, what had he said? Something about a snake?

He kissed her lips, smiling against her mouth. "You seem much more relaxed than you were when I came in."

"Uh... yeah." In some ways. In others, she was antsy as hell.

"Do you need anything?"

Her eyes opened, and she found his only an inch away, dark, warm, and sparkling with delight. "I do," she whispered. "I need you to love me."

"Fuck, baby, I do. I love you. Let me show you how much. Let me make you feel good."

Yes.

"Your only job is to lie there and fucking enjoy. And as much as I love the sexy sounds you make, you need to save that voice, so no screaming, okay?"

"Shit," she whispered. Could she do it?

"I stop the first time you shout."

Looked like she had to try. "O-okay. I'll be quiet."

"Good girl." Jinx gave her a playful wink and disappeared beneath the covers. He shoved her shirt up and kissed his way along her stomach.

Harper sighed. She wished she could do this every day for the rest of her—

Her eyes flew open. *Holy shit.* She could do this for the rest of her life. He was hers, and she was his.

She loved him.

She trusted him.

And she was free.

She was free to spend the rest of her life by Jinx's side, in his bed, and on the back of his bike.

With her heart doing flips in her chest, she closed her eyes again and relaxed into his touches.

For the first time, she didn't feel the heavy press of regret and betrayal.

She was exactly where she was supposed to be.

Happy and in love.

Epilogue

Harper stood at the water's edge, letting the salty foam of the surf wash over her painted toes. The sun heated her exposed skin. Sweat dotted her forehead and ran down the small of her back. She wore a skimpy black bikini her incredible friends forced her to buy because they knew her boyfriend, her ol' man, would lose his mind when he saw her in it.

And lose his mind he had. Harper had barely put the thing on before he peeled it back off.

Overhead, seagulls called to each other. All around her, people laughed and played in the gulf. Back on the beach blanket, her chosen family sat eating, drinking, and soaking up the simple joy of an afternoon on the beach.

But it wasn't simple for Harper. Exactly eight years ago this day, she'd been arrested for a crime she'd never been a willing participant in. That day changed her life forever. Life had been beyond hard for so many years. In her wildest fantasies, she couldn't have imagined standing here today, blissful and free.

She'd built impenetrable walls around her heart to protect herself from further pain.

But then, she hadn't anticipated Jinx.

He'd been the unyielding force that managed to blow through her defenses. He called her Prickles, but his patience, kindness, humor, and bold personality plucked every spiny thorn she possessed, revealing her soft core. She opened up to him in a way that initially terrified her but became vital to her existence.

Jinx was more than the missing portion of her heart. He was the final piece of her freedom. The freedom to be herself, to love and be loved.

He was her soul.

She inhaled a final hit of the sea air, then turned around and started for their blanket. As she made her way there, a wolf whistle rang out.

"Yeah, baby, strut your stuff."

Rolling her eyes, Harper swayed her hips and sashayed like she owned a catwalk.

Her friends cheered.

Jinx yelled out, "That's it. Work it, baby."

This was another gift he'd given her—the ability to be playful and let her hair down and be silly. It was the most incredible feeling, and she embraced it as she posed.

"Hell yeah, that's my sexy lady." Jinx hopped up from the blanket and ran toward her. The man was hot in his swim trunks with all that tattooed skin on display. There wasn't a single woman who walked by who didn't cast her appreciative gaze in his direction. But he never returned it, making Harper feel like she lived on top of a mountain.

"Let's go get wet!"

Her eyes widened. "What? No. I'm not ready to go in."

"What do you mean? You're at the damn beach. We're getting wet."

She held her hands out to ward him off as she backed up. "No, Jinx. Not yet. Let's have a snack first."

His grin grew impish. "Snack? You know you can't swim for forty-five minutes after eating." The closer he got, the quicker he moved.

"Jinx..."

She picked up speed, shuffling back as she laughed.

All of a sudden, he attacked like a linebacker going for the tackle. He crouched and launched forward, tossing Harper over his shoulder before she had any idea what was happening.

"Jinx," she shouted, laughing.

"We're going in." He ran toward the water as though holding a stuffed animal instead of a fully grown woman, bobbing and weaving around other beachgoers.

"Woohoo," Liv yelled. "You know you love it, Harp."

She laughed so hard it was nearly impossible to breathe. Water splashed up as Jinx ran into the surf. "Oh my God, don't dunk me!"

"What? I didn't hear you?" He flipped her off his shoulder and dropped her ass first into the water. She sputtered and sank like a stone. When she popped up a second later, Jinx had his back to her and his arms raised. "All hail the king!"

Harper wiped the hair off her eyes as a huge hunk of seaweed floated by. She smirked and bit her lip to keep from laughing as a plan fell into place.

While Jinx was still distracted by his success at dunking her, she grabbed the seaweed. He was still crowing like a champ, not paying any attention, which made this so easy anyone could have pulled it off. She grabbed the waistband of his trunks, pulled the elastic out, and dropped the smiley green plant straight down the back of his pants.

Jinx screeched and danced around. "Holy shit! Oh my God, what the hell is that?"

On the beach, their friends cracked up at their antics and how his voice went up a few octaves.

"Didn't take you for a soprano," Spec hollered from the shoreline.

Harper doubled over, laughing so hard her stomach

cramped.

"You!" He turned toward her. "Get it out. Get it out *now*."

She couldn't have even if she wanted to. She couldn't even straighten up from her hilarity. "Oh my God." She wheezed as she spoke. "I can't breathe."

"You better not be expecting me to do mouth-to-mouth."

That only made her laugh harder.

"What the hell is this?" He fished around in the back of his shorts until he found the seaweed, then pulled it from his trunks. "Seaweed? Really? This shit is slimy as fuck."

"Sorry?"

He snorted. "Oh, it's on, baby." Then he charged, taking them both down.

They played in the water until the sun indicated the late afternoon hour. Their friends joined them for an epic splash fight, and the laughter and smiles continued all afternoon. Eventually, their stomachs growled, and their skin itched from the salt.

Hands down, it had been one of the best days of her life—fun, carefree, and full of love.

All thanks to Jinx.

JINX SAT IN the sand with Harper between his legs. She rested her back against him as they watched the sun dip below the horizon. He couldn't remember a day this incredible. Hell, the last few months had been nothing but bliss, at least where Harper was concerned.

If he had his way, it would never end.

He'd gotten so damn lucky, finding his soulmate. It almost didn't seem fair. There he was, riding a high, living the best moments of his life with nothing but blue skies on the horizon while one of his brothers suffered the opposite fate. He'd been furious with his brother in the aftermath of the attack on club property. Lock was the reason Harper got hurt.

Twice.

Fuck, she'd almost died because of Lock's choices. He'd come close to beating the shit out of his brother and demanding Curly take his patch.

But Harper was a far better person than him. She'd talked him down and helped him realize how much pain Lock was in and how his choices and actions were a direct result of suffering. Lock would be entering rehab in a week. If Jinx was at an all-time high, Lock had hit his lowest point. He hadn't forgiven his brother yet, but he'd get there.

He wasn't about to question his good fortune. Nor would he take it for granted.

"Thank you," Harper whispered.

He kissed the top of her head. "For what, baby?"

"This. Everything. My life."

His heart flipped over.

Yeah, he'd never take this life for granted.

"Your life? Shit, Harp, that's all you. Don't give me credit for your hard work." He tightened his arms around her, anchoring her to him. Her skin was warm and soft, if a little sandy.

The damn bathing suit nearly gave him a heart attack when he'd seen it. It was nothing more than a few pieces of string and swatches of fabric. Absolutely sinful. He'd fucking loved it until they got to the beach and realized every male's eyes went straight to her. Then he'd nearly knocked a few heads together and plucked out some of those eyeballs.

Harper was his, and those assholes needed to know it. He should get Tracker to ink a big Property of Jinx across her forehead.

She'd go for that.

Right?

Maybe not.

But he did have a better idea to progress their relationship and stamp some ownership on her. "Move in with me," he whispered in her ear.

His Prickles would have stiffened in his arms not long ago, sputtered, and panicked. Harper would have gotten all growly and turned him down.

Now, she gasped and looked up at him with shining eyes. "Really?" she whispered.

"Fuck yes. You're there all the damn time anyway. So why the hell haven't we made it official? I hate sleeping without you. I hate eating without you. I hate showering without you. If you don't move in with me, you're condemning me to a life of hating everything."

She chuckled. "What about Lock? Aren't he and Caleb supposed to stay with you when he gets out of rehab?"

Jinx sighed. "He's not doing great, so they're extending his time. I don't know when he will be released, and I can't put my entire life on hold for him. Move in with me. We'll cross the Lock bridge when we come to it. I'll still have plenty of room for him and Caleb."

"You're sure?"

He scoffed. "Fuck, Harper, yes, I'm sure. I want you with me all the damn time. The few nights we spend apart suck. I just... I need you."

She peered up at him with his favorite smile. The one she only gave him—special, sexy, full of love and affection. "Same. I'd love to move in with you."

"Fuck yes." He said the words on an exhale as tension bled from his body. Even though he'd assumed she would agree, a sliver of doubt remained.

They kissed, then resumed watching the sunset. A family of four walked through their field of vision, laughing and gathering shells in the water.

"You want that?" he asked as he watched them.

Harper's breath caught. She didn't pretend to

misunderstand. "Yes. I think I do. Someday."

The thought of Harper growing round with his child had his dick hardening. Yeah, he could envision that future. "Me too."

"Really?"

"Yeah."

"I didn't think about those things for so long because I thought they were off the table for me. But you've shown me that nothing is out of my reach anymore. You've given me the life I never dared to dream about."

Christ, when she said things like that and gave him those glimpses into how bleak her existence had been, he felt his heart crack. But she always repaired it in the same sentence by expressing how much she loved the life they were building.

"Never stop dreaming, baby. I'll make every damn one come true for you."

As she'd already done for him.

Thank you for reading JINX. Please read on for a preview of ZACH, Hell's Handlers MC Book 1.

Zach Preview

Tennessee 2008

It was finally fucking over.

Or maybe it was just beginning.

Either way, years, *years* of busting his ass, taking shit, and being treated like a worthless maggot were finished.

The vote was unanimous.

He was finally a brother.

Well, he was ninety-nine-point-nine percent of the way in. They couldn't just vote him in and chuck him the patch he'd been salivating over for the past two years. No, they had to throw him one last challenge, and a bitch of a test it was.

A branding. The Hell's Handlers Motorcycle Club emblem. On the left forearm. It was as important as the patches on the leather cut each brother wore. So important, if a man was tatted on his left forearm he couldn't even prospect. No, the emblem had to be seared into clean skin, so anyone and everyone would know who belonged to the motorcycle club.

And if being branded wasn't bad enough, there were rules that went along with the barbaric ceremony.

Every brother had to be in attendance. Heckling, ribbing, waiting to see just how much the new member wanted to be a part of the life. Waiting for them to crack.

No screaming.

No tears.

No passing out.

A grunt of pain was allowed, but beyond that, any outward show of weakness would null and void the unanimous vote to end the prospecting period and make him a fully-patched member of the Hell's Handlers MC.

He wouldn't make a peep. They could cut his fucking arm off and beat him with it and Zach still wouldn't utter a sound. That patch was his, and the only way he'd give it up was if some lucky motherfucker managed to pry it from his cold, dead hands. Even then, he'd haunt the bastard and wear the thing as a spirit.

A shrill whistle cut through the raucous laughter and drunken male partying around a huge bonfire. The fire was necessary because the night air was barely butting up against forty degrees. And, of course, the guys made him stand around shirtless while he waited for his fate.

Usually, the sound of fucking made up much of the party's noise, but not tonight. This was just for the men, brothers in all but blood. At least this early part of the night. After Zach got his patch, they'd bring in the club pussy and he'd have his pick of the litter. One, two, hell even three women if he wanted. He'd earned it, watching brother after brother partake in the sweet privilege that was not bestowed on prospects. Club pussy was for patched members only.

And now he was one.

His dick twitched in his pants but died the moment his president spoke. "Okay, fuckers, listen up."

All around him, his soon to be new brothers lowered their drinks and gave their leader, Copper, their full attention. At twenty-nine, Copper was young to be in the role of club president, and since he'd been at it for almost four years, he was officially the youngest leader in the club's near fifty-year history.

"We're just minutes away from welcoming another brother into the club. Shit, Zach's been one of the best prospects we've ever had. Tough as fuckin' nails, pulls more than his own weight, never runs his mouth, loyal." A puff of steam drifted from Copper's mouth as he spoke to the group.

The prez wasn't one to be fucked with. A good few inches over six feet, with a beard the color of a dirty penny, and plenty of hair to match, he was mean as a starving pit-bull. But Copper had the respect of every man in the club. Not just because he held the title of president, but because he'd earned it, dragging the club from the brink of disaster and making it a thriving brotherhood once again.

Zach blew on his hands, trying to infuse some warmth into the frozen digits. Damn, it was colder than a witch's titty and standing around shirtless for the past half hour hadn't helped anything.

"Just one more test of this asshole's strength before he gets to be one of us. Ready, boys?" Copper waved Zach over to the mountain of wood crackling and spitting sparks. Sticking out of the bonfire, a long branding iron roasted away, just waiting to scorch some of Zach's skin.

Shouts of encouragement and a few hecklers betting on how much of a pussy he was and what octave his scream would hit reached him as he made his way to the fire and his waiting president. Careful to keep his expression neutral, Zach drew up next to his prez and paused. Wasn't that the whole point? Act like he wasn't scared. Wasn't about to shit his pants in anticipation of what would probably be the worst physical pain he'd ever experienced.

Fuckin' Copper's facial hair split and his teeth gleamed in the flickering fire. Prez lived for this bull. And if he didn't, he sure acted like he did with that shitty grin of anticipation. "Anything you want to say first?"

Zach shook his head while he bounced on the balls of his feet, hitting his pecs as hard as he could. Maybe if he could get some pain going somewhere else, the burn of the iron wouldn't be so bad.

"Won't work," Copper said, as though reading his mind. "Tried the same thing when I was in your spot. Ain't nothing gonna make this shit any better." He bent and retrieved a bottle from next to his foot. Zach had no idea what was in it, moonshine probably. "You know the drill. Bottle in your left hand. Ten seconds to drink as much as you can. Hold your arm out straight. I'll mark ya. No dropping the bottle. No spilling. No screaming. No puking. Stay on your feet for two whole minutes. Then you're a fuckin' brother."

Zach nodded. His chest rose and fell in a rapid rhythm as his breathing increased and the blood raced through his veins. After blowing out a breath, he grabbed the bottle and brought it to his lips, tilting his head back and opening his throat as much as he could.

Some of the nastiest hooch he'd ever tasted flooded his mouth and streamed down his throat, burning a path to his stomach. Fitting really, since he was about to be burned all to a crisp anyway. Somewhere in the distance, he could hear his soon to be brothers whooping like a horde of wild baboons, but he managed to drown out most of the noise. All but the sound of Copper counting down from ten.

"Three...two...one...arm!"

Zach tore the bottle from his lips and extended his arm. Unable to look away, he stared in fascinated horror as the glowing end of the iron made contact with the thin skin of his forearm. There was a fraction of a second where his eyes registered the flesh-to-iron connection, but the pain hadn't yet reached his brain.

And then it did.

All-consuming, searing pain like he'd never experienced

fired through his nerve endings. Though the spot being branded was no bigger than a silver dollar, agony seemed to encompass his entire being until he couldn't recognize where it originated from. Then there was the audible singe accompanied by the stench of melting flesh. He wasn't expecting that.

Blinding pain was a phrase he'd heard before, but in that moment, he lived it. Darkness clouded his vision, and he slammed his knees back, determined not to succumb to the blissful oblivion that hovered just out of reach.

All around him, men screamed and hollered, but he couldn't make out their cries over the rushing in his ears. Nostrils flaring with each forceful inhalation and exhalation, he mashed his teeth together, probably pulverizing the enamel, as he fought to remain conscious.

Then, the nausea hit. Instead of helping to lessen the pain, the damn moonshine sloshed in his gut and started a trip back up his esophagus, just as disgusting the second time around.

His eyes locked with Copper's. The grinning bastard was definitely enjoying it. All the more motivation to remain standing, quiet, and avoid vomiting the moonshine all over.

Copper pulled the iron away and tossed it to the ground, but it did nothing to diminish the agony. After what seemed like an eternity, Copper pulled his gaze away and checked his watch. Seconds ticked by slower than the thickest motor oil dripping from an engine. Finally, he looked at Zach again and this time his smile was genuine, welcoming. "Two minutes, brother."

Brother. Sweeter fucking words had never been spoken.

Copper grabbed him by the elbow and lifted his throbbing arm. The pain was still there, but now the rush of excitement at achieving his two-year long goal overrode the worst of it. That, and the moonshine was kicking in.

With a loud cry of triumph, Copper held up Zach's branded arm. "Say hello to your newest brother, men." Cheers rose up all around.

Zach swayed on his feet as pain and nausea still warred for victory over his consciousness.

Copper whistled, reigning in the crazy. "He's now to be shown the same respect any other brother receives. He's going to make a damn fine addition to the club."

Zach's chest constricted as pride surged.

"Proud of you, brother," Copper said, for Zach's ears only. "You were one hell of a prospect, and you'll be one hell of an addition to the club."

"Thanks, Prez."

Raising his voice again, Copper turned to the rowdy crowd. "Now someone get Zach a beer and some pussy. The man's waited long enough."

They wouldn't be giving him any pain medication for the burn, but losing his dick in a club girl should take care of the last of the discomfort.

Brothers converged on him from all angles, slapping his back and welcoming him. Not only would the moment be burned into his skin forever, but it was seared into his brain as well.

Best night of his life.

He was in.

Now it was time to set his sights on an executive position.

Enforcer would do quite nicely.

Thank you for reading JINX. If you enjoyed this book, please leave a review on or Goodreads.

Other books by Lilly Atlas

No Prisoners MC
Hook: A No Prisoners Novella
Striker
Jester
Acer
Lucky
Snake

Trident Ink
Escapades

Hell's Handlers MC
Zach
Maverick
Jigsaw
Copper
Rocket
Little Jack
Joy
Screw
Viper
Thunder

Hell's Handlers Florida Chapter

Curly
Spec
Tracker
Frost
Jinx

Mayhem Makers Series
Solo Rider
Series Page

Blue Collar Bensons
First Comes Loathe
Shock and Aww

Audiobooks
Audio

Join Lilly's mailing list for a **FREE** No Prisoners short story.
www.lillyatlas.com
Facebook
Instagram
TikTok

Join my Facebook group, **Lilly's Ladies** for book previews, early cover reveals, contests and more!

About the Author

Lilly Atlas is an award-winning contemporary romance author. She's a proud Navy wife and mother of three spunky girls. Every time Lilly downloads a new eBook she expects her Kindle App to tell her it's exhausted and overworked, and to beg for some rest. Thankfully that hasn't happened yet so she can often be found absorbed in a good book.

Printed in Great Britain
by Amazon